# THE SHADOWMAN RISES

The shadowman. Cassell thought of the
man with the mocking voice as that; an
invader of his sleep, a completely separate
entity from the *persona* of Jonal Cassell.
To do otherwise meant he accepted the
shadowman, the taunts of revenge and killing, the brutal, living tableaux of murder,
as some hitherto unrevealed portion of his
own mind. He could never accept that; it
went against everything Tula stood for. It
opposed the very moral fiber that was
Jonal Cassell....

*In another world, in the distant future,
the incredible adventure begins....*

# SHADOWMAN

by

## Geo. W. Proctor

FAWCETT GOLD MEDAL • NEW YORK

SHADOWMAN

Published by Fawcett Gold Medal Books, a unit of CBS Pub-
lications, the Consumer Publishing Division of CBS Inc.

ISBN: 0-449-14350-3

Printed in the United States of America

First Fawcett Gold Medal printing: June 1980

10  9  8  7  6  5  4  3  2  1

To Lana, thank you for being.

# SHADOWMAN

# ONE

Death stalked Tula.

Though not *the* Death, skull-faced, shroud-cloaked, scythe clutched in skeletal grasp, who eventually lays claim to all men, he was death just the same.

As with any planet, Tula knew *the* Death, felt and understood all its manifestations. The death weaving his way through the throng crowding the Avenue of Reason was unknown to the inhabitants of Tula. He was incomprehensible to the citizen representatives and the spectators entering the great, domed Assembly Hall of the Supreme Council. This death was alien to the planet, unheard of in Tula's fifty-year existence. He was death in its most perverted form—death sprung from Cain's loins—mankiller—assassin.

He walked freely amid the milling crowd gathered for the annual assemblage of the Supreme Council. His only cloak was that the concept of man-killing-man was beyond the comprehension of Tula's populace. His single charade was the forged media credentials pinned to his lapel. Not that the ruse was necessary. The thought of such deception was also unknown on Tula.

9

The assassin, code name Black Sheep, smiled when he entered the Assembly Hall. There were no identification checks, no guards to question his purpose there. For the first time in a long career of death-dealing, he was almost free of the nagging burden of caution.

Almost.

Fifty such assignments, as he preferred to call them, had taught him caution was the primary tool of his trade. Even on this planet, this enigma, caution was a necessity, perhaps more so. If the inhabitants of Tula found the assassin beyond their concepts, Black Sheep found it impossible to accept their utopia, a single sphere of peace amid a universe of chaotic violence.

He refused Tula and the lulling serenity permeating the planet. He denied the sense of false security it created within him. Such a world could not exist. Caution told him there was more to Tula than his senses perceived, something buried deeply beneath its unnatural masquerade of nonviolence. Man could not live with man as he appeared to do here. If fifty assignments taught Black Sheep anything, they tutored him in the natural relationship of man to man.

Now, because there was no apparent reason for caution, the assassin overcompensated. His senses came alive. He was totally aware of the Assembly Hall, the crowd—his purpose.

He wandered over the main floor of the building, slowly working toward the speaker's platform. There was no rush. This assignment was planned second by second, detail by detail. Now was the time to be casual, to mingle, to nod and smile at those around him who nodded and smiled, to greet those who greeted him.

It was also his last opportunity to survey the Assembly Hall. Occasionally, his gaze rose to the two tiers of spectator balconies ringed above the main floor of the auditorium. Arched over all hung the great dome, a canopy of steel and stone. More important were the catwalks suspended beneath, radiating like spokes from the dome's center.

Black Sheep allowed himself a moment of self-confidence. There was no doubt in his mind. He had selected the perfect position to carry out the assignment. The catwalks provided an overview of the whole Assembly Hall.

More nods, smiles, and greetings, and he stood beside the speaker's platform. Unnoticed by those around him, Black Sheep casually inspected one of the myriad of microphone wires running to the main podium. True to his plan, a wire was loose.

Stretching the black line tautly along the side of the podium, he withdrew a roll of tape from a pocket. He tore six eight-centimeter strips of the plastic and carefully secured the wire to the podium. The tape appeared no different from the tape used on the other microphone wires.

Black Sheep smiled. He expected no trouble during this stage of the operation, and none occurred. He knew his trade well and was prepared for the unexpected. The six strips of explosive tape on the podium's side were his backup, a precaution should his initial course of action fail.

But he was not accustomed to failure. Failures were not tolerated in his line of work.

A glance at his watch and Black Sheep eased away from the speaker's platform, losing himself in the growing crowd that pressed onto the floor. Precisely ten minutes later, he pushed through a double-doored exit at the rear of the auditorium. Walking along a well-lit corridor, he came to a maintenance elevator, entered, and pressed a button marked for a service level above the second balcony.

Once outside, he slipped a tattered floor plan of the Assembly Hall from a pocket and stepped down a curving passageway. Following every minute detail of his assignment plan, he hastened his strides, furrowing his brow while he studied the blueprint. Only on occasion did his eyes dart up to note a door marked NO ADMITTANCE—AUTHORIZED PERSONNEL ONLY, and the blue coveralled maintenance person standing beside it. All was as it should be.

"Damn!" Black Sheep forced frustration and agitation into his voice. He stopped beside the man. "I'm lost! My C-camera crew is supposed to be on walk 18Z, and I can't find them. Can you help me, citizen?"

"No problem." The maintenance man smiled and reached for the floor plan. "Let me show you. It's only a bit farther down this corridor."

The man's finger began to trace the route on the blueprint. Black Sheep nodded, following the instructions for a moment, then glanced around. They were alone, as the assassin knew they would be.

"Fine, I see where I managed to lose myself in this maze," Black Sheep said. "Now, if I could ask another favor? I need to know where Service Tube 12B is."

"Hmmmmmm?" The man leaned over, scrutinizing the small print on the floor plan.

In an instant, Black Sheep threaded a slim, silver wire from the sleeve of his jacket. And in the next moment, he twisted the garrote tightly around the neck of his first victim.

The man struggled, fighting to free himself from the strand noose crushing his esophagus. It was in vain. He died, eyes bulging, tongue hanging loosely from his mouth.

Exhilaration coursed through the assassin, almost sexual in nature. Success was near.

Dragging the body a few meters down the service corridor, he opened a maintenance closet. He stripped away the dead man's coveralls and donned the blue jumpsuit. After stuffing the body into the cramped closet, he returned to the door stenciled NO ADMITTANCE.

Beyond lay the catwalk. His gaze ran along the ramp. Halfway to the center of the immense dome was his chosen position, a platform of spotlights directed at the main podium. In a crouched run, he covered the distance to the lights and dropped behind them.

Ten minutes passed. The lights of the Assembly Hall dimmed, and the spotlights flared, beaming down on the podium. The crowd below hushed as the first speaker rose and began his address.

Black Sheep paid no attention to the words droning over the public address system. In the white glow spilling from the spotlights, he began his final preparations. Peeling open the front of the jumpsuit, he extracted three dull-blue objects from the pockets of his own suit. Deftly, his fingers matched threads to grooves, twisting and screwing the three parts to one.

A pleased smile played over his lips when he hefted the lightweight pistol. There were disadvantages to an Ubra 470, but he had used the weapon before—with success. Its miniature rocket projectiles were silent and deadly. The Ubra also lacked the giveaway beam of an energy weapon.

Delving into his pockets once more, he drew out a barrel extension and attached it to the muzzle. Likewise, he produced a T-shaped metal stock that he screwed into the pistol butt and a telescopic sight for the barrel. The Ubra was now a rifle. He snapped a clip of five explosive cartridges into its butt, and it was armed.

Black Sheep lifted the weapon, stock nestled firmly into the hollow of his shoulder, and leveled it at the podium below. The speaker's head filled the sight, cross-hairs meeting directly between the man's eyes. Black Sheep curled a finger around the trigger. He felt another rush of exhilaration. It was perfect. Everything was perfect.

He relaxed, lowering the Ubra to his side. His target had yet to take the stand.

He reached into his pockets and emptied them, pulling out a small manila envelope and a dull black box no larger than a pack of cigarettes. With the latter, he

13

eased open the lid and placed it on the catwalk so he could see the single white button at its center. One tap of a finger would bring the back-up system into play, detonating the explosive tape on the podium.

Tearing open the envelope, he removed the photograph within—Jonal Cassell—his target.

Black Sheep studied the full shot of his target. He knew every physical detail of the compactly built man in the photo. Cassell stood one-point-eighty-three meters and tipped the scales at eighty-four kilos. A tendency toward an overweight problem eliminated by daily exercise, Black Sheep recalled from Cassell's personal profile. He scrutinized the angular face, framed by a thick mop of brown hair that was a bit too long to be stylish. The assassin had memorized each feature of that face: the thin mouth that seemed too small; the narrow nose; the light brown pinhead mole on the right cheek; and the hairline crowsfeet beginning to show at the corners of deep, green eyes. Black Sheep would have recognized Cassell even if he accidently passed the man on the street, which was exactly why he carried the photograph. Black Sheep trusted nothing to memory when it concerned a target.

Applause erupted from the floor below. Black Sheep peered over the catwalk. A new speaker was introduced, a woman. It wasn't time yet.

He turned back to the photograph, scrutinizing it. He cared little about the history of a target. His job was to eliminate a man, not know him personally. To delve too deeply into the character of a target was dangerous. Too much knowledge of a man could result in personal involvement, even empathy. Either meant inefficiency.

Black Sheep knew more about Jonal Cassell than he liked. As with most assignments, those who hired him felt it imperative that he know the target intimately. Thus he knew Cassell as a man—thirty-nine years old, Earth Standard; married, wife's name Ailsa; no children, preference, not biological; former geophys-

14

icist for Zivon Development Conglomerate; and now a representative on Tula's Supreme Council. Cassell headed the powerful, self-reliance faction of the council's membership, the Autonomy Party, which sought planetary independence from Zivon.

Black Sheep shook his head. What good were such facts to him? They only served to muddy his real purpose for being on Tula—to kill Jonal Cassell.

Worse, Black Sheep's employers deemed it necessary to justify their actions to him. Why should he care that they sought to block the movement for autonomy on Tula by assassinating a party kingpin? Did such knowledge steady his finger on a trigger? He never understood why those buying his services had to explain their reasoning to him, guilt perhaps, or a rationalizing of their self-righteousness.

It did not matter. Black Sheep never let such things interfere with the task at hand.

Laughter rolled up from below. He leaned against the catwalk's rail and looked down at the crowd. They suspected nothing, no hint of apprehension among them.

He felt his earlier need for caution return. Glancing over his shoulder, he sought imagined guards hidden in the Assembly Hall's darkness. That there were none was disquieting. It wasn't right. No planet could be estranged from the rest of the universe. On any other world, a governmental convention, even the smallest conclave required a security force, normally a small army, armed to quell a simple civil disturbance or wage all-out warfare, whatever the situation demanded.

His two weeks on Tula did not convince him the planet was real. A world without human violence was impossible, an anomaly.

Yet, there were no guards.

Nor was there a civilian police force anywhere on the planet's surface.

Tula could *not* exist!

Applause broke from the crowd again. Immediately,

15

Black Sheep's attention returned to the podium. A man and woman, emerging from the shadows behind the speaker's platform, approached the microphones.

Black Sheep swung the Ubra to his shoulder while the pair mounted the platform. He recognized the smiling face that filled the telescopic sight, but double-checked the photograph beside him—Jonal Cassell.

Automatically, his finger slid to the rifle's trigger. Keeping Cassell dead center of the scope, he followed the man and woman to the podium. Applause and cheering reverberated within the Assembly Hall.

The hairlines of the scope crossed between Cassell's eyes. Black Sheep tightened his finger, curling it around the trigger, and smoothly squeezed off a shot.

Even before his mind registered the faint hiss of the escaping projectile, he realized his target moved. Cassell stepped back, his head turning to the woman at his side.

The man's jaw exploded, showering flesh, blood, and bone over the podium.

Black Sheep's pulse raced, hammering in his temples. But he suppressed the panic that threatened to rise within him. He lifted the Ubra's barrel a centimeter, crosshairs on the man's forehead. As his finger squeezed down a second time, a woman's head entered the scope, blotting out Cassell's face.

Black Sheep did not watch the results of the second shot. He knew what an explosive charge to the temple would do. Instead, he searched for Cassell in the scope, but could not locate his target. The man had collapsed behind the podium.

Lowering the rifle, Black Sheep reached down and pressed the white button to his back-up system. The explosion rocked the hall. The podium and a majority of the speaker's platform vanished in an actinic glare of red and yellow.

There was no time for him to evaluate the damage.

Black Sheep pushed to his feet and ran back down the catwalk. He had discarded the blue jumpsuit and made his way from the building before the house lights flooded the interior of the Assembly Hall.

# TWO

Pain— Awareness. Simultaneously, they came to Jonal Cassell.

Pain, real pain, writhed within him. Shooting rivers of liquid fire raced through every neuron of his body. Synapses transformed to white-hot super novae, consuming axon and dendrite of each nerve cell.

He stirred, arms groping, legs twitching spasmodically. Explosions of agony detonated within him. His brain screamed in anguished protest. He stopped, lying motionless, enduring the endless torment.

"Doctor, Doctor!" The urgent voice of a woman penetrated his awareness. "He's coming to!"

Cassell forced his eyes open. A blinding glare engulfed him, swirling. Another blast of agony rippled to his brain. Nausea washed through him in hot flushes. He fought the sickening waves, slowed the spinning maelstrom of light that sought to suck him back into the numb security of unconsciousness.

The pain localized, centering in his right eye. No! *Socket!* There was no right eye, only a socket. He had but one eye . . .

And the left eye?

What was wrong with it? Cassell was brutally aware of the blurred vision of his remaining eye. Everything was vague, without edges, a fuzzy white nothingness. He could not focus. Had he lost true sight? Was he blind?

Panic overrode the never-ceasing barrage of pain. He twisted his head. A dark patch broke into the field of white. He stared. The blotch of darkness sharpened in clarity, until he recognized it for what it was, a door, painted green. Relief suffused through him. He could still see.

Basking in the relative security of that realization, he allowed his gaze to wander. More whiteness, then a clock came into view. The whiteness was a wall, he now saw. Below the clock, a row of shining, stainless steel machines lined the wall. They were vaguely familiar, but their purpose eluded him. They were pleasing, their angular bodies so bright and polished in contrast to the flat white of the wall, like a rank of automatons rigidly at attention for military inspection.

Military inspection? The strangeness of the comparison was perturbing. A military did not exist on Tula. Why did he think of it now, after all these years?

Downward Cassell's single eye traced. There was a woman beside him, lying on her back atop some type of bed or table. The intricate, floral pattern of her caftan-style dress was beautiful. Ailsa wore a dress like it when they left home that morning.

*Ailsa!*

His mind railed in shock. He remembered now. All of it came rushing back in a tormenting deluge—the convention of the Supreme Council—the Assembly Hall—the spotlights—the applause—his speech—the awful roar of thunder—pain—blackness.

He jerked his head, trying to see the woman's face. His neck did not respond; it would not move. Something restrained him, restricted his muscles. He rolled his eye upward to the limits of its socket. Again his vision blurred, not in reaction to the stabbing pain, but distorted by a thin layer of gauze lipped over the edge of his brow. For the first time since regaining consciousness, he was aware of the tight cocoon molded around his body.

Bandages! He was encased in bandages. The machines, the room—he was in a hospital!

Ignoring the renewed swells of pain, he strained against the confining tightness. The bandages gave a fraction of a centimeter, enough for him to see his wife's face. Her head lay tilted back, the black mass of her hair tumbling over the edge of the table in a dark, tangled cascade. She stared up at the ceiling, unmoving.

"Jonal, Jonal?" A man's voice echoed in his ears. "Can you hear me, Jonal?"

*Ailsa.* Cassell forced the throbbing length of an arm to rise, to reach out and take his wife's hand. His fingers, awkward in their bandages, closed around hers. He squeezed to reassure her.

"Jonal, it's Ragah. Can you hear me?" The man persisted, nagging him. "Jonal, everything is going to be all right. The doctors are here, Jonal."

Cassell squeezed Ailsa's hand again. There was no response.

Cold, even through the layers of gauze, he could feel the coldness. He tightened his hand around hers, fighting back the fear held in those cold, stiff fingers.

"Jonal, the doctors say everything will be all right." The man assured him once more. "It's going to be all right."

Ailsa was dead. Cassell could not escape the lifelessness he held in his hand. Not even the pain would hide the truth. Ailsa, his Ailsa, was dead. Tears welled in his eye, misting his wife's motionless face. Ailsa was dead. Why?

"What's wrong? Can't he hear me?" The voice went on. "I thought you said . . ."

"Mr. Tvar, please!" Another voice answered the man.

20

"Everything will be fine. You've got to give us time. This man has been through hell. It's a miracle he's still alive. Give us time to help him. We've got to get him into an Accelerated Growth Module."

Cassell felt a hand on his, prying open his fingers, slipping Ailsa's cold hand from his grip. He closed his eye, holding it clamped tightly while tears still welled.

Ailsa in the morning, snuggling warmly against his side; Ailsa in the afternoon, the brilliant colors of the garden surrounding her; Ailsa in the evening, gazing from the balcony to the sea; Ailsa at work, determined, logical, sitting at the comp-con console; Ailsa at play, laughing eyes sparkling; Ailsa in the spring, alive with the budding greenery of the forest; Ailsa in the summer, nude on the white beach, body golden in the sun; Ailsa in the fall, bulky gray sweater, hair disarrayed by the wind; Ailsa in the winter, white furs bundled around her, nose and cheeks red with the biting chill; Ailsa the girl, delicate and vulnerable, hiding in his arms; Ailsa the woman, warm and sensual, giving and taking with passionate hunger; he had lost them. Ailsa was gone.

"Nurse, the injection. We've got to get this man into the AG Module."

Gone.

"Jonal, I know you can hear me . . ."

Gone.

". . . we don't know who did this to you. But we'll find him, Jonal. We'll find him."

Gone.

"Mr. Tvar, please! It's useless. He can't hear you."

Gone.

"Yes, he can. I know it. He's conscious. Jonal, it's Ragah. Everything is going to be all right, Jonal. We'll find the man who did this."

Gone.

Cassell opened his mouth to scream, to unleash the agony tearing at him. Pain blasted through his face. His jaw! It was gone!

21

"Jonal, Jonal?"

"Mr. Tvar, can't you see he can't hear you? Every centimeter of his body is burned, half his face was blasted away in the explosion, and he's lost an eye, possibly both. He's breathing at the moment, and that's more than we expected."

"Doctor, the injection."

Cassell felt a pinprick against the throbbing of his arm.

"Now, let's move this man out of here and get him where we can do some good."

There was a scurry of feet. The table lurched beneath Cassell, moving. The pain lessened. His body was going numb. The injection, he thought, his mind adrift in a syrupy fog, was taking effect.

"Jonal, just hold on. Everything is going to be all right. We'll find the man. I promise you, we'll find him."

The fog thickened, solidifying to a black sheet. Jonal Cassell slipped back into unconsciousness.


Bron Cadao fed the coded transmission into the computer. On the surface, the message was innocuous, a simple agricultural report on Tula's grain crop. Not even the most trained investigators would suspect it. However, the right eyes within Zivon Development Conglomerate would understand.

Cadao leaned back in his chair and sighed aloud. He was tired, tired of Tula, tired of keeping tabs on Jonal Cassell's recovery in the Accelerated Growth Module, tired of the daily reports on the situation.

He should have refused assignment on Tula, but they convinced him that ten years on this world would be easy, no problems. He couldn't believe he had fallen for that old line. He was a fool for joining the agency in the first place, a fool to the tenth power for coming to Tula. If he could hold out two more years, he would take early retirement and lie back on a nice, fat bank account. Field service *did* pay well.

That was still two years in the future. Now was Tula,

22

and the planet was getting to him. For eight years he had stuck it out, maintaining his cover. He sighed again, with longing. It would be nice to hear someone call him by his own name—Bron Cadao—but as long as he remained locked on Tula, he and his cover were one, even down to the name.

Then there was Cassell.

He cursed aloud, his words echoing off the walls of the empty room. When Cassell first started getting planetwide attention, Cadao knew the man would have to be eliminated eventually. His superiors should have listened to him and allowed him to arrange an accident for Cassell back then. But, no, they did not want one of their men involved. They rationalized away the threat Cassell presented, saying interest in independence would fade, the Autonomy Party would fall flat on its ugly face. Tula had it too good under Zivon control. The inhabitants would not want to change that.

His superiors had blown it. Now the situation was going to get worse before it got better. Just how much worse nagged at Cadao. It would be easy to see that Cassell's AG Module failed, a short-circuited relay perhaps, or one mislabeled half-liter of contaminated blood. He had used them both before, and they worked. But his superiors refused to condone that now. It was too dangerous. If he were discovered, he was a direct channel back to them. The whole Tula Project would go down the drain, shot to hell.

Cadao glanced down at the list of commodity prices in his hand. Carefully, he redecoded the message for the tenth time, his latest directives. He found nothing new. It told him to sit tight and maintain his surveillance of Cassell. It also warned that Zivon was sending a team to Tula to instigate an investigation into the assassination attempt and Ailsa Cassell's murder. There were assurances that the assassin, Black Sheep, could not implicate him, Zivon, or the agency, should the man be apprehended.

His superiors were getting sloppy. They failed with

Black Sheep, and now everything was up in the air. They fell back to their wait-and-see stance.

Cadao preferred action. But what could he do? After all, he was just an errand boy. He held no delusion about his importance in this matter. So, he would do as he was told, sit tight, wait, and see.

# THREE

"They come, Gyasi. I can see the head of the procession turning by the fountain. Soon Adum Saht will be ours. It is a glorious day for the *Raeysa,* the children of the most exulted one."

Jonal Cassell turned to find Chiad standing, dark head poked over the parapet. Grabbing the seat of the youth's wrinkled trousers, he yanked.

The boy's feet flew out from under him. Chiad flopped to the tar roof on his back, grunting as the air was jarred from his lungs. For a moment, he lay there, dazed by the unexpected fall. Then with a soft moan, the youth pushed to his elbows and stared at Cassell, his expression a mixture of wounded pride, anger, and surprise.

"Do that again, and I'll use this on you." Cassell hefted the rifle laying at his side. "Do you think the *Kiatos* are blind?"

"Pardon my error, Gyasi," Chiad said in a whisper. His head lowered, chin resting on chest. "I was caught in the glory of the day and forgot our perilous position

25

for a moment. For one of the *Raeysa*, ridding the Golden Throne of Adum Saht is a glimpse of the promised salvation of our people. Gyasi, you must understand the importance of the work you do here this day. You must realize you are the burning arm of our Lord. Gyasi, a whole world awaits..."

Cassell turned the youth off in his mind. Chiad was like every other person on Talald III, a religious fanatic. *Raeysa* or *Kiatos*, it did not matter; they were both alike. For three weeks, since his arrival on the planet, Cassell had listened to the *Raeysa* and their pious rantings. All religious fanatics were the same. They bored him. They were no different than any other type of fanatic. But fanatics had their good points. They were what kept him alive, or at least the dirty work they needed done did.

He rolled to his stomach and peered through the lattice work of the parapet. The street below could have been a scene lifted from one of a thousand historical holodramas depicting Earth's Arabia at the turn of the Eighteenth Century. In fact, it probably was. Reactionary worlds such as Talald III often adopted a fragment of Terran society to represent the "golden age" the planet was supposed to recapture. It was easier to accept the romantizied histories of holodramas than face the brutal reality of Earth's pre–World Combine civilizations.

The white stucco buildings, the domed temples, and the slim spires of the city pleased Cassell. They fitted a desert world. On Talald III, one could never escape the desert. Even here at the heart of the city, the morning breeze carried the smell of flint from the desert, an odor all the exotic gardens on Talald III would never mask.

"...you see. Adum Saht and his followers pollute the very heart of the universe." Chiad slid beside him. "The crowd gathered below honor Adum Saht's ascent to the Golden Throne. They are ignorant of the truth. The *Kiatos'* propaganda machine is efficient. They completely hide the shining core of the *Balietid* from the masses. Gyasi, do you . . ."

*Gyasi.* Cassell was struck by the oddness of the name. Chiad called him Gyasi. It wasn't his name, but it seemed suitable for the occasion. He liked it.

"Look how they flock to him, Gyasi." Chiad tilted his head to the growing crowd on each side of the street below. "In their ignorance, they sing praises to the false one. But you, the burning arm of our Lord, will help us show them the true path, Gyasi."

For an eighteen-year-old boy, Chiad rambled on as though he were a fully ordained priest of the *Raeysa*. Normally Cassell worked alone, but the *Raeysa*'s demand for his job to be completed only four weeks after first contacting him on Gavis made the young native of Talald III an unavoidable necessity. Three weeks on a planet was not enough time to learn all that a man of his profession needed to insure success.

Two lines of yellow-robed priests moved in front of the crowd on each side of the street. The inner files held little concern for Cassell. They were only show, part of the pomp. Each man carried a large brass bowl filled with rose petals, that he sprinkled onto the street as a carpet for the feet of Adum Saht.

However, the outer row of priests was an entirely different matter. The milling spectators knew this and edged back when they approached.

These were the *Kiatos-Cinba*, bodyguards of the most-blessed Adum Saht. Each priest carried a two-meter staff of ironwood. The rods appeared innocent enough, but Cassell had inspected one of the walking sticks that the *Raeysa* had stolen for him. Each staff concealed a high-powered, pulse-beam laser, a weapon the *Kiatos-Cinba* would, and did, use on any man, woman, or child they suspected even harbored a thought of injuring their religious leader.

"See how they pervert the teaching of the *Balietid?*" Chiad said. "The *Balietid* is very exact in prescribing

27

that orange blossoms are to precede the most-holy of feet..."

A resounding chorus of trumpets blared, drowning out the youth's voice. Framed in a diamond-shaped window of the lattice work, Adum Saht entered Cassell's field of vision. The man, robed in golden silks and trailing a train of peacock feathers, strolled casually between the rows of yellow-frocked priests. The crowd cheered as the man raised his hands in blessing.

"The miscarriage of a dog!" Chiad cursed with hate-filled vehemence. "His very presence taints the perfection of our people. Now he'll feel the burning arm of our Lord!"

Firmly gripping the rifle, Cassell rose to his feet and stood, staring over the parapet of the roof. He swung the rifle to his shoulder, right eye pressed against the sight. The crosshairs centered on Adum Saht's neck. If the *Raeysa* wanted the man's head, that was exactly what Cassell would give them.

He tightened a finger around the trigger and squeezed.

Through the scope, Cassell saw the dark hole appear in the man's neck. A fraction of a second later, the explosive projectile detonated, ripping head from torso.

The burning arm of the Lord had struck. And that arm was Jonal Cassell. His temples pounded with excitement. His chest heaved with labored breaths. The thrill was an ecstasy that transcended all carnal pleasures. This was what brought him to Talald III, not the money the *Raeysa* paid. This was the pleasure—the kill.

Cries of horror wailed below. The crowd screamed in terror, bringing Cassell from that orgasmic moment. He dropped behind the parapet. Chiad grinned widely, admiration in his dark eyes.

"It is done!" The youth reached out and clasped Cassell's shoulders. "Today you did the Lord's work!"

"It's not over," Cassell replied. "The *Kiatos-Cinba* are still down there. And there's nothing as blood-thirsty as a bodyguard who has failed its task. We've

28

got to get the hell out of here. In another minute they'll be swarming all over this roof."

Chiad nodded. "We've planned your escape well. Come, the others are waiting to get you off-planet."

"Here, kept this as a souvenir." Cassell held out the rifle to the boy. "I thought you might like to show it to your grandchildren one day."

Chiad's grin widened as he took the rifle and caressed it to his chest. "Gyasi, I will never forget this day, or you."

The youth started to rise. His movement was what Cassell waited for. Grasping the boy by the waist, he lifted Chiad into the air, head and chest rising above the parapet. Chiad screamed.

While Cassell remained safely hidden, the *Kiatos-Cinba* did the rest. Light flared. Flesh sizzled as the priests' lasers lanced into the boy. Cassell felt Chiad stiffen and jerk with each piercing beam that sliced into his body.

Cassell held him there for a moment, letting the *Kiatos-Cinba* unleash their wrath. Then he heaved Chiad, rifle still clutched to his chest, over the parapet. There was a sickening thud when the body hit the street below, followed by a victorious cry from the priests.

The *Kiatos-Cinba* had their assassin. Even if they suspected the boy, by himself, was incapable of killing Adum Saht, they would be distracted long enough for Cassell to make it off-planet, which was all he wanted.

In a crouched run, Cassell hurried toward the door leading down from the roof. He did not need the *Raeysa*'s aid to get off Talald III. He never left his escape in the hands of others. In an hour, he would be safely tucked away aboard a freighter headed toward Earth, no more than another merchant marine.

Cassell's hand touched the doorknob. Pain exploded, penetrating every cell of his body. He screamed.

—There, Jonal, you understand the *why* of it.

*Who?*

29

Only laughter answered him as Talald III dissolved in blackness.

Bron Cadao sat and waited.

# FOUR

Cassell floated, endlessly adrift in a sea of amniotic fluids. Consciousness fled him, but there was perception. He felt the pulse of the umbilical cord connected to his navel, two arteries flowing with life-giving nutrients, one vein carrying wastes from his body.

Content, assured by the constant thump-a-thump rhythm in his ears, he floated. The darkness around him was total security, hiding him from the frightening dreams that invaded the periods of sleep.

—Poor little Jonal has finally achieved the goal of all men, hasn't he? Returned to the womb. Come now, surely a grown man has better things to do with his time, even in a place such as this.

*Who?* The mocking voice did not answer him. *Who?*

Cassell floated, no longer content. Then there was sleep and the dreams, the terrifying dreams.

He woke to feel his world tilting. The warm, caressing ocean drained, receded, leaving him naked and vulnerable. He shivered. Light penetrated the darkness. Cold air washed over his wet, bare flesh. Hands touched him, pulled, bringing him closer to the light.

31

"He's breathing," a voice said in the darkness. "Pulse is normal."

"Switch off the auto-heart and sever the cord as soon as it stops pulsing," another voice said. "He looks good."

"After all the work we've put in on him, he'd damn well better look good."

"Hey, you two, quit wasting time. Get him up to Recovery. He's their problem now. We've got other patients down here who need us."

"Son of a bitch! You'd think this unit was the whole world, if you listened to him."

More hands touched Cassell, pulling him downward, rolling him to his side, to his back.

"He's right. We're through with this one. He belongs to Recovery now. Let's get this table to the liftshaft."

"Talking about Recovery, there's this new nurse in Section A I wouldn't mind recovering with. He's something else."

"Jenica, you've got a one-track mind!"

"Right, and I'd like to find out what track that nurse is on."

"Uhhhh," Cassell tried to find his voice. His vocal cords felt thick, unresponsive. "I . . . ahhhhhh."

"Hey, he's coming out of it."

He tried to speak again with the same garbled results.

"Move it! Get him back under! If he comes to down here, there'll be hell to pay with Recovery!"

"Pleeaassee . . ." He managed to form a single word before his tongue got in the way.

Something cold and hard pressed to his arm. There was a sharp hiss and a stabbing instant of pain.

"There, that should keep him for another hour or two."

"Plee . . ." It was no use. Everything swirled again. Everything darkened, drawing him back into unconsciousness.

Bron Cadao stood by the liftshaft when Jonal Cassell arrived in Recovery. He was agitated and disgusted.

Letting the man live only complicated matters. Why couldn't his superiors see that they would eventually have to eliminate this man? Even now, he could arrange an accident for Cassell, but his superiors still balked. If they waited much longer, it would mean another messy incident like the Black Sheep foul-up.

Still there was nothing he could do, except wait.

—Now this is the way you should kill him, Jonal.

A man stood before Cassell, silhouetted in a harshly bright light. He glimpsed the man's features when he moved his head, but not enough to identify him.

—Jonal, are you listening? We might not have much time, and, if I'm going to instruct you in the delicate art of the garrote, I think it best if you listened.

The voice was vaguely familiar, like the voice of an acquaintance one has not seen in ten years. But Cassell could not see the man's face. If he would just turn to the light a bit more.

—Now the real beauty of the garrote is its silence. Others might tell you it's too awkward, but . . .

*Who are you?* The man frightened Cassell. There was something about him that Cassell hated, an instinct-level reaction to his presence.

— That isn't important right now. At the moment, I've got to prepare you for him.

*Him? Prepare me for what?*

— To kill the man who tried to blow your head off, of course. Now the best garrote is . . .

*I don't give a damn about your garrote.* It was ridiculous. Who was he? *Leave me alone.*

— Perhaps you're right. A garrote might not be the best thing for this. What about a knife? A knife is always good for close work. And, there's a certain satisfaction . . .

*Who the hell are you? Why are you doing this? I don't care about your garrote, or your knife! All I want . . .*

—Jonal, you can't seriously be thinking about a pistol or a laser? It's got to be a knife or a . . . Oh! Now I

33

understand! How stupid of me. Your bare hands, you want to kill him with your bare hands. Strangle him, or beat him to death. The truly personal touch this situation demands.

This was insane. What was a man like this doing on-planet? *I've no intention of killing anyone. I came to Tula to escape the madness of Earth.*

—Jonal, I believe you're serious. What have they done to you?

*They? No one's done anything to me.*

—Haven't they? Take a look at yourself, Jonal. Take a good look. A man has tried to kill you, take off your head with an explosive projectile, succeeded in killing your wife, and you can sit there and calmly tell me you're not going to try and kill him? Do you really think they haven't changed you?

*Ailsa! Oh god! Ailsa!*

—Now, are you ready to listen?

*Go to hell! Leave me alone. I don't need you. I don't want to listen to your vile ideas!*

—This is going to be harder than I thought.

*Get out! Leave me alone!* Cassell cried, tears for his dead wife filling his eyes. *Don't you understand? I don't want your help. I don't need you!*

—We'll see.

He wiped ineffectually at his eyes and looked up. The man was gone.

*Ailsa! Why?*

The face of an unknown man hovered over Cassell when he woke. The man smiled broadly. Cassell weakly returned the gesture while taking in the fact he was flat on his back in a hospital bed.

"Good morning, Mr. Cassell. I was afraid it would be hours before you came around. The team down in the Accelerated Growth Unit gave you a stiff injection when you started to come to," the man said. "You might feel groggy for a while, until you get the drugs out of your system."

34

"Jonal." The head of Ragah Tvar poked beside the man. Cassell smiled at his friend and political aide Ragah looked small, childlike, and vulnerable, as though he had suffered the injuries rather than Cassell. "You don't realize how good it is to see you again. I thought we'd lost you when ..."

"Mr. Tvar, I think you'd best let me talk with Mr. Cassell first," the man said, a touch of irritation in his voice.

"Yes, of course." Ragah backed off like a punished puppy. "I was just excited. Sorry."

Unobtrusive Ragah, Cassell thought. The man would never change. He was a follower, loyal and obedient.

"Feel like sitting up?" The man looked back to Cassell, who nodded. The bed started to rise beneath Cassell's shoulders. "Thought you might. You've been lying in one of our AG Modules for a long time, a month to be exact."

Elevated in a full sitting position, Cassell got a complete view of the room. It was small, but private. His bed, two chairs, a small table, and a holo set were its only furnishings. However, a large window to the right of the bed overlooked the rugged coast of Tula's East Sea. Waves broke on the rocks below.

"There, that should be better," the man said with another smile.

"Much better," Cassell replied with a glance to the stranger. His gaze returned to the ocean. White spume was flung into the air as a wave crashed onto the rocks. Another wave rolled in and more spray flew against the sky.

Ailsa and he watched the sea at night from the balcony of their home. They both found comfort in the rhythmic lapping of the waves on the white sand beach. Now, the ocean was strangely disquieting. He saw it from a new perspective, glimpsed another of its faces—violence.

"Mr. Cassell, would you prefer that I close the window?" The man moved to the foot of the bed. "It seems to disturb you."

"No." Cassell shook his head. "I've always liked the sea."

"Very well," the man replied, pausing for a moment while Ragah seated himself in one of the chairs. "Perhaps I should begin by introducing myself—Dr. Onan Parlan."

Again the man paused, as though expecting a reply. But Cassell said nothing. The resulting silence was more uncomfortable than if he had made some nonsensical remark.

"Mr. Cassell, I know of no delicate way to get to what I need to know," Parlan said, his eyes staring intensely at Cassell. "Do you remember what happened to you?"

"Yes, some," Cassell said. "Ailsa and I were at the Assembly of the Supreme Council. We were introduced and had just taken the podium. Something hit my face, then there was some type of explosion. After that, I don't recall anything. I think I was knocked unconscious."

"There was an assassination attempt," Ragah said, hushing when Dr. Parlan glanced at him.

"You don't seem surprised by that." Parlan turned back, an eyebrow raised. "On a nonviolent world such as ours, I'd think that would come as quite a shock."

"I remember," Cassell replied.

"Remember?"

"Yes, hearing Ragah talking to me," Cassell said. "He kept saying he would find the man."

A puzzled expression wrinkled Parlan's face, but he did not press further. "You're a lucky man, Mr. Cassell. When we first brought you here, we weren't sure you would survive. The assassin did everything but kill you. You were struck by a rocket projectile with an explosive charge. You lost an eye and your jaw when it hit..."

Cassell remembered now, the white room with the

36

green door, the clock, the machines. But he had both eyes now, and his jaw.

"... apparently there was some type of explosive device rigged to the podium. That was also detonated," Parlan said. "You lost a leg in that, and the majority of your body received third-degree burns."

*A leg?* Cassell did not recall that. But he did remember the pain, the awful, devouring pain.

"If you'll allow me a bit of pride," Parlan said, "I think the team here at the hospital performed nothing short of a miracle in patching you up. We cloned most of the replacement parts in an AG Module, while keeping you alive in another. In the past month, you've undergone a series of fifty delicate operations. All of which were successful, as I think you'll see."

Parlan walked to the table and lifted a mirror, which he handed to Cassell. "There won't be any scar tissue."

Cassell studied the face in the mirror. It belonged to him, even down to the hazel-green right eye. He detected a subtle change in the skin texture and tone of his jaw, pinker, smoother, infant-like. He touched his chin, exploring with his fingertips.

"Nothing to worry about," Parlan said. "In a month or so, you won't be able to tell the new flesh from the old. It will match perfectly with the rest of your skin."

"And the eye?" Cassell asked.

"You tell me."

"It seems all right." He closed his left eye and stared around the room with the right. "I can see with it."

"I don't think there will be any complications." Parlan smiled reassuringly. "But if there is any trouble, let us know immediately. That applies to everything. You've just been through quite an ordeal. There might be problems readjusting to a normal life after what's happened. Our staff can also help in that area, if you need them."

"Such as my dreams?"

"Dreams?"

"The time I was in the AG Module," Cassell said, "I dreamed."

Parlan's forehead furrowed, but the doctor did not comment. Cassell needed no urging to continue. The dreams disturbed him.

"I don't know if I remember them all," he said. "They were of other worlds. Some I've heard of vaguely, Lanatia, Vertos, Palla. Others are unknown to me, Talald III, Gyon, Sarthum. But all the dreams involved assassinations."

Parlan's expression remained unchanged as he listened, but Ragah leaned to the edge of his chair. Both men seemed to have more than a casual interest in what he said. Their attention was discomforting, but he wanted to tell someone about the dreams, needed to tell someone.

"The dreams varied. Sometimes I was a spectator, in others, the assassin," Cassell said. "In some cases, everything was clear, as though I were an actor in a holodrama. The others were vague. I remember the names of the victims too . . . Adum Saht, Javas Garridan, Ragnar Oles, Bina Fanett, Tymon Priest . . ."

Cassell's voice trailed off. He did not like recalling the dreams. They were nightmares, violent. Like every inhabitant of Tula, he had come to this world, made it his home, to escape the violence that ate away at every other planet where Man had settled. To find such thoughts, even if they were dreams, within his own mind terrified him. It bordered on insanity.

"Disturbing, but I really don't believe it's anything serious," Parlan said. "An obvious reaction to what happened to you. And a normal reaction for a man who suffered the shock you did. I suspect Mr. Tvar's comments to you before you were placed in the AG Module increased your anxiety. Your mind wasn't able to grasp what had occurred."

Parlan cleared his throat and cast a reprimanding glance at Ragah. "I don't believe you should let these dreams disturb you at this point. However, if they persist, it might be wise to consider the possible need of a psycho-reconditioning session or two."

Cassell nodded. He was relieved, having just told someone about the dreams seemed to have taken a tremendous weight from his chest.

"Now, gentlemen," Parlan said, walking to the door of the room, "I've other patients to tend. Mr. Tvar, please don't stay too long. Mr. Cassell needs rest, and I don't want him exerting himself." He turned to Cassell. "And that's what I want you to do—rest. I'll look back in on you later to make sure that's exactly what you're doing."

With that, the physician left. For a moment, neither Cassell nor Ragah spoke. Cassell's gaze moved back to the window. Outside a bank of gray clouds rolled in from the east. The water below lost its blue-green color, turning a dull slate-gray.

"Jonal," Ragah rose from his chair and walked beside the bed, "I can't tell you how glad I am you pulled through this. Everyone in the party has been concerned. Without you, there's no hope of pushing through independence."

"You're exaggerating my importance to the party, Ragah." Cassell forced himself to smile. He did not want to talk politics. The Supreme Council was the furthest thing from his mind. But Ragah was like that. He was well-meaning, his concern was genuine, but his one undying passion was the party. He lived, ate, drank, slept, and loved the party.

"After the attempt on your life, the council postponed the assembly until you recover," Ragah said. "No one else in the party felt they could take your place. We..."

Cassell stopped listening. Dr. Parlan avoided mentioning Ailsa. Cassell was frightened, remembering. The white-walled room with the green door had not been a fragment from a dream. The image of Ailsa lying on the table, staring at the ceiling, was etched on his mind. He felt the coldness of her hand in his, the lifeless rigidity of her fingers. *It had not been a dream.*

"Ailsa is dead," he said, looking at his friend. It was a statement rather than a question.

Ragah stopped in mid-sentence, eyes downcast. "Yes. She was hit in the temple by the assassin's second shot, Jonal. There was nothing the doctors could do."

*God!* Cassell could not suppress the shudder that ran through him. *An explosive charge! Ailsa, my beautiful Ailsa, what have they done to you?*

"Funeral services were held two weeks ago," Ragah said. "Everyone in the party attended. The holo networks carried the services. All Tula mourned her."

"Why, Ragah, why Ailsa? Why not me?" Cassell could not stem his tears. "What did she do? Why murder her?"

"I don't know, Jonal," Ragah said with a slow shake of his head. "We're trying to find out why anyone would want to kill either of you ... who on Tula is capable of ..."

Alone, he was alone. The brutal reality was inescapable. Ailsa was gone and he was alone.

"... The Company sent us a team of investigators from Earth. They've been helpful, done everything they could," Ragah said. "Four days ago they found the man who did it, Jonal. They've been interrogating him ever since, but he hasn't said a thing, not even under drugs. He's being held at the Zivon Building. They put locks and bars on the doors and windows to serve as a makeshift prison, since we didn't have anything like that here. There're also guards ..."

The assassin had been captured. What did that matter? Did it bring Ailsa back to him? Cassell rolled to his side, burying his face in a pillow. He cried, his whole body shuddering.

Later, when he could cry no more tears, and only the hollow emptiness remained within him, he remembered hearing Ragah leave the room. He was grateful for the privacy.

Outside, the waves still broke upon the shore.

Bron Cadao grinned broadly, his gaze coursing over the decoded message. His transmission of Cassell's medical report, with its mention of the man's dreams, achieved the desired results, kicked them right where it hurt. He could tell by the wording of the reply that his superiors were incredulous, but too scared not to react. Cassell was a walking time bomb that could blow Tula apart at the seams. They could not allow that.

Unless Dr. Onan Parlan could be convinced to pull Cassell in for psycho-reconditioning, he was ordered to take matters into his own hands, at his own discretion. His superiors had done the unheard of; they supplied him with the names of two other on-planet field agents to assist him, should it become necessary.

Cadao slipped the message into a disposal unit and leaned back in his chair, hands locked behind his head. First, he would talk with Parlan, taking it slow and easy to avoid arousing the doctor's suspicion. If that did not work, it would be time for action.

# FIVE

Cassell stood on the beach, watching the tide come in. It was early morning, or late afternoon. He was not sure; the sky was overcast with flat, gray clouds.

—I really don't know what to say, except you frighten me, Jonal.

*You!* Cassell jerked around. No one was there, only a voice. *I frighten you! Who are you! Why do you keep bothering me?*

—Just think of me as a kindred spirit, Jonal, one who knows you better than you know yourself. And, yes, you do frighten me. Why else would I have left you alone this past week? I mean, talking with that Dr. Parlan about all the things I've shown you, and telling him about what I've said.

*Go away. I thought I was rid of you.*

—Parlan's talk of a "session or two of psycho-reconditioning" and your passive acceptance of letting someone play with your mind really got to me. I didn't know how to handle it. It's taken me ten years to find a way to talk with you. I didn't want to lose that. So, for the last week, I've sat back and observed Parlan and you. Now, I think we'd better talk about the assassin. It's time you did something about him.

*Leave me alone. I won't listen to you. You're just a bad dream.*

—Bad dream! Quite amusing, Jonal. I've been thinking the same thing about you for a long time—ten years as a matter of fact. But this is no dream. We both know that, don't we?

*I don't know anything. I'll talk with Parlan as soon as I wake. The reconditioning sessions will wipe you away.* This was insanity, and Cassell knew it. Who ever heard of a man conversing with a dream? He *did* need psychotherapy.

—Go ahead. You're completely sane, Jonal. The sessions won't help. I'm here to stay. I know the way to get to you now, and I won't forget it. Accept that. It's the truth. You might be able to hide from me for a short while, but I'll be back.

He did not like the sound of the voice. It mocked him.

—No, Jonal, I'm not taunting you. I admit you disgust me most of the time, but I accept you for what you are. All I ask is that you do the same for me. There's no reason why we can't be friends. I can help you, if you let me.

*A figment of my imagination, that's what you are, a figment of my imagination.*

—Not very original. I expected better from you, Jonal. You'd make it a lot easier on yourself if you'd accept me for what I am.

*Which is nothing but a bad dream, a residual effect of my injuries.*

—You don't believe that, so why say it? Everything I've shown you is quite real. Check on it.

*Where?*

There was no answer. Cassell twisted around, trying to find the man who spoke to him.

*Where should I check?*

Still no answer. He sat down on the white sand and stared out across the gray sea. Waves ran lapping fingers up the beach, licking at his feet.

The loud hiss of an opening door brought Cassell from sleep. Bright lights flared above him, blinding him for a moment. He blinked in confusion, while his eyes adjusted to the harsh glare.

He lay naked atop a hard, cold examination table that had not warmed a degree in the past five hours. The seemingly unending series of tests, probes, prods, X-rays, scopes, and a myriad of other intimate examinations of his new-old body had taken more out of him than he realized. He recalled Dr. Parlan and two assistants leaving the room after a long and uncomfortable exploration of his nether regions. He had closed his eyes and apparently napped.

Voices came from beyond the glare of the lights, but Cassell could not locate their owners. It was just as well. He did not want to contend with any further probings or questions. Every joint in his body was beset by niggling discomfort. He stretched a bit to relieve the aches of lying motionless for so long. It didn't help.

The discomfort was not in his body, but in his mind— tension stemming from anxiety. After a week's absence, the shadowman of his dreams, or at least his voice, was back.

The shadowman, Cassell thought of the man with the mocking voice that way, as an invader of his sleep, a completely separate entity from the *persona* of Jonal Cassell. To do otherwise meant he accepted the shadowman, the taunts of revenge and killing, the brutal, living tableaux of murder, as some hereto unrevealed portion of his own mind. That he could never accept. It went against everything Tula stood for; it opposed the very moral fiber that was Jonal Cassell.

"Well, Jonal, I can't find a thing wrong with you," Parlan's voice came from beside him, a welcome interruption to his disturbing reflections. "I don't see any reason for keeping you here a moment longer. The sooner you vacate your room, the sooner we can move in someone who really needs it."

Cassell sat up and took the white robe the doctor offered him.

"Put this on and I'll walk you back to your room. I had Mr. Tvar bring you some clothes this morning. As soon as you're dressed, we'll get you checked out," Parlan said. "According to all our tests, you're a perfect specimen of physical health. I think it would be best if you went home instead of lying around in a hospital bed. Getting back to familiar surroundings will be a greater aid to full recovery than anything we can do for you here."

"That's the best news I've heard all week," Cassell said with a grin as he followed Parlan from the examination room. "I admit I've felt like I'd contracted a terminal case of boredom the past few days. I'm ready to get back to doing something useful."

"Slow down, don't be in such a hurry," the physician replied when they entered Cassell's room. "You're not ready to walk out of here and pick up where you left off. You still need to take it easy and rest. Every muscle in your body is out of condition, and I don't want you pushing yourself. Stay away from real work, mental or physical. Get plenty of mild exercise. Build up slowly. Understand?"

"Rest, mild exercise, no work." Cassell nodded. He found clothes laid out atop the bed and started to dress.

"I mean it, Jonal," Parlan said. "At least for two or three weeks, I want you to take it easy."

"Right," Cassell replied. "I'll stake out a place on the beach and live there, take numerous, casual strolls, and swim a bit."

"Don't overdo it on the swimming," the doctor said, "or the walks."

"Yes, sir," Cassell answered as he finished dressing. The feel of his own clothes, after a week in hospital

45

robes, was marvelous. "Do I have to call down for a cab?"

"No, we'll have one waiting for you," Parlan said. "However, before you leave, there's one more thing I want to discuss with you . . . your dreams."

Cassell tensed with apprehension. A cold finger tapped the base of his spine and tickled upward. His thoughts froze on the dream, and the shadowman's last words—"Check on it."

"Have the dreams continued?" Parlan asked, staring intensely at him. "Are you still having them?"

"No," Cassell replied without hesitation. "I haven't had one since the AG Module, since I talked with you about them."

Guilt flushed through him. He lied. Why? There was no reason for lying to Parlan. He had never lied before in his life, not even the usual little white lies between husband and wife. Yet, now, it seemed the right thing to do. He knew what Parlan's reaction would be if he told the physician about the dream in the examination room. Reconditioning seemed too drastic a measure to take because of a few nightmares. If the dreams persisted, then he would seek help, but not now.

"Good, good," Parlan said, visibly relaxing. "It was as I thought. The dreams were just a minor side effect of shock. However, if they should come back, let me know immediately. We'll schedule a few sessions to eliminate them."

*And play with my mind.* He shocked himself. Reconditioning was nothing new for him, or for anyone on Tula. He had gone through sessions both here and on Earth. It was an accepted psychiatric tool, a necessary therapy. It was a safeguard to check antisocial behavioral patterns. Why should he now consider it meddling with his mind?

"If they return, I'll contact you," Cassell said. He would, *if* the dreams worsened. For now, he could handle them. The shadowman's last words still nagged at him. There was something he wanted to find out before he let any psychiatrist put him through the remolding of psycho-reconditioning.

"Then, I see no reason for keeping you any longer," Parlan said, holding out his hand. "Just follow my instructions and be back here in two weeks for another physical."

Cassell shook the physician's hand, nodded, and walked from the room, feeling an uneasy relief. Taking a dropshaft to the hospital's ground level, he exited the building through the main lobby.

Outside, Tula's single sun hung low in the western sky. Evening approached rapidly. Cassell felt a twinge of disappointment. Parlan's examinations robbed him of most the day. He refused to let it dampen his spirits. He was out of the hospital. For the moment, it was enough.

He sucked in a deep breath, filling his lungs with fresh air. A sharp saline odor assailed his nostrils—the smell of the sea. The biting tang of brine irritated him, bringing back the last scene of the dream—waves lapping up the beach, washing over his feet. He pushed the disturbing tableau from his mind and stepped to the edge of the shuttle ramp. A bubble cab approached, stopping before him. "Jonal Cassell," a speaker on the side of the cab called.

Extracting his identification card from a coat pocket, Cassell pressed it to the cab's ident-plate. The door swung upward to admit him, and he slipped onto the couch inside. He punched out the coordinates of his home on the driver console, then leaned back and closed his eyes. The cab lurched, beginning to move toward its programmed destination.

*Check on it.* He could not shake the shadowman's taunting challenge. The dream haunted him. Despite its vagueness, the disembodied voice, it seemed more vivid than all the dreams he had while in the AG Module. He remembered every word of it, as though the dream had been a conversation with a business associate, or a friend.

47

He should have mentioned it to Parlan. The dream gnawed at him, twisting his insides into cramped knots. He needed reconditioning. He could recognize the early stages of mental imbalance, insanity. He needed those psychiatric sessions to overcome the shock of losing Ailsa and the attempt on his own life.

*No.* He shook his head. Psychiatric remolding would be wrong, at least now. He could not risk the mental probes, the memory erasures, until he satisfied himself that the shadowman was wrong. He had to get to the computer at home before he called Parlan. After he proved his dreams wrong, he would get help.

The cab slowed perceivably, interrupting his chain of thought. He opened his eyes and sat up with a curse. His voice reverberated within the plastic bubble.

The vehicle was apparently one of the older models, programmed to take the most direct route between two points. The cab now entered the administrative district of Farrisberg, the very heart of Tula's capital city. Newer cabs were programmed to travel the most expedient route to a destination, which for Cassell would have been one of the outer concourses ringing Farrisberg. The traffic in the district would add a half hour to his trip home.

Muttering another expletive, he sank back in the seat. There was nothing he could do about the delay, except endure it. His gaze wandered to the buildings outside the bubble-canopy. Farrisberg was a model city, clean and orderly, as was everything on Tula. The towering structures were constructed of steel and stone, not a strip of plastic to be seen. Something few of the colonized planets could claim.

Residential areas were outside the actual city. The green country beyond Farrisberg's administrative district provided unlimited space for the construction of homes. Or the ground beneath the countryside did. The majority of Tula's personal dwellings were underground, leaving the surface free, maintaining the planet's natural ecological balance.

The populace of Tula had Zivon Development Conglomerate to thank for that. Zivon Development Conglomerate, Zivon, the Company. Tulans had many names for it, all of them spoken with a reverence that bordered on religious awe.

Zivon, "vigor and alive," it came directly from one of Earth's ancient, and now dead, languages. But for Tula, the Company was the giver of life and vigor. Unlike the majority of exploration and development combines constantly seeking new planets for financial exploitation, Zivon was a philosophy. Its goal was utopia, a perfect world where men of peace could live in harmony. While other combines ruthlessly stripped a planet of its valuable resources during the fifty-year colonization period, leaving the inhabitants to make do with what remained, Zivon planted the seeds of paradise.

To be sure, the Company found financial gain on Tula. Cassell did not fool himself by thinking profits were not a motivation for Zivon. On a resource-rich world such as Tula, profits were always a major concern. A combine, even Zivon, could not settle a planet for purely philanthropic reasons. Zivon received their profits from iron, copper, silver, uranium, and timber. Real wood was a high-priced commodity on Earth and a hundred other planets. When Tula gained independence, the planet could maintain a healthy economy based on the exportation of timber. Careful management of Tula's forest-covered continents would mean a resource that would never be depleted.

Zivon made their profits; Cassell would never deny that Tula more than rewarded Zivon's investments in the planet. But there was more to Zivon than financial interests. That something extra was what made Tula what it was. The Company believed in the people of Tula and their goal to build a world free of the violence and the insanity that normally plagued any of Man's enterprises.

Cassell remembered the strict psychological screening he had undergone to win a berth to Tula. The testing and retesting lasted a year. One in ten thousand were selected; one in ten thousand were found acceptable for Tula. He had never forgotten the joy, the moment of supreme satisfaction he felt when he received his acceptance ten years ago. Tula was a noble experiment, one to which Jonal Cassell had dedicated the past ten years of his life. The most noble of Man's ventures, and a successful one for fifty years. Not one violent act marred the planet's history.

Or had not, until Ailsa's murder.

The pain returned. No matter where his thoughts wandered, they eventually revolved to the same point—Ailsa. Parlan had warned him not to dwell on her death, but he could not stop himself. Ailsa was dead, and he was alive. It gnawed at him. He knew he must accept her death and begin again. There was no other way to survive. He could not just give up.

Cassell turned his attention to the walkways connecting the buildings outside, trying to hide from the memories of Ailsa. It was shift change. Crowds flooded from the structures, moving toward the bubble cab ramps.

The scene was familiar. For eight years, shift change had been an integral part of his day-to-day life. That was before he was elected to the Supreme Council and took the chair of the Autonomy Party.

He scooted closer to the cab's transparent canopy, peering at the crowds. There was no rush, no bustle. No one fought to reach the ramps before his co-workers. There was no pushing, no shoving, no angry faces, only polite smiles and a steady, leisurely pace.

The scene bothered him. It held a certain lifeless quality he could not define. These were human beings, men and women, people who had just finished a four-hour work shift, people who shedded the confines of their offices and returned to their homes and personal lives. Yet, there was no rush, no hastening of feet to hurry them to the arms of wives, husbands, families, lovers.

It was incongruous. Somewhere, amid the thousands, there should be one disgruntled expression, a displeased frown, a wrinkled brow. Cassell searched the faces, but could not find one. There were only smiles and unheard mouths, lips moving in pleasant conversation.

How many times had he walked from his office amid such crowds? How many times had he moved from work to the cab ramps, idly chatting with colleagues, and thought how peaceful it was, how fortunate he was to live in such an orderly fashion?

Why did it seem passive now, sapped of vitality?

Cassell clamped his eyes closed, holding them tightly shut. What was happening to him? Had he already lost his sanity? He clutched his knees, shivering. What was wrong? All his thoughts were tainted with doubt. He had to get hold of himself, take a grip on reality.

He forced himself to look outside the bubble once again. His trembling passed. There was nothing wrong with the crowd. It *was* peaceful. These were the actions of human beings, not animals clawing their way to freedom. This was the way Man was supposed to behave. This was the essence of all that was sane.

The Zivon Development Conglomerate Administration Building entered his field of vision. He tensed. Uneasiness returned, knotting inside him. Ragah said Ailsa's murderer was under guard within the building. The man who had killed his wife was there.

He sat up, hands shooting for the buttons of the cab's control console. He stopped himself, fingertips hovering above the panel, the coordinates of the Zivon Building repeating over and over in his mind.

Cassell dropped back to the couch, feeling the cab accelerate. What would be the use of it? What good would it do to see the man? It would not ease the emptiness inside him. It would not bring Ailsa back.

Outside, the buildings thinned. The cab picked up speed, rapidly entering the forested countryside surrounding Farrisberg. Cassell took a deep breath and steadied himself. Parlan was right, he needed rest. He needed to forget. Away from the city, on the beach, it would be easier to gather his thoughts and make plans for a future without Ailsa.

The thought of the man back in the Zivon Building refused to leave him. The man was not even in a prison; there were no prisons on Tula. The planet now had a three-million-plus population and not one prison, or jail cell. The fact spoke well of the success of Tula, and Zivon.

At the same time, it troubled him. As with the crowds during shift change, it seemed incongruous. No matter how stringent Zivon's screening of colonial candidates, it was logical to expect that at least one misanthrope would manage to find his way on-planet, one sociopath loose like a wolf in a pasture of lambs.

The cab slowed, swinging onto a small ramp leading from the main concourse. It shot through a leafy tunnel of interlocking tree limbs arched above the cab's track. Abruptly the dense foliage fell away, and Cassell stared out over the ocean. The bubble cab track now bordered the top of a thirty-meter-high cliff. Below, a stretch of white sand met the sea.

A sharp beeping tone resounded in the bubble cab. A blue light winked on the console. A prerecorded voice spoke, "One minute to arrival. Please remove all personal articles from the cab when disembarking."

Out of habit, Cassell reached down for his attaché case. He smiled. He was his only personal article this trip. The thought did not ease his discomfort.

Another beep and flashing blue light, and the bubble cab halted. The door swung open, and Cassell stepped out onto a concrete slab six meters from the edge of the cliff. The cab door closed behind him, and the cab whirred off, leaving him alone in apparent wilderness.

The untamed terrain was deceptive. Ailsa and he

had carefully landscaped the area above their home to provide the illusion that Man had never touched the land. Only the concrete slab on which he stood destroyed the effect. And perhaps Ailsa's rose bushes. Roses were not native to Tula, but Ailsa had managed to convince Zivon shipping officials to smuggle her two cuttings from Earth.

A dull ache throbbed in Cassell's chest as he remembered his wife nurturing the cuttings, caring for the plants as though they were infants. Ailsa's efforts were successful. The cuttings were now bushes, and in bloom. He could see his wife grinning with pride while she examined each of the deep red blossoms. Below was Ailsa's garden, a carefully disguised hothouse hidden within Tula's bedrock. The exotic flowers there were constantly in bloom and Ailsa had loved them. But she deemed only the roses beautiful enough to plant on the surface. Her gift to a world she loved.

Cassell turned from the two bushes and walked to a metal pole protruding from the center of the slab. Atop the meter-high rod was a black box. This he opened and placed a hand on the ident-plate within. A second later there was a hiss, like the sound of escaping air. Beyond the slab, the ground opened, a wide circular hole, the mouth of the dropshaft leading to his home. Cassell stepped into the aperture and gently sank downward.

Their home was worse than the rose bushes. Ailsa was everywhere, her ghosts lingering in a chair, beside the tapecase, at the balcony. The bedroom brought the most pain. The intimacies, the passion, the love they had shared seemed to hang in the air. The temptation was there to stand and stare, to relive each moment of his life with Ailsa.

The tears in his eyes and the tightness in his chest told him it was wrong. He could not live in the past. And for all the aching and hurt within him, Ailsa was now part of the past. He was the present; he still lived.

It sounded good, strong and confident. And he knew

he would eventually convince himself of that fact, and live with it. But now, the past was too dear; it held him too close. Ailsa had died more than a month ago. But for him, a month floating unconscious in an AG Module, her death had been but seven days before.

He considered calling Ragah Tvar and arranging to stay with him a few days. It would be easier than living with ghosts. But he could not find the willpower to break away from the house. He wanted to be there. Yet, he was afraid of the memories he found in every room.

Sleep, if he could sleep, he would avoid the painful memories. Tomorrow would be a fresh start, easier to accept the house.

Beside the bed, Cassell found a vial of sleeping pills. Popping its top with a thumb, he tapped it against his palm. The contents spilled into his hand. He stared blankly at the green and yellow capsules for a moment. Ailsa and he had used them on occasion as a mild aid to overcome tension. Twelve capsules in all. It would be so easy. First sleep, then an end to all the pain— forever. So simple to take all twelve, no more than a few swallows, then a never-ending sleep.

He dropped ten of the capsules back into the vial and recapped it, unsure why he did so. Perhaps it was *too* easy that way. Perhaps death frightened him more than loneliness. He swallowed the remaining two capsules, sleep not death, then sat on the edge of the bed.

*Check on it.* The shadowman's momentarily forgotten challenge echoed back. Cursing under his breath, Cassell reprimanded himself for taking the capsules without first completing what he had returned home to do. There was still time before the drug took effect.

Rising, Cassell walked into the library and seated himself at the console of a small personal computer. He ran his fingers over the keyboard, punching out a series of commands. A moment later, the terminal screen blinked, displaying the words, FARRISBERG

LIBRARY LINK COMPLETE—REFERENCE BANKS AVAILABLE.

His fingers punched the keyboard, quickly calling for memory retrieval cross-reference, general category ASSASSINATIONS. He then paired victim names with planets: Adum Saht—Talald III; Javas Garridan—Lanatia; Ragnar Oles—Vertos; Bina Fanett—Palla; Tymon Priest—Gyon; Paulles Nught—Sarthum.

Cassell sucked at his teeth and held his breath nervously. He was frightened, afraid that the information retrieval system would verify his dreams, even more terrified that it would not. His palms sweated, and his temples throbbed.

The screen winked. Its message filled the terminal:

ADUM SAHT—TALALD III
Religious leader of the desert planet Talald III, whose assassination, 378 T.S., sparked a five-year civil war between the Balietid factions, Raeysa and Kiatos, on that planet. Assassin's identity unknown, suspected to be off-worlder hired by the Raeysa faction. Never confirmed.

378 T.S., twenty-one years ago Earth Standard. Cassell's pulse quickened, his fright squeezing at his chest. The screen blinked again, and the second message flashed:

JAVAS GARRIDAN—LANATIA
NO ASSASSINATION REPORT. Javas Garridan, president of Xythine Combine, died in a hovercraft collision during a routine inspection of Xythine Combine holdings on planet Lanatia, 3098 L.S.

Nineteen years ago Earth Standard. A hovercraft with tampered guidelevers, Cassell recalled from one of the dreams. He knew every detail of the collision, and it scared him.

## RAGNAR OLES—VERTOS
Ragnar Oles, sole owner of the Oles Copper Mines on the planet Vertos, was stabbed to death by his wife, Lian Oles, during a marital dispute, 56 V.S. Wife was later ruled insane. Oles' holdings were inherited by their only child, Paz Oles.

Subtle psycho-reconditioning plus an overdose of the hallucinogenic drug Patis were all that were needed to convince Lian Oles her husband intended to murder her that night, Cassell thought. The authorities never suspected. Paz Oles paid through the teeth, but he had inherited his father's estate nineteen years ago Earth Standard.

## BINA FANETT—PALLA
NO ASSASSINATION REPORT. Bina Fanett, onetime popular holodrama starlet on the planet Palla, committed suicide by leaping from her penthouse apartment, 1189 P.S.

Seventeen years ago Earth Standard. All it took was a simple push, Cassell thought. Fanett had overplayed her hand, used her blackmail threats on a lover who was too powerful to be bothered by her petty ploy.

## TYMON PRIEST—GYON
Tymon Priest, political leader of Gyon Independence Party, killed in an explosion at his residence. Hired assassin thought to have placed the explosive device, no confirmation, 69 G.S.

Fifteen years ago Earth Standard. Cassell remembered Priest. He shared a kinship with the man. Only he had been luckier. He still lived, despite an assassination attempt.

## PAULLES NUGHT—SARTHUM

Paulles Nught, suspected killer of eight hostages during an attempted robbery of the Sarthum Credit Exchange, was acquitted of charges following a long, controversial trial. Paulles was later found murdered, his body mutilated, 575, S.S. No suspect apprehended in the case.

The husband of one of those hostages had paid well for Paulles Nught's death thirteen Earth Standard years ago. Cassell vividly recalled the horror of his dream, Nught screaming as he butchered the man—alive.

The terminal blinked and went blank.

Cassell stared at it, numbed. The dreams were true—all of them. His mind swirled. How could it be? He tried to think, grasping for any explanation, but there were none. None of the incidents were important enough to be picked up by the media for interplanetary transmission. He had never been to any of the planets. He had only read of a couple, and then superficially.

The shock of the discovery was too much to contend with at the moment. He could not sort it out. He needed to talk with someone, tell him what he had found. Ragah? Parlan?

He pushed from the console and stood. The room reeled.

*Damn!* The sleeping pills were taking effect. He felt dizzy, disoriented. He moved toward the living room, using the walls for support. He was so relaxed now, nothing seemed to matter. He could contact Parlan in the morning, after he slept. His mind would be clearer then; he could fit all the pieces together.

He found the couch and stretched out atop it. The

cushions felt good under him, restful. He closed his eyes and relaxed, forgetting the computer, the house, and the ghosts.

The terminal screen died, a flat gray-green eye that stared blankly at Bron Cadao. The man ran a hand over his neck impatiently. He did not like what he had just seen. Parlan was a fool! Cassell was still worried by those dreams. That the man had not mentioned it to his physician indicated the situation was worsening. Had it not been for Cadao's foresight to link into Cassell's home console, he would have never known about it—until it was too late.

However, Cadao still had everything under control. Soon, the problem would no longer exist. First, he would have to take care of the library reference banks, then he would contact his two fellow field agents. Within twenty-four hours, Jonal Cassell would no longer threaten the security of the Tula Project.

# SIX

—You continue to astound me, Jonal.

Cassell turned. The fog wrapped about him like a tenuous, milky cocoon for an instant, then dissipated. He stared, attempting to part the mist with his gaze. The voice's owner remained hidden.

—If it didn't frighten me so, your foolishness would be a source of never-ceasing amusement.

The fog thinned to reveal a man's dark silhouette. Cassell's stomach churned; something twisted and knotted itself deep in his gut. Unreasoning fear shot through him. He pivoted on the ball of a foot and froze. A cold, panicked sweat prickled over his skin. The shadowman still stood before him, half-veiled by the wavering mist.

—The sleeping pills were stupid, sheer lunacy. Drugs dull the senses, Jonal. You need to be totally alert. You'll fail otherwise. Even here on Tula, the odds are stacked against you. When the opportunity presents itself, you have to be ready. You have to strike before they suspect anything. If you don't, you'll never get away with it. One chance, that's all you'll get.

*I'm not going to do anything.* He did not have to ask what the shadowman was talking about. His nightmare visitor knew but one topic—killing Ailsa's murderer.

—You will. It might take a bit more time for you to accept that fact, but you will. You felt it today when you passed the Zivon Building. When the time comes you will...

*No! I just wanted to see him ... to question him ... to find out why! There was nothing else. I could never...* The act the shadowman urged remained beyond the limits of reason.

—...kill Ailsa's assassin.

*Never. I just want to understand why. I could never kill. Never!* Cassell clamped palms over ears to shut out the shadowman. The nightmare voice penetrated his defenses and echoed in his brain.

—Why, why, why! Stop deluding yourself. You know the whys of it. Didn't I show you that? Your own computer verified everything. Now you have to accept that it's time to take matters in your own hands, so to speak.

*I won't! I couldn't!* His arms dropped to his side, hands clenched in tight fists, then spasmodically opening, fingers like rigid spikes, and snapping shut in a desperate rhythm. The shadowman chuckled, a low, throaty, nasty sound. *You're wrong. I could never kill.*

He felt his tormentor's unseen eyes skewering through him like a silver pin that transfixed a live insect to a velvet board. He squirmed under the mocking smirk he imagined warped the vision's shadow-cloaked face. Again he pivoted away. The nightmare persisted; the shadowman remained in front of him.

—Accept it, Jonal. Make it easier on both of us. You can feel it now. Accept it.

*No, damn you! I don't feel anything!* Yet, something moved within him. Dark and awakening, it uncoiled and writhed in his chest. No! The shadowman confused him, distorted the truth.

—Your thinking is muddled, Jonal, but it has nothing to do with me.

*And who are you?* Cassell eased closer to the silhouetted man. He reached out. The fog rippled away from his hand in expanding circles as though a stone had been tossed into a mirror-smooth pool. The concentric rings quavered over the shadowman, fracturing his image. Cassell's hand opened and closed on empty air, again and again.

—Jonal, you're straying from the purpose of our talk.

*Your talk.*

—If you want. It really has no bearing on the situation. What is important is, when do you intend to see the man who butchered your wife?

*Tomorrow.* He did not bother denying his intentions. Though he was not sure why.

—For now, that's enough. It's a beginning, a step in the right direction.

The fog thickened to obscure the man. Again Cassell's hand plunged into the mists. Rippling rings undulated before him.


Torrents of massaging water abruptly stopped when the shower heads automatically shut off. A moment later air blasted from a series of jets inset on the cubicle walls.

Cassell shivered. Ailsa always set the air temperature too low. She insisted it was invigorating, that the warmer drying setting he preferred left her lethargic. This morning he agreed with her. Despite the gooseflesh that covered every centimeter of his body, the cool air was exactly what he needed. Last night's sleeping pills had been too much. He had overslept and managed to drag himself into the shower with a head that throbbed like a record-breaking hangover. Ailsa's cold air peeled back the groggy layers blanketing his brain. Briskly, he rubbed his hands over arms and legs to hasten the evaporation. He smiled as new life tingled into leadened limbs. Today he needed to be totally alert . . .

. . . The smile faded. *Totally alert*—the shadowman's words. Reality hammered home. The drug had done more than left him drowsy. For a moment, he forgot that Ailsa was . . .

Or was it another indication of mental collapse?

The air jets died with a protesting hiss; the door to the shower cubicle slid open. Cassell stepped out. Ailsa's ghosts waited.

Spectres rose to greet him from every corner of the dressing area, reminders of the woman whose life he once shared. Combs, brushes, a tidy shelf of cosmetics, a dressing mirror, surrounded him, pressing in. Gently he ran a hand over a row of neatly hung clothes. The fabrics, synthetic and natural, even those used in her work coveralls, were soft and flowing, sensual to his fingertips.

And all were empty and lifeless.

Cassell closed his eyes and struggled to swim above the engulfing tide of memories. They belonged to another time, the past, whether he wanted it or not. He breathed deeply to steady himself. A musky sweetness hung in the air. Like a coy fragrance clinging to a lover's pillow, it lingered in his nostrils. Tears welled beneath his eyelids.

With sudden resignation, he brushed the wetness from his cheeks, turned, jerked a change of clothing from a row hanging opposite Ailsa's, and quickly slipped into them. She was gone, dead. He could not change that. Memories would not bring Ailsa back. He had to accept it. He had to.

Determination did nothing to lessen the pain as he walked through the other rooms of the house. It had been a mistake to return here so soon. Ailsa was still too alive. He needed time before he could face and conquer her overwhelming presence within their home. To remain would only drive him closer to the edge.

The computer screen across the living room drew his

attention. He remembered. The shadowman. New doubts rushed forward in a relentless assault. The threads of reality strained. He had to talk with someone, to sort through everything and find the answers.

*Answers?* Were there any answers? An irrational certainty told him answers existed. He just needed help in finding them. He couldn't turn to Ailsa's and his mutual friends. They would be worse than the house, their sympathetic smiles, their uneasiness as they strived to comfort him. Parlan? He recoiled from the thought of seeking the physician's aid. Psycho-reconditioning frightened him. Electronic probes could erase doubts and eradicate memories, but nothing would be solved, no answers found. *Totally alert,* the shadowman's image rolled in his mind. He had to remain totally alert.

Who?

*Ragah Tvar.* Cassell found security in the thought of the man. Others could aid him more, he was sure of that. But could they be trusted? Every name among friends and business associates held a nagging doubt with it. He reached for the tri-phone and punched Tvar's number.

While he recounted the dreams since their first occurrence in the AG Module, Cassell watched the skepticism grow in Ragah's expression. Politely the man tried to disguise his disbelief, but it seeped through despite all his attempts to retain an open mind. How else was he supposed to react? Cassell was not sure, but not like this. He stopped in mid-sentence.

The unexpected silence drew Ragah's questioning gaze. "Jonal, is something wrong?"

"You don't believe a thing I've told you." Cassell sank back into his chair, feeling defeated. "I'm sorry I bothered you. There doesn't seem to have been any need for you to have come here."

"You were right in calling me." Ragah leaned forward, sincerity written all over his face. "You needed a friend, and I'm here to help. I understand your want to get away from the house. Ailsa has been dead for over a month, and I can still feel her here. For you, it must be unbearable. You should get an apartment in Farrisberg . . . stay there a month or two, until you can face coming back here. You know, you're welcome to stay with me until the apartment release comes through."

Ragah, ever afraid of offending, neatly sidestepped the issue of whether he believed what he had heard, Cassell noted. It was like his friend. Cassell took a direct route. "What about the dreams?"

Ragah glanced around nervously, his gaze eventually coming to rest on the floor. "I don't know. But I think you should see Parlan. Perhaps it's like he said, the dreams stem from your inability to accept Ailsa's death."

"Murder, my wife was murdered!" Cassell snapped, surprised by the sharp edge to his voice. He tried to calm himself, but Ragah's disbelief irritated him. "And the shadowman? The things he told me weren't just dreams. I told you about the computer. How do you explain that?"

"I don't know, Jonal." Ragah's eyes refused to meet his. "I don't know."

"Neither do I," Cassell said. "That's why I need your help."

"I'll do whatever I can, but I'm not sure I can help." The man looked doubtful. "Parlan could . . ."

"No! I don't need Parlan." Cassell shoved from the chair, shouting. "Perhaps later, but not now. I've got to have answers, work this out somehow."

"But psycho-reconditioning . . ."

"Won't give me any answers." Cassell walked to the computer unit. "Ragah, I don't know what to do. Maybe you're right and Parlan is the answer. But I've got to come to that conclusion on my own. Right now, going to Parlan seems wrong, too drastic."

Ragah rose and came to Cassell's side. He reached

out and squeezed his friend's shoulder. "All right, I said I was willing to help. What do I do first?"

Cassell smiled with gratitude when he turned to the computer and keyed a link to the Farrisberg Library reference banks. When the gray-green screen commanded him to proceed, he once again paired his dream victims' names with their homeworlds. "I want you to study these and see if you can detect some connection between them."

The screen blinked:

ADUM SAHT—TALALD III
No existing information available.

Cassell stared incredulously at the terminal. He felt Ragah's gaze on him. The screen fluttered:

JAVAS GARRIDAN—LANATIA
No existing information available.

"There must be something wrong. Some electronic foul-up . . . blown circuits . . ." Cassell watched the display terminal wink once more to proclaim no information existed on Ragnar Oles of Vertos. His fingers stabbed at the keys, repeating his call for information retrieval.

Four times the screen's luminescent letters denied any knowledge of Adum Saht, Javas Garridan, Ragnar Oles, or Bina Fanett.

"Jonal . . ." Ragah said softly.

Cassell shoved him aside. For the third time he punched the six names into the computer. For the third time, the screen replied that no such information existed.

"I don't understand. Last night . . . it was . . ." Cassell staggered back, his gaze riveted to the terminal. From thin air a sledgehammer had fallen. Taut, tauter, reality's threads stretched.

"Jonal." Ragah took his arm and led him to a chair. "You've got to take it easy. You've gone through hell."

*And lost my mind along the way. Last night, it was so real. It couldn't have been just another dream. Yet . . .*

"Jonal, you need to rest. Coming back here was too much for you." Ragah sounded muffled, a kilometer away. "I'll call Parlan."

*Parlan?* A day or two more in the hospital, then everything would be back to normal. Like the sleeping pills, it would be so easy to accept the reconditioning. Too easy. Remove the questions in a bath of chemicals and dancing electrons, then there would be no need for answers. So easy.

He glanced at the computer. The information was there last night. *It was there!* He knew what he had seen. It had been there. He had no explanation for the lack of information today, but he *knew* what he had seen. It did not make sense, but neither did Ailsa's murder. Parlan could not give him the answers he wanted. There was only one man on Tula who could.

Standing, Cassell moved beside Ragah, who stood at the phone, and slammed his palm down on the CANCEL bar. "I'm not ready for Parlan."

"Jonal, you need help," Ragah protested, while Cassell punched out a request for a bubble cab.

Cassell turned to his friend. Ragah's eyes widened with uncertainty. The smaller man retreated a step. *Am I that frightening? Is insanity that apparent?* Ragah reached for the phone again. Cassell knocked his arm away.

"I don't want to hurt you," he said. His right fist rose, clenched and threatening. "But if I have to, I'll stop you. We're going to the Zivon Building."

Ragah's face paled, and he backstepped farther, visibly shaken by his friend's threat of violence. More frightening, Cassell realized, was the fact that he would have struck Ragah had it been necessary.

"All right . . . all right, Jonal. I said I'd help you." Ragah swallowed. "I'll go with you, but I don't think . . ."

"That you'll go is enough." Cassell grabbed his friend's arm and ushered him to the liftshaft that led to the surface.

Cassell leaned back, letting the bubble cab's cushioned seat fully support his weight. Above the cab's transparent canopy, fluffy white clouds floated lazily across a blue sky. Despite the hurricane wiping through his brain, he felt an inward calmness. He was taking action, not just sitting and bemoaning the twisted circumstances that sought to ensnare him. Whether the course he took would prove of any value was of no concern. The action, moving off high center, was what was important.

His gaze moved to Ragah, seated opposite him within the cab's cramped confines. The man's color had returned, and, at least outwardly, he seemed to have conquered his fear. Cassell knew better. At the first opportunity, Ragah would call Parlan and report in detail everything that had happened. Then there would be no choice, he would have to undergo psycho-reconditioning. Still, there was Ailsa's murderer. If he could get the answers he needed...

He caught Ragah's attention. The man cleared his throat. His lips parted as if to speak, then closed. His Adam's apple bobbed a couple of times, and he finally said, "Jonal, do you really think seeing this man will accomplish anything?"

"I don't know," Cassell replied. "At the moment, it's the only thing I can do."

"Zivon has an investigative team here to handle this," Ragah said. "What can you do they can't?"

"Nothing probably, but . . ." He did not finish. Ragah would not understand. The same complacency he had noticed in the workers during shift change yesterday now dulled his friend's face, an unnatural, unquestioning acceptance. "Ragah, why was Ailsa killed?"

The smaller man's forehead creased with puzzle-

67

ment. "Someone was trying to kill you. Ailsa's death was an accident."

"*Why*, that's what I've been asking myself over and over, but I've never really thought it through," Cassell said. "Ailsa died instead of me, yet why would anyone want me dead?"

"Your leadership of the Autonomy Party," Ragah answered. "I think that's obvious."

"Which means someone, or something, wanted to stop, or at least impede, the vote on independence."

"Something?"

"Who would benefit the most if Tula's autonomy were blocked?" Cassell challenged with an intense stare.

Ragah's eyes widened, and he slowly shook his head. "No, you aren't implying Zivon had anything to do with Ailsa's murder?"

"Can you think of anyone who has more to protect? Zivon's got a profitable monopoly sewn up on Tula. If Tula's electorate were to choose to govern themselves, Zivon would suddenly find itself in competition with other combines wanting a share of our trade," Cassell said. "The loss of a planet seems to be motivation enough to order an assassination."

"Jonal, you can't believe that!" Ragah's expression reflected the sacrilege Cassell suggested. "Zivon is built on the concept of nonviolence. You truly can't think the Company was involved in Ailsa's murder?"

"No . . . no," Cassell admitted to himself as much as to Ragah. "That's what is so damn frustrating. If not Zivon, then who—and *why*?"

Ragah leaned forward as though Cassell's line of reasoning had penetrated. "Perhaps someone within Zivon's Tula administration? An individual whose position is threatened by independence."

"Perhaps," Cassell mused aloud. The possibility was valid, more palatable than Zivon being involved. Still, the Company had a financial monopoly on Tula.

The bubble cab slowed, entering Farrisberg's business district. Ahead rose the Zivon Building. White in the late afternoon sun, the structure towered over all the city's buildings, Tula's heart since the planet was colonized fifty years ago.

Cassell studied the building. Its exterior provided no insight to the questions convoluting through his head. Zivon had everything to gain by stemming the independence movement, but he could not conceive of the Company ordering his murder. Zivon held the real means to successfully eliminate anything they opposed—Tula's economy. They had no need of violence, just quietly tie a few purse strings. Much cleaner and much easier.

*If not Zivon, then who? And why?*

Was the flaw in his reasoning something or someone overlooked? A member of the Autonomy Party could want him out of the way, hoping to take over the party's leadership. Or was his own ego, his own self-importance, standing in the way of seeing the real motive? Ailsa? Was this a case of simple jealousy, a former lover seeking revenge? Worse, had the assassin achieved his purpose? Had Ailsa been the killer's target and he the one who had gotten in the way? Cassell let an over-held breath hiss through his teeth in frustration.

"What is it, Jonal?" Ragah eyed him carefully.

"Nothing, just a stupid thought." Cassell admitted to himself that his rambling web of reasoning was tenuous. Any Tulan seeking to harm either Ailsa or himself would be detected during their yearly psycho-profile evaluation; antisocial tendencies eliminated via psycho-reconditioning. Zivon returned to the forefront of his suspects.

The cab announced their approaching destination. It swung from the main concourse and trundled down a single slot to halt before Zivon's administrative complex.

Inside the building, Cassell produced his identification card and announced his intentions to an information clerk. In turn, the clerk, who wore the lapel nametag ARS ESTIN, took the plastic card, pressed it to a vidcom screen, and repeated the request. He then directed Cassell to a line of chairs near the lift and dropshafts at the center of the building's lobby. With Ragah at his side, Cassell took the offered chair and waited.

Ten minutes later a slim, stone-faced woman in Zivon Security Branch yellow approached. Without so much as an introduction, she asked for Cassell's identification, verified it, then escorted Cassell and Tvar to a liftshaft. Twenty levels up, they exited. An overweight woman in a muted brown suit stood obviously waiting for their arrival. She tilted a head of thinning black hair, and the woman in yellow walked down a hall to take a position to one side of a door already guarded by a man in similar yellow coveralls. The woman in the brown suit looked at Cassell and smiled:

"Citizen Cassell, I'm honored by your visit. The name's Leig, Vrinda Leig, Zivon Security Terra, assigned to investigate your wife's murder."

"No official authorities from Earth?" Cassell asked, surprised to find Zivon employees handling the investigation.

Leig's smile drooped to a wounded pout. "Zivon holds colonial jurisdiction in this matter. Terran police can be called in if it is deemed necessary. Company policy, however, is to conduct such investigations without outside interference if at all possible."

"Is it possible?" Cassell felt invisible walls being thrown up around him. The woman's association with Zivon had all the signs of a cover-up. Suspicion and irritation crept into his voice. "And if it is, when?"

Leig's ego-bruised expression hardened to a defensive one. She replied sharply, "It's difficult to judge ho‐‐ long a matter such as this will take. Progress has been made, Mr. Cassell. We apprehended your wife's murderer when he attempted to leave Tula posing as a media representative. Had my team not been . . ."

"Citizen Leig, that was a full week ago." Cassell cut

ner short before she launched into an account of the capture and the efficiency of her investigation. "Has anything happened since then? What have you learned from the prisoner?"

The woman's mouth opened, then closed as though she decided verbal strong-arm tactics would be useless. She stared at him a moment or two, then said, "Come into my office."

Cassell and Ragah followed the woman into a room opposite the door guarded by the two in yellow. Motioning for them to take two chairs within the small office, Leig stepped behind a desk and pressed several buttons on a side console. The lights dimmed and a vidcom screen on the wall came alive.

"This is your wife's murderer," Leig said.

The vidcom revealed a lone man stretched atop a portable cot. In the background, a barred window was visible. Cassell studied the man. He did not know what he expected a murderer to look like, but this man seemed too young, too thin, too frail.

"Looks too young to be such a bloody bastard, doesn't he?" Leig said. "But we've got positive identification on him. Plus he was still carrying the gun used to kill your wife when we picked him up."

"And?" Cassell turned to the investigator.

Leig's eyes darted away and she shook her head. "I'm afraid that's it. We don't know his name, age, or homeworld. We speculate he's a hired assassin, probably Terra-born by his accent. But there's nothing definite. We've got visuals, voice prints, and fingerprints fed into every police computer available and haven't come up with a thing."

She paused, but when Cassell said nothing continued, "Always try the criminal records first, just in case, to save time. If we have to tie into the general population banks, it could take a year or two before we came up with anything. I wouldn't be surprised if the police don't have anything on this one. He's young. Might not have a record yet."

Cassell looked back to the vidcom. "What about him?"

"Haven't been able to get anything out of him," Leig replied. "I've got a team of the best investigators in the business on this case. We tried every legal method of interrogation, and some not quite so legal. The man can't tell us anything."

"Can't?" Cassell asked. "Or won't?"

"Can't. He's apparently undergone something similar to what Tulans refer to as psycho-reconditioning," Leig said. "The method's been used before, especially in cases of murder for hire. Erasure of short-term memories is a fairly simple process."

Cassell sensed the invisible walls creep closer together, hemming him into a neat, inescapable box.

"As best as we can tell, the man has no memories of what happened," Leig said. "He has no memories of killing your wife, or a maintenance man whose body was found in the Assembly Hall."

"Are you sure?" Cassell asked. "Can he somehow be faking a memory loss?"

"I'm as sure as anyone can be in a case like this. There is documentation of a few individuals who have resisted mental probes," the woman replied, "but I think that possibility can be ruled out here. He's been examined by five psychiatrists. They concur; he's undergone reconditioning of some sort."

Cassell rose in an attempt to shake the claustrophobic presence of the invisible walls. It could not end this way. Everything hung in the air, unanswered. Somewhere a loose end dangled. Whoever, whatever, was behind Ailsa's murder had overlooked something. All he had to do was find it.

"What do you intend to do now?" Cassell stared at Vrinda Leig. "Someone has to be responsible for the man's memory erasures. What about that person?"

"We're doing everything we possibly can," Leig assured him. "But this investigation will take time..."

"Time to forget!" Cassell made no attempt to disguise

his mounting suspicion. "Once out of the public eye, it will be easy to bury my wife's murder in bureaucratic red tape."

"Cassell, Zivon has no intention of concealing anything," Leig said with an appropriate display of indignation. "We want to find those responsible for your wife's murder as much as you do!"

Cassell tuned her out. Words were empty; he wanted results, something tangible. The vidcom screen flickered, electron tracks tracing the image of a lone man in a makeshift prison cell. "I want to talk with him."

The woman glared at him, her dark eyes smoldering at the contempt he flaunted in the face of her authority. Yet, she nodded. "He's in the room across the hall."

Cassell felt their eyes, Ragah, Leig, the two yellow-clad guards, sensed their smug satisfaction at his failure. In an hour he had been unable to get even a simple "yes" or "no" answer to his questions from Ailsa's killer. The man just sat there on the edge of his cot, that smirk curled on his lips—a taunt that spoke of his self-confidence, secure in the knowledge that he had been well-protected.

"Cassell." Leig's hand touched his shoulder. "It's useless. You had better leave now."

"In a moment." He brushed the hand away, his eyes never leaving the assassin. "Whom were you working for? Who hired you?"

The man lazily lifted his head and looked to Leig. His cocksure smirk twisted his mouth. "I'm tired. Take this citizen away and leave me alone."

"Come on, Cassell." Leig gripped his shoulder again.

It could not end this way, Ailsa's murder erased from her killer's mind. Someone, something, was responsible; they could not escape this easily. He would not let it end here.

"Cassell, I want you out of here." Leig's fingers tightened with determination. "I gave you your chance, now get out."

The taut threads of reality unraveled. The dreams, the shadowman, the computer. Each tightly woven strand snapped like a violin string, the terrible rent resounding in his mind. Ailsa was dead. Someone had to pay.

Alien sensations, desires—anger, hate, rage, revenge—coursed through the frayed fibers of his brain with the explosive impact of pure sodium touching water. Warm, pliant flesh suddenly lay beneath his palms. He heard a startled cry of terror. His hands closed, squeezing into the vulnerable neck he clutched. The cry died in a desperate strangled gurgle.

Shouts hailed from over Cassell's shoulder. Feet scrambled over the polished tile floor. He closed them off and focused his total consciousness on the closing windpipe beneath his fingertips. He reveled while the man's eyes bulged wide, wider. A shower of blows hammered against his face. Hot, thick moisture trickled from his battered nose to fill his mouth with the taste of rusty salt. He ignored it all. *Someone had to pay.*

A sledgehammer slammed into his spine. He gritted his teeth and cursed, shaking off the jarring impact. Tighter his fingers clenched in an attempt to force themselves into the pliant throat. Hands tore at him, pried at his wrists. He screamed out against them. They persisted.

His hands came free, fingers rigidly sliding from bruised flesh. He tumbled back; arms yanked and tugged at him.

"Get him out of here!" He recognized Leig's voice. "Get a doctor in here to look at this man!"

Cassell felt himself jerked upright, shoved backwards. A tempered calm suffused through the mental storm, awakening him to his surroundings. Leig huddled by the cot to help her choking prisoner rise. The man's eyes opened, and he gingerly rubbed at his neck. *He lives—Ailsa's murderer still lives!* Cassell groaned.

Through the door, they dragged him. His back thudded solidly against a corridor wall, and the two-yellow clad guards held him there, pinned beneath their com-bined weight.

"They should lock this one up, too," the woman said. "I thought this was supposed to be a nonviolent world."

"Don't be too hard on him. That bastard in there killed his wife. I'd probably do the same thing if I were in his position," the other guard said. "I've got him now. You'd better get a doctor."

Before the woman could answer, Cassell heard Ra-gah. "I'll do it. Jonal's under a physician's care. He'll . . ."

*Parlan!* Panic etched deeply. Cassell heard a voice scream, "Noooooo!"

The voice was his own. His knee jerked up and buried itself in the male guard's groin. A moan of pain tearing from his lips, the man folded, then crumpled to the floor. The woman's head jerked around to meet Cassell's descending fist. She joined her companion, two yellow blotches staining the corridor's white tile.

Cassell ran.

# SEVEN

Cassell stopped. His lungs burned, and his legs ached with knotting cramps. He stood. How long, or where, he was unaware. Eventually, he turned full circle to examine his surroundings with dull, unseeing eyes.

*Running?* It tickled into his consciousness, a minor sensation like the flick of a feather's tip. *Why?* It seemed of no consequence, yet it sat there a half-remembered wisp of something. He reached for a shattered fragment. Liquid, it slipped through his mental fingers.

He did not mind. More important was the aggravating itch on his upper lip. He considered it a moment before lifting a hand to scratch. His fingertips felt a thick, sticky moisture. Idly, he glanced down.

Blood.

Cassell trembled. It rushed back in a deluge. He moaned, his cry quavering and wild. The Zivon Building! The prisoner! The guards! He thrust them away, unable to accept the madness that swept through him in a drowning torrent. His thumb rubbed small circles in the blood coating his fingertips. *Must be a mess.* He had to clean himself before he attracted attention.

Around him, buildings poked above the leafy tops of trees. Irony rippled across his lips, the vague hint of a smile. He still held an inkling of sanity. He knew where he was. A kilometer from the Zivon Building, he stood in a small park at the middle of Farrisberg. Years ago, he spent his lunch breaks here. The park provided a welcomed change from the monotony of office routine. Now, it felt right, firmly set in the secure past, unchanged.

He surveyed the park again. He was alone. Apparently Leig's guards had not followed. For the moment, at least, the park offered him shelter.

He walked to a small pavilion at the park's center and entered the rest room. In a wall-length mirror hung over a line of sinks, he carefully examined his face. Blood caked his nostrils and upper lip. Pressing the top of a faucet, he released a steady flow of water. He cupped his hands under the cold stream and bathed his face several times.

He looked into the mirror again and nodded. With the blood gone, he appeared human, better than he had expected. Both nose and lips were swollen, but he could live with them. Gently, he tested his nose with a fingertip. Tender, yet he found no serious damage.

Drying his face, Cassell turned his attention to his clothes. Surprisingly, they were unbloodied. Rumpled and wrinkled, they looked as though he had spent a rough night in them. However, they were less likely to attract attention than had they been splattered in red.

Satisfied with his appearance, Cassell left the rest room. He stopped outside the pavilion and drank deeply from a water fountain to remove the dry cotton left balled in his throat from his flight. Glancing around and still finding himself alone, he started walking with no particular destination in mind. At the back of his thoughts was the possibility that Leig and her guards might be searching for him and he should keep on the move. The prospect of being a hunted fugitive really did not bother him. He needed to think and walking helped.

Like a man peeling away the layers of an onion, he sifted through the scattered fragments of the day, carefully, trying to bring everything to a manageable level. On the surface, it was no more than another of the shadowman's convoluted nightmares. Only this was real. He had attacked Ailsa's killer. He realized he would have murdered the man had he not been torn from him. That the man's life was not enough meant nothing. It would have been a start. He could still feel the yielding flesh squilching up between his fingers. It felt good, right, not in sensual terms, but with the righteousness of vengeance.

*Good? Right?*

Deep within himself he sensed a grinding rumble. *Good?* It horrified him. *Right?* The very feel of the thought revolted him. Good and right found hand in hand with the violence he secretly nursed. It rent the fabric of his existence. A life's abhorrence to human cruelty splintered like cheap plastic veneer to bare the deep-seeded core of reality he harbored with guarded relish. He desired revenge. He wanted to inflict on another human being the suffering he endured. More terrifying was the very heart of that fiery core. He wanted vengeance for himself, not out of love for Ailsa, not in guilt that she died instead of him—but in pure selfishness to satisfy an inner need to return violence with violence.

Tremors mounted to full-fledged quakes that buckled the foundations of his sanity. His life lay naked, every aspect row atop row of intricately twisted crochets. What seemed simple and clear a month ago now made no sense. Unaware, he had been invaded, conquered, used, then discarded.

*How?*

78

A vision of the exploding podium erupted in his mind. He scurried back in a cowed retreat. Ailsa's death offered nothing but a dead end, no relief, only those two elusive questions—WHO? WHY? The answers appeared more distant than ever.

Like a loop of tape fed into a reverberation system, Zivon repeated over and over in his mind. All avenues dovetailed into Zivon. Perhaps the Company stood as the obvious answer, perhaps his own devotion to Tula obscured his reasoning, perhaps . . . he had no valid reason for his denial. He simply could not accept Zivon as the force that shredded the fabric of his life.

Ragah had to be right. An individual wanted him dead, someone within Zivon or the party who would gain from his death. He steadied himself and sought the rational amid the jumbled straws of irrationality. He grasped at logic to shield him from the swirling vortex of insanity that sucked him downward.

Someone with off-world contacts, he snared one fragment of the spinning flotsam. Leig suspected the assassin came from off-planet, Terra because of his accent. That meant money, enough to bring a hired killer halfway across the galaxy, then arrange the reconditioning the murderer had undergone. Could an individual arrange that? On Earth it would be simple. But on Tula? The risks of discovery were too immense. Again, the annual psycho-profile evaluation required of every Tulan loomed like a barrier of solid granite, dead ending the mental avenue he traveled. The sessions were thorough, specifically designed to detect aberrant behavior. Corrective reconditioning was mandatory.

Which left . . . conspiracy?

He choked back the thought. It careened to the same conclusion, Zivon. The Company's planetwide organization could arrange everything needed, and nobody would ever suspect. Who else could shield a criminal psychiatrist, slip an assassin on-world undetected?

And the Farrisberg Library reference banks, his list

of victims and planets? Tula's computer network belonged to Zivon. They controlled it, continually fed new information into it—and ordered programs erased.

Cassell shook his head. That morning he had been so certain about what he had seen on the terminal. Now, could he be positive? For a man who dreamed of murder, had attempted to strangle a man, hallucination was just another symptom of a deteriorating mental . . .

*No!* The information had been in the reference banks last night. Today it wasn't!

That left one alternative. The information had been tampered with. Someone selectively erased the computer program, eliminating his assassination victims from the library's memory. And that pointed to more than money being involved. It meant power, access to the inaccessible.

It also meant they watched him, monitored his activities. For the names to be erased, someone had to know that he had retrieved those seemingly unrelated bits of the computer's memory, information that somehow presented a threat.

The shadowman? Cassell's nightmare tormentor slipped into the picture. If the elusive "they" held the resources to wipe out a killer's memory, then they could have been capable of tampering with his mind while he recovered in the AG Module.

It fit. They faltered in their attempt to kill him, now they attacked on a new front. Disgustingly clear, his focus sharpened. Weave a thread of insanity into his mind, and they could accomplish what the assassin's bullet failed to do. *Had accomplished!* Once his attack on Ailsa's killer was leaked to the media, Jonal Cassell, member of the Supreme Council, leader of the Autonomy Party, would be discredited, branded totally insane.

A cold sweat prickled over him, heat flushed his face. Had he been manipulated that easily? Less than a day after his release from the hospital and he performed his programmed task like an unthinking, obedient zombie.

The clarity blurred. Neatly placed pieces spun away in total disarray. Everything happened too fast and was too alien. It seemed so logical, and, at the same time, it made no sense.

Cassell looked around him, seeking to draw assurance that some sanity remained from the material substance around him. He had wandered a half kilometer from the park. Evening cloaked Farrisberg in a flat gray. Here and there workers late for shift change hurried to their destinations. Already bubble cabs from the residential districts shuttled passengers into the city to patronize the varied restaurants and theaters.

Estranged and a light year away, he no longer belonged to the peaceful world about him. Ragah was right; Leig was right. His own stability wavered. Tula was a dream of perfection that had found a reality. The wrongness came from within, not from without. He needed Parlan and the psycho-reconditioning. The investigation of Ailsa's murder should be left to Leig and her team of professionals. What could he do, except . . . try to kill the only lead in the case?

Vividly the afternoon's incidents flashed through his mind. Every minute detail became a brand of burning madness, the contorted workings of a deranged mind.

—You took a step on your own, and now you can't accept it. Disgusting. Jonal, for a man who leads one of this planet's most powerful political parties, you act like a child.

Cassell froze, his body rigid. *The shadowman?* He wasn't asleep. He didn't dream.

—Right or wrong, you did what anyone would have done when confronting the man who had killed his wife. Why do you think police normally don't allow such confrontations? They don't want to be responsible for another murder. Only on this cockeyed world would authorities even contemplate letting you close to the killer.

81

It was not his imagination. He was awake, and he heard the shadowman. Cassell jerked around. His eyes darted about in a frantic search for the voice's owner. He found no one.

—Too bad you botched it. Strangulation was totally inept. You didn't have enough time to do any real damage, just choked the bastard a bit. A hammer fist to the temple, an upward palm slammed to the nose would have been effective. But it's too late now. They'll never let you close to him again.

Cassell trembled. He drew himself in, trying to escape the disembodied voice. This couldn't be happening. It couldn't be.

—Don't worry about it. Leig's prisoner isn't the one you really want. He would have been nice for openers. But the ones you have to find are those who paid for his services. That's where we'll concentrate your efforts.

Was he beyond Parlan's help?

—Forget this insanity crap! You're clouding the real issue. You've got to find the answers.

"Answers?"

—The ones that are eating at you.

It was insanity. His fingernail grasp of reality slipped.

—Dammit! Stop whining! This whole screwed up world is insane, not you. Look around. Tula can't exist. Man can't live this way. Find the answers, Jonal. Find them.

"Where? How? I don't know what to do."

—Yerik Belen has the answers. Find Belen, Yerik Belen, and you'll find the answers.

"Yerik Belen? Who is he?" The shadowman did not answer. Cassell knew no Belen. He called to the shadowman, "Who is Yerik Belen?"

"Can I help you?" A woman spoke, and a hand touched his shoulder.

Cassell spun around, suddenly aware that he had been speaking aloud to the shadowman. People gathered about him; they stared and whispered among themselves. His own doubts were reflected in their questioning eyes.

"Is there anything wrong?" the woman asked.

Cassell shook his head numbly. Ten meters down the walkway, an empty bubble cab sat poised by a ramp. He pushed through the crowd and moved toward the vehicle. He knew what to do now. Dreams did not talk to stable men, voices did not materialize out of thin air. He would return home and call Parlan before it was too late to salvage the last shredded remnants of his sanity.

"I've seen him before," a man's voice followed him. Another answered, "On the holo. That's Jonal Cassell."

His feet hastened. He ducked into the vacant cab and punched his home coordinates into the driver console. Cassell then sank down into the couch, unable to quiet the spasmlike shudders that shook his body.

The ground irised open. Cassell stepped into the dropshaft and gently floated into the living room of his home. He took one step and stopped. Two men dressed in hospital green sat on the sofa. Somehow it did not surprise him. Ragah and Parlan covered all bases.

"Cassell," the taller of the two said, more of a statement of recognition than a question, when they rose.

"No need for haste," Cassell replied. "I was going to call Parlan. I've decided he's right. I do need psycho-reconditioning. I was ..."

Both men reached inside their green smocks. Metal glinted in their hands when they pulled them free.

Cassell needed only one glance to recognize and react to the pistols. His arm swung back, palm slapping the light panel beside the dropshaft. Instantly, darkness blanketed the room. He dropped to the floor.

Two fiery blossoms hissed in the blackness. Something thudded into the wall behind him. Thunder exploded and splinters showered his back. *Explosive projectiles!* He hugged the carpet closer.

"The liftshaft!" He recognized the taller man's voice. "Cover it."

Feet shuffled toward him. Cassell rolled away, still keeping himself near the light panel. The feet stopped; so did he. For long minutes, with only the sound of his heart thumping like a bass drum in his ears, he mentally pictured the darkened living room. One man stood by the sofa roughly two meters away. The other guarded the liftshaft less than a meter from where he lay. The only items he could possibly use as weapons were across the room, and those were no match for the pistols. Besides, the man by the sofa successfully blocked movement in that direction. He could do nothing but wait.

Near the sofa, something moved, black against black in the dark room. Cassell listened to the approaching footsteps. He sucked in a deep breath, and drew himself into a tight crouch. Closer the carpet-muted steps came. He tensed, judging distance by sound.

A step away, he leaped. Upward his left arm swept before him. It slammed into the man's extended gun hand and drove it over his head. Light flashed and another explosion resounded. Simultaneously, Cassell drove his right palm toward the unseen face. Hard, his body weight behind the blow, he struck on target. He felt the crunch of broken bone, the nose give way, then slide up into the man's brain cavity.

Together, they toppled to the floor. Cassell's fists pounded into the man's temples. Again the pistol fired. The taller man's fingers tightened in a knee-jerk reflex to death. Then he was still.

Running a hand along the dead man's arm, Cassell pried lifeless fingers from the gun. His own palm cradled the solid security of the pistol butt. A finger rested lightly on the trigger.

"Wal?" Cassell's second assailent whispered. "Wal?"

"Yeah." Cassell muffled his voice against an arm. "He's dead."

"I'll get the lights."

Crouching, Cassell lifted the gun and honed in on the black shadow that moved against the room's darkness. He closed his left hand around his right wrist to steady its trembling.

The lights flashed on, their harsh glaring flooding the room. In a heartbeat, Cassell sighted on his assailant's forehead, saw the man's bewildered expression, saw his gun hand begin to rise. Smoothly, Cassell squeezed the trigger.

The pistol fired, its recoil throwing his braced arm upward. A dark hole appeared between the man's eyes. The would-be killer jerked back. Then the projectile exploded. Cassell turned away from the shower of gore.

Pressing a finger against the jugular of the man beside him on the floor, Cassell felt for a pulse. There was none. Dead—both men were dead. He had killed them!

His whole body quaked. That the two would have taken his life had no meaning. He had killed. He commanded his fingers to uncurl from the pistol butt. They refused to move. He wanted to scream, but his voice froze within his throat. He had killed. *I had to!* His brain rejected the necessity of his action.

"I had to!" he screamed aloud.

Something penetrated his terror-tormented mind. Like nagging, half-heard whispers it came to him. He listened, trying to discern the words. Disjointedly, his head cocked from side to side.

From the corner of an eye, he caught blurred movement. He swung around, pistol leveled against a new attack. Two men stood by the dropshaft. Their faces whitened. *Fear? Horror?* He blinked. *Ragah and Parlan.* He stared at their moving lips, straining to hear their undistinguishable whispers.

Ragah stepped toward him, but was halted by the physician's raised arm. Then Parlan slowly moved forward with an outstretched hand.

"Jonal..." Cassell heard his name whispered. He

twisted his head to one side, unable to make out the other words.

Parlan came closer, cautiously kneeling before him. "The gun, Jonal. Give me the gun."

Parlan's lips conformed to the whispered sounds, but the words seemed to come from another source. Cassell stared at the doctor, unable to comprehend what he wanted.

"Relax. I'm not going to hurt you, Jonal." The whisper continued, sounding more like Parlan's voice. "Just relax. I've come to help you. But you've got to give me the gun first."

Cassell relaxed, uncertain, but incapable of moving through the haze fogging his mind. Parlan could help. He was a doctor. He would help.

—Jonal, don't let him have it!

The shadowman screamed at him. New terror coursed through his brain.

—Don't trust him! Get out of here! Run, Jonal, run!

Parlan's hand closed about his. Cassell's fingers relaxed, and the gun slipped from them. A weight lifted from his mind and body.

"Now, Jonal," Parlan said in reassuring tones, "I'll give you this, and you'll start to feel better."

Cassell saw the hypodermic, felt the hot spike of pain as compressed air emptied its contents into his arm.

"Count backwards from one hundred," the doctor said.

*Ludicrous.* Two men lay dead on the floor of his home and Parlan wanted him to count backwards. He wasn't insane, but Parlan was. Cassell wanted to tell the physician that.

—Fool! Fight it, Jonal. Fight it!

Cassell no longer listened. He closed his eyes and slept.

Impatiently, Bron Cadao waited while the communiqué came through the computer. In all his time on

Tula, nothing had ever gotten this far out of hand. Cassell still lived, and two of the agency's operatives were dead.

The man shook his head in total disbelief. How could Cassell have taken them? Both were trained and capable, or they would not have been on-planet in the first place. Whatever their mistakes, the results were quite evident; mistakes he had no intention of repeating if his superiors had not changed their minds once again.

The possibility of their indecisiveness bothered Cadao more than the prospect of having to kill Cassell himself. If his superiors were stupid enough to allow Zivon to send a team of investigators to Tula, they were stupid enough to do anything.

Cadao regretted having informed them that Cassell was now in Parlan's care. It was just the sort of information they needed to change their minds once again. The chance that Cassell could be saved via reconditioning was the sort of thing they had been grasping for since Black Sheep botched his assignment.

To allow Cassell to live would be a mistake. Surely even they could see that. He had killed two men. Cadao managed to cover up the incident as best he could, but too many people knew too much.

The computer stopped and stuck out a paper tongue. Cadao ripped it off and decoded his instructions. A pleased smile played lightly on his lips. His superiors had not proven the fools he thought them to be—at least not this time. They reconfirmed the previous orders. He was to kill Jonal Cassell.

Unlike his two former co-workers, he would not be sloppy. A few adjustments to Parlan's equipment and the Jonal Cassell problem would be eliminated. It would be quick and clean, accidental electrocution by a faulty psycho-reconditioning unit.

Cadao's smile grew.

# EIGHT

—Time is running out, Jonal. You have to pull yourself together and get the hell out of here.

The shadowman stood silhouetted before a glaring light. Cassell felt too drained to turn away from him.

—You really handled yourself quite well against those two men. It's taking time, but you're learning. However, you fell apart after that. Stupid, Jonal, very stupid.

*I killed them.* He knew the nightmare visitor would never understand how the killings tormented him, completely destroyed a lifetime devoted to nonviolence. *I killed two men.*

—Hell, yes, you killed them. If you hadn't, you wouldn't be here whining about it. It was either you or them. What else could you have done?

It sounded right when the shadowman said it, better than when he told himself the same thing. The two had been waiting to kill him. What else could he have done?

—Letting Parlan get his hands on you was a bad mistake. Now, you've got to do something about it before it's too late. They've tried to kill you twice. They won't stop until they succeed. While Parlan's got you, you're a sitting duck. You've got to keep on the move.

*Yes,* Cassell answered, doubting his sanity. Everything the shadowman said sounded logical. That was what frightened him.

—Sanity! Insanity! Jonal, can't you get it into your head, there's nothing wrong with you. You're sane. Can't you grasp that? *They* are the ones you've got to watch. They butchered your wife and are trying to kill you.

*But who are "they"? Why is all this happening to me? What have I done?*

—Find Yerik Belen.

*Who is Yerik Belen?* It was the second time the shadowman had urged him to find this Belen. The name meant nothing to him.

—Find Yerik Belen. Everything will be answered then.

*Where? Where can I find this Yerik Belen? Who is he?*

—Earth, Jonal, you'll find him on Earth. Find Yerik Belen and then you'll understand everything.

The light flared. The shadowman's silhouette went fuzzy around the edges, then faded. Cassell stood alone, left with a name resounding in his brain—Yerik Belen.

The buzz of swarming insects echoed down the well, enveloping Cassell. He retreated deeper into the pit. The drone intensified, punching holes in the comforting fabric of sleep. He floated upward.

—Caution, Jonal. Be careful. They'll be watching you.

He glanced around, unable to locate the shadowman. Upward he swam toward the light at the top of the well. The persistent buzzing took the shape of words:

"It's difficult to accept—two men. Any indication of what sent him over the edge?"

Cassell opened his eyes to narrow slits, while he

feigned sleep. Once again, he lay in a hospital room. Parlan and another man stood at the foot of his bed. He closed his eyes and listened.

"He's had reason enough," Parlan said. "I should have caught it sooner. The indications were there since he experienced dreams in the AG Module. I never thought he was homicidal. To kill those two attendants without provocation, I..."

*Without provocation? What about the pistols?* Cold realization tapped at Cassell's spine. Parlan had not seen his assailants' other weapon. Had Ragah? He doubted it. Finding him crouched beside the men would have been a total shock to both Parlan and Ragah. They would have been fully occupied with helping him, not attempting to discover what had occurred. He suppressed the urge to leap from bed and explain that the two attendants intended to murder him. Without the other pistol, he had no proof. The other gun would no longer be on the floor of his living room, he realized. The disposal of something so small would be easy for anyone capable of erasing library memory banks.

"Don't blame yourself. We've never confronted a case such as this on Tula," Parlan's companion said. "You know the problem now, and that you can correct it is all that is expected of you."

"I suppose you're right," Parlan answered in a subdued tone. "Still, I feel I share in his actions. Two men would be alive now had I acted when the symptoms first surfaced."

The irony was inescapable. Cassell was hard-pressed to hold back the sarcastic chuckle that rose in his throat. He lay flat on his back, fearing for life and sanity while his physician lolled around in a puddle of guilt and self-pity.

"How long has he been under sedation?" the other man asked.

"Two days," Parlan said. "Being uncertain how many sessions will be required to reestablish his normal character patterns, I want him well rested before I begin treatment."

The other man laughed softly. "I know at least ten of our colleagues who wish they were in your position. You'll have one hell of a monograph to present at the next medical association conference."

"I hadn't thought of that," Parlan said. "Remind me to arrange for a tape crew to cover the sessions tomorrow morning."

Cassell had heard enough. His life had just been reduced to the subject of a scholarly treatise to be authored by a neurotic psychiatrist. He stirred, stretched, and yawned. Blinking, he glanced around beneath leadened eyelids. The two men turned to him. Parlan smiled and walked beside the bed.

"Feeling better?" he asked. "You've been asleep for quite a while."

"A bit drowsy." Cassell maintained his charade. He blinked a few more times and blankly gazed about as though noting the room for the first time. "Where am I?"

"In the hospital, under my care again," Parlan said "Do you recall anything . . ."

"Two men attacked me in my own house." He had not meant to let that slip. He did not want Parlan to know just how lucid he was.

Parlan glanced at his colleague. The other man raised a disbelieving eyebrow and almost shook his head until he noticed Cassell's gaze on him.

Parlan's head turned back to his patient. He cleared his throat as though at a loss for words, or uncertain whether to press the subject further. "Mr. Tvar has informed me that you've been keeping your dreams from me."

He knew Ragah would tell the physician everything. But learning that his friend had actually done so left Cassell feeling somehow betrayed. Ragah had done what he felt was right; the same thing he would have done had their positions been reversed. It did not ease the abandoned feeling.

"I think it would help if you talked about it, Jonal," Parlan said, a pleasant bedside manner smile still plastered on his face. "It would make matters easier if we could get to the heart of your problem."

Cassell sucked his teeth with disgust and rolled away from the man. He wondered whether the doctor was sincere or merely delved for additional details to flesh out his forthcoming monograph on the deterioration and collapse of one Jonal Cassell.

"Very well," Parlan said. "Perhaps tomorrow you'll be ready to discuss your condition."

*With you drilling electronic probes into my brain.* He heard Parlan walk to the foot of the bed. The physician and his companion whispered. Cassell wanted to say something, to let Parlan know the subject of his monograph would never allow himself to be dragged into the psycho-reconditioning chamber. Deciding a verbal outburst would be foolish, he remained silent.

"I'll send an orderly in with a dinner tray," Parlan said while he and the other physician walked to the door. "I'll look in on you tomorrow morning."

When the two exited, Cassell rolled to his back and stared at the ceiling. Parlan had not mentioned the reconditioning scheduled for tomorrow. Apparently the psychiatrist did not intend to tell him what was planned, preferring to keep his patient ignorant. *A bit sadistic, twisted,* Cassell thought, *like everything in my life.*

—You're not going to let him do it, are you?

*Not you! Go away, I don't need your interference!* Cassell closed his eyes and held them clamped tightly. He feared to look around the room and find no one there.

—You need someone. This is a mess, Jonal.

It was. Whenever he managed to find some sense in all that occurred, the shadowman intruded. And there was no sense to the shadowman, except...Cassell

92

shuddered, denying everything about his mental invader.

—Don't withdraw, Jonal. You can't hide from the facts. If you don't get your ass out of bed, Parlan will get his claws into your brain tomorrow morning.

Cassell squeezed his eyes tighter, trying not to hear, not to feel, not to think.

—That's an intelligent answer, Jonal. Ignore everything and it will go away. It won't work. Tomorrow, Parlan is going to crawl into your mind with his probes. He's going to bathe your brain with chemicals. Subtly, he'll mold and rearrange you. Of course, when he's through, you won't realize what has happened. Everything will seem perfectly normal. But things will have changed. You won't be the same.

*I know, dammit! I know!* Parlan could help him, could shore the walls of his sanity. But at what price? Minor erasures were an integral part of reconditioning. How did Parlan intend to remold his psyche? What memories would his probes neatly sever? His dreams and the shadowman certainly would be stripped away. Ailsa's murder? He feared that would not be enough. The psychiatrist would delve further, wiping away portions of his life with Ailsa. He could not accept that. Memories were all that remained for him.

—That is if *they* allow you until the morning.

Cassell did not ask for clarification. The two attempts on his life had failed, and there was more than enough time for a third before morning. This time, they might succeed.

—You're beginning to get the picture. If you lay around here moaning and groaning, you won't see tomorrow. And if by some chance they do let you live, after Parlan gets through—you won't be you!

*I've got to get out of here,* Cassell finally admitted.

—The sooner, the better.

*Yes. Yes.*

—Remember, Yerik Belen. Find him and you'll understand everything.

93

Cassell opened his eyes and pushed to his elbows. Across the room was a closet. He threw back the covers, slipped from the bed, and walked to it. Inside a single rack stood bare except for a few clothes clips. Parlan took no chances. It was difficult for a man to consider an escape when his only clothing was a ridiculous robe that left his hindcheeks bare to the world.

The door to the room swung open. A nurse with food tray in hand was halfway through when an arm shot out to block his entrance. Another man stepped in front of him.

"Sorry, no one's allowed in there except Dr. Parlan and myself," the human barricade said firmly. "This one's a certified case for the brain blender. Killed two men. Unless you want to be number three, I'd let Alf take that into him."

"Don't be stupid," the nurse with the tray protested. "Alf, I'm quite capable of . . ."

Alf eased his fellow nurse back. The door closed, muffling their voices. Cassell cursed. His guess about a guard was correct. Parlan had placed a watchdog outside the room to assure his patient did not wander away.

Closing the closet, Cassell scrambled back into bed and slipped the sheet up around his neck. When the door opened again, he had once more assumed his drug-groggy pose. He gazed at the approaching Alf through half-opened eyes.

"Here you go, Mr. Cassell." The nurse-guard smiled, placed the dinner tray on a bed table, and rolled it forward. "Dr. Parlan had the kitchen prepare you something special this evening. There's your normal hospital fare. But if your stomach can handle it, there's also a nice hunk of meat here."

It was easy to see why Parlan selected Alf for guard duty. The man was *big*. His loose-fitting green tunic could not hide the powerful physique beneath. The nurse was obviously a devotee of body sculpturing. Muscles like the ones he sported did not come naturally, but through hours of progressive resistant exercise. The strength in each arm rippled with the slightest movement. Attached to each massive arm was a hand the size of a ham, a thick, meaty paw.

"Let me raise the bed some, then you can dig in." Alf touched a button on the bed's side. The upper portion of the bed lifted Cassell into a sitting position. The big nurse smiled again. "Looks good, doesn't it?"

Steamy aromas drifted up from the tray to tantalize Cassell's nostrils. Vacantly, his eyes rolled downward. Despite his drug-stupor charade, everything Alf offered looked more than palatable. His stomach rumbled. He recalled eating a light breakfast before visitng the Zivon Building. That had been three days ago. He had every reason to be hungry.

—And the condemned man ate a hearty meal.

The shadowman taunted and Cassell ignored him. His fingers closed around a plastic fork on the tray.

—One bite and it might be your last, Jonal.

Cassell dropped the fork. Paranoia coursed through him like poison from a ruptured cyst. It would be easy for whoever was trying to kill him to poison the food. For an instant, he considered slinging the tray across the room to remove its temptation. Instead, he sank back into the bed.

—That's good. Keep calm. No need to arouse the gorilla's suspicion.

"Come, Mr. Cassell, surely you're hungry," Alf said. "If you don't eat this, I guarantee I will."

The nurse lifted the fork and speared a couple of vegetables. He pressed the food against Cassell's lips. Cassell fought the urge to open wide and inhale the savory-looking morsels. Instead, he sat there, staring through the nurse as though the man were not before him. Persistent, Alf tried again with a bite of meat and received the same results.

"All right." Alf finally gave in with a shrug of his shoulders. "I'll leave this here. If you get hungry, just eat what you want." He walked to the door and turned back. "If you need anything, I'll be outside."

Cassell's attention returned to the food. The urge to shovel heaping forksful into his mouth bordered on the uncontrollable. He told himself his fears were ridiculous, irrational paranoia. Still, if Parlan did not believe the two men had attempted to kill him, the physician would have not taken any precautions in the meal's preparation. He shoved the bed table away, removing the temptation it presented.

—Good. Now get yourself out of this deathtrap.

Cassell eased from bed again and moved to the windows. As with most of Tula's buildings, the hospital was climate controlled. Built solidly into the wall, the windows did not open. They existed for lighting purposes only. He rejected the idea of breaking the glass after a glance outside. The room was several floors above the ground, eliminating even the age-old holodrama escape via bedsheets knotted together.

He turned his back on the windows and surveyed the room. The only exit was the door, and Alf quite efficiently guarded that avenue. Find clothes and remove Alf, if he could accomplish those two simple tasks, he could . . .

*Alf*. Cassell smiled. Hastily he glanced about the hospital room again. Atop a bedstand he found what he wanted, a white plastic water pitcher. He hefted the container.

—Too light.

Even filled with ice and water, the pitcher had little weight. But he did not want to kill the nurse, only daze him. It would do.

Cassell set the container back on the stand and returned to bed. Reaching out, he tipped the dinner tray over the edge of the bed table. It hit the tile floor like a crashing cymbal. Plastic dishes shattered in splintered shards; food splattered in messy globs and streaks.

Alf burst through the door before the racket subsided. He stared down at the spilled tray. Then, hands planted firmly on each side of his waist, the nurse looked up at Cassell for an explanation.

"The toilet," Cassell mumbled as though his tongue were still drug-thick and sluggish. "I was trying to get to the toilet."

Alf shook his head with disgust. He pointed to a door to the right of the bed. "Get out on the other side. I don't want you tracking through this mess."

Disjointed and jerky as he could manage, Cassell scooted across the bed. Alf watched his feigned struggle to untangle his legs from the sheets for a minute before crouching to gather the shattered plates from the floor.

Quietly, Cassell slipped from the bed and lifted the pitcher. He shoved the corklike lid tightly into the container's mouth and skirted around the foot of the bed until he stood directly behind the nurse. Upward, he jerked the pitcher high, then swung down. Solidly, it slammed atop the nurse's head. Plastic cracked, splintered. Water and ice showered from the shattered container.

Still crouched, Alf swayed. A massive hand shot out, preventing him from sprawling face-down on the floor. He groaned, his other fleshy paw rising to rub his head.

Dumbfounded, Cassell watched the nurse slowly rise and turn to face him. The big man should have gone down. Alf blinked as though unable to comprehend what had happened. He blinked again.

Before Alf could gather his wits, Cassell found his. Balling a fist, he struck, a hard-swung upper cut that connected with the nurse's chin. Despite all the muscular meat he carried and an obviously thick skull, Alf's jaw was glass. He grunted. His eyes rolled back to display their whites, and his knees gave way. The man collapsed, out cold.

With desperate determination, Cassell wrestled Alf's hospital uniform from his one-hundred kilograms of dead weight. He tossed away the skimpy robe and pulled on the uniform. It was a size or five too large

97

and stained with the remains of his spilled dinner, but it would suffice.

Ripping a sheet into strips, Cassell securely bound the nurse's arms and legs, then stuffed a gag into his mouth. He made no attempt to heave the unconscious man into the bed. The last thing he wanted was a sprained back from trying to lift the muscular man. He turned to the door.

—Unless you intend to hoof it, you'd better have an identification card.

Cassell stopped in mid-stride, realizing the shadowman was correct. He patted the uniform's pockets. Empty. Before panic took hold, his gaze ran to the foot of the bed. There, neatly labeling one of the bedposts was his own identification card. He grinned and slipped the card from the metal frame holding it.

Outside the room, he moved down a corridor unheeded by passing doctors and nurses. A dropshaft brought him to the cab ramp outside. He found a call button and summoned a bubble cab. Hands in pockets to hold up the oversized trousers he wore and gazing into the night sky above, he did his best to appear inconspicuous and calm, knowing any moment someone would enter a room on the hospital's upper floor and discover Alf.

Minutes that ground like hours crept by before the lights of a bubble cab swung from the concourse and pulled before him on the ramp. Cassell stepped in, his fingers playing over the driver console.

When the cab sped away, he turned to watch the hospital and Farrisberg disappear in the night.

*Find Yerik Belen.* The shadowman's words echoed in his mind.

# NINE

A minute, an hour? Jonal Cassell huddled within the relative security of the bubble cab unaware of time's passage. The thought that he should evade those seeking to kill him toyed lightly in his mind, but the transparent canopy shelled about him stood as a barrier against the world outside. It took no effort to tell himself that only this was real, beyond the cab's bubble dwelled a maniac's nightmare. It was simpler to randomly tap the driver console, then lean back and watch the blinking stars overhead.

—It won't work, Jonal. You've had your rest. Now it's time to decide.

*You were easier to handle as a bad dream.*

—And you've wasted too much time. Someone is going to miss Alf.

*Or check on my condition, or Alf will regain consciousness and free himself.*

—You're too vulnerable in this cab. You need to arrange passage off Tula.

*To Earth?*

—To Yerik Belen.

*To Yerik Belen.*

—You'll need clothes and currency.

*That means returning home!*

—You'll have to risk it. Anyone who can tamper with the library memory banks will surely have access to the transportation computer. Using your identification card is like wearing a homing beacon around your neck.

He saw the shadowman's point, but he did not like the idea of entering his home again. Anyone searching for him, Parlan or those trying to kill him, would go there first.

—I said it was a risk. You need computer access to get currency, and that means going home.

Cassell considered waiting until the banks opened in the morning and discarded the idea. He doubted "they" would allow him that much time.

—Just hope you've got any time left at all.

He reached up and punched his home coordinates into the bubble cab.


He drifted down the dropshaft, temples throbbing like a runaway bass drum, body taut and tensed to meet whoever waited below. He found only blackness. He stood within the dark living room afraid to even breathe, and listened. Despite the conjurings of his imagination, he heard nothing, not even the house's normal creaks and groans.

—Jonal, stop wasting time.

He pressed a palm against the light panel. Light cut the blackness. Cassell blinked to accustom his eyes to the glare. The room was empty—more than empty. A crawling sensation moved up the back of his neck. Something was wrong.

Remaining motionless, he let his gaze travel about the room, unable to locate the source of his unrest. Nothing seemed out of place, nothing appeared different . . .

. . . and that was the problem. He had killed two men in this room, spilled their blood. Yet, there were no dark stains on the deeply piled carpet.

Cassell ran a hand over the wall, remembering the deep-gouged craters left by the would-be killers' explosive charges. He found no hint of the violence that had ripped holes in the walls, nor a trace of the repairs that had been obviously made. Every reminder of what had transpired that night had been erased. Why? What reason would anyone have for covering up what had happened here? If the elusive "they" were trying to discredit his leadership of the Autonomy Party, then why conceal the fact he had killed two men?

—Jonal, there isn't time. You've got to get out of here.

His gaze covered the room again, still unable to discern any trace of his struggle with the killers. With a disbelieving shake of his head, he walked into the bedroom. He pulled a fresh suit from a closet rack and stripped away Alf's hospital uniform. Quickly dressing, he then pulled a small piece of luggage from the closet and opened it on the bed.

—Forget it. You can buy what you need later. Time is the one thing you can't buy.

Cassell tossed the suitcase back into the closet and returned to the living room. Memories still clung about him, but the ghosts were gone. Ailsa's spirit had left. The house felt totally empty, a series of connected, lifeless rooms. He squeezed his eyes closed tightly to hold back the tears of frustration that welled beneath his eyelids. Breathing deeply to steady himself, he forced his eyes open and stepped toward the liftshaft. Time was precious and could not be wasted on lingering memories.

—Currency, Jonal. Don't forget the money.

*Damn!* He turned back to the computer console. Slipping the identification card into a slot on the terminal's side, he linked into the Credit Exchange. A second later

101

tne screen blipped alive with a complete statement of Ailsa's and his personal accounts.

—More than you need.

Cassell's fingers hovered above the keys ready to withdraw the total sum.

—Leave a portion.

*Why?*

—You'll need to use your identification card a bit more.

*They can trace me through the card!*

—Trust me, Jonal. You're still new at this. You want them to trace you, at least for a while.

Cassell did not question the shadowman's riddles. His fingertips tapped the keys, requesting the withdrawal of three-fourths of the amount in the accounts. The screen blinked as it recorded the transaction. From a slot beneath the terminal, several perforated sheets of standards in various denominations shot out. While he tore the sheets into separate bills, Cassell linked the computer with the library reference banks, then summoned any information available on Yerik Belen.

—Time, Jonal. If they've found Alf, they'll come here first.

Cassell ignored the empathic urging and stuffed the standards into a pocket. The display screen flickered to announce the memory banks held no information on Yerik Belen. It did not surprise him.

—Satisfied? Now summon a cab!

Cassell did.

*Two hours! Two goddamn hours!* Bron Cadao dropped into a chair in front of the computer console. Cassell had a two-hour jump on him. This time there was no one to blame except himself. He should have foreseen something like this, but Parlan told him Cassell would be under sedation until the first psycho-reconditioning session.

*Damn!* Cadao winced; pain lanced through his right forefinger when he stabbed at the code keys. He had

102

bent back a fingernail, tearing it away from the quick. A trace of red seeped beneath the nail. Sucking at the throbbing finger, he finished his computer request with a cautiously moving left hand.

The screen brightened to tell him the link to the transportation system was complete. He then requested bubble cab records for the past two hours, keyed to Cassell's identification card. A moment later the information flashed onto the screen.

Cadao smiled. Cassell had used a bubble cab twice. The first trip indicated a meandering jaunt from the hospital that eventually ended at his home. The second was from his home to a theater in Farrisberg.

Cadao leaned back, eyeing the two reports. Both spoke of disorientation, confusion, a lack of decision. That was good. Cassell apparently still was unaware of the threat he posed to the Tula Project. The man was frightened and on the run. That meant erratic flight, an attempt to evade any pursuers. It also meant sloppiness.

He was willing to let Cassell run for as long as he wanted. The man would tire quickly and allow himself to be lulled with self-confidence, assured he had shaken any followers. When Cassell stopped, unable to flee any longer, Cadao would act. Until then, he would sit and wait, letting the computer do the legwork.

Following the shadowman's advice, Cassell used the standards to book passage on a sub-orbital, hypersonic shuttle from Farrisberg to New Druka. Arriving in the city, he avoided the bubble cabs and walked.

During recent months, his party campaigning had brought him to the city on several occasions. Then he saw New Druka as a totally different entity from Tula's capital. Now, he recognized what were once dramatic distinctions as only an outward facade. To be sure, architectural variants existed, New Druka preferring low, sprawling structures, while Farrisberg was a city of towering spires. The differences ended there. The two cities might have been built from the same set of blueprints, the architectural diversity programmed to relieve monotony. Administration complex, commercial district, industrial section, residential areas, all neatly arranged in a repetitious pattern.

And New Druka's citizenry? Cassell watched them from a window of a small cafe during the morning shift change. Any one of them could have been suddenly transported to Farrisberg and never notice the change.

—Earth, Jonal. You have to arrange passage and . . .

*Find Yerik Belen! I know. But first, I've got to lose myself.*

—What is that supposed to mean?

Cassell chuckled, pleased to discover the shadowman did not know every intimate detail of his mind. *You'll see.*

—Jonal, I was hoping that you had grown to trust me enough to openly share your intentions. Haven't I proven myself to be a friend?

Did he detect the hint of a bruised ego in the shadowman's voice? Cassell smiled smugly. He was capable of needling his uninvited companion.

—Since you choose to refuse me your confidence, I'm forced to explain the details of your plans. Following this meal, you intend to check into a local hotel, using your identification card. After that, you will again use the card to book passage aboard the next cruiser bound to Earth. Shall I continue?

Cassell's smug smile fell. He finished his breakfast, then walked to the nearest hotel. The shadowman hummed a cheery tune, while he cursed under his breath.


Twelve hours and Cassell had not used his identification card. Bron Cadao sat confused, irritation mounting. Where was the man?

It hit him like a collapsing brick wall.

He had been on Tula too long. He was becoming as placid and trusting as those who surrounded him. Ca-

104

dao's fingers danced across the terminal's keyboard. He cursed aloud when the records of Cassell's bank accounts appeared. *Damn!* He should have frozen the accounts when Cassell entered the hospital. It was too late now.

He summoned a planetwide credit search. A half-hour later, the terminal flashed to reveal Cassell's registration in a New Druka hotel. It blinked again. Cassell had also used his identification card to book passage on an Earth-bound cruiser.

"Son of a bitch!" Bron Cadao quickly coded a message to his superiors. Not waiting for their answer, he booked himself on the next shuttle to New Druka.

Jonal Cassell awoke when the shuttle's cushion field touched the runway with a sudden jolt. Another jarring thud, a softer bump, and he felt the landing gear touch the tarmac. The shuttle rumbled in vibrating protest. Reentry shields slid back from the craft's windows. Outside, the glaring lights of the Epai Spaceport fought back the night. Cassell gave Tula's largest commercial port a hasty glance, then looked at his watch. Eighteen hours had passed since leaving Farrisberg. The cruiser on which he had booked passage was scheduled to leave New Druka in six hours.

—That little maneuver has bought you at least that much time. With any luck you'll be off-planet before then.

The shuttle taxied to a tunnel ramp. Cassell rose and moved with the other passengers when they exited the craft. He did not like relying on luck. Yet he had nothing else. Within the terminal's main lobby, he found a vacant information booth. He entered and requested a list of Earth-bound vessels with passage available.

—A freighter would be best.

Agreeing, he amended the request. The display screen flashed a list of five freighters destined for Earth

105

within the next twenty-four hours. The *Carrie Ann* headed the list with ten berths still vacant.

—She's almost perfect!

The disqualifying "almost" was the fact that the freighter's passenger shuttle was scheduled to lift off in thirty minutes. There wasn't enough time. *Onadi's Romp* left in two hours; still not enough time to complete everything that had to be done.

Cassell's gaze dropped to the third ship listed, the *Tommy John*. Its passenger shuttle was scheduled for six in the morning.

—With stops for freight at Lanatia, Tai, and Javol, final destination Earth.

An indirect flight would be longer, Cassell realized, but it was what he wanted. They would expect him to take a direct route. The possibility that he could disembark at any of the three planets would also serve to confuse any pursuers. While he did not like the fact the ship left after the New Druka cruiser, there was nothing to do about it.

### ADUM SAHT—TALALD III
Religious leader of the desert planet Talald III whose assassination, 378 T.S., sparked a five-year civil war between the Balietid factions, Raeysa and Kiatos, on that planet. Assassin's identity unknown, suspected to be off-worlder hired by the Raeysa faction. Never confirmed.

Cassell felt a pocket of sanity open to envelop him as he watched the terminal screen blink out information on Javas Garridan, Ragnar Oles, Bina Fanett, Tymon Priest, and Paulles Nught.

—Hope it makes you feel better.

He ignored the shadowman's sarcasm. He felt relieved. The information contained in the Epai reference banks proved the Farrisberg Library had been tampered with. "They" did exist, he was certain of that

106

now. That their identity remained hidden, that he still did not know whether they were a single person or a tight-knit organization did not lessen the relief he found in confirming their existence.

—You're sane. I've been telling you that all along.

*What about you?* His growing acceptance of the shadowman's constant presence tended to veil the truth. The shadowman's mere existence indicated something was ajar within his brain.

Cassell's attention returned to the computer. He punched out a request for the past week's media reports keyed to his own name. After several minutes, the screen announced a complete lack of any news stories pertaining to Jonal Cassell. He frowned, perplexed. If "they" were trying to discredit him, why hadn't they reported the killing of the two men? Like the repairs in the living room, he could not grasp why they covered up the killings. It did not make sense.

—Jonal, time is precious. Introspection is fine, in its place. At the moment, the problem at hand is getting you aboard the *Tommy John*.

*Which is exactly what I intend to do now.*

Cassell opened the public computer booth and stepped back into the dimly lit cocktail lounge. While his eyes adjusted to the lack of lumination, he surveyed the three-level lounge. By accident, he apparently had selected one of the bustling nightspots in Epai. Patrons clustered around every table. His gaze honed in on a man who weaved an unsteady path from the rest room to a floating, circular bar. The man took a seat away from the other customers and waved to the bartender. Cassell crossed to the bar and sat a stool away from the man.

When his requested glass of a mild, violet wine arrived, Cassell sipped it casually and listened to the man bend the bartender's ear. The young woman politely nodded to the less-than-sober man while he explained he was a minor accountant with Zivon's Ara administration, stationed in Epai for two weeks, a member

107

of an auditing team running quarterly checks on the Company's profits.

—You've got a good eye, Jonal. I think you've found your man.

Cassell did not have time to answer. The man rose on wobbly legs to announce he had exceeded his limit and now intended to return to his hotel and sleep off his mistake. Cassell followed him outside, watching the accountant hail a bubble cab, then stumble forward and fumble unsuccessfully as he attempted to enter the vehicle.

"May I help?" Cassell moved to him.

"It appears I've had a bit too much this evening." The man grinned sheepishly and nodded for Cassell's assistance. "I need to go to the Epai Elite."

"The Elite? I'm heading there myself." Cassell helped him through the canopy entrance. "That is if you don't mind some company?"

"To be honest, citizen, I would appreciate some aid in getting back to the hotel." The man managed to slur his words while Cassell took the seat opposite him. "Here, the cab's on me."

The man fumbled inside his coat a few seconds, finally extracting his identification card from an inner pocket. He handed the card to Cassell who fed it into the cab's driver console. The cab acknowledged the destination and jerked forward. The console ejected the card. The accountant leaned forward to retrieve it.

—Now, Jonal!

Cassell swung, his fist hammering into the man's chin. Without so much as a groan of surprise, the accountant crumpled back into his seat, unconscious.

—He'll be out until noon tomorrow.

Redirecting the cab to the spaceport, Cassell pulled the identification card from the slot and glanced at it. Doron Tem. Not a name he would have chosen for himself had he the opportunity, but it provided the new identity he needed. He dropped the card into his pocket.

Ten minutes later the bubble cab halted before Epai

Spaceport's main terminal complex. When he stepped from the vehicle, Cassell dropped his own identification card into the console, then punched out the coordinates for his home in Farrisberg. He backed away to watch the canopy close and the cab slide away into the night. For a moment guilt tugged in his chest at the thought of Tem awakening in the morning, half a continent away from Epai, and nursing a sizable hangover.

—Forget him. He'll be all right. You just taught him a lesson in the dangers of alcohol.

Cassell turned and stared at the terminal entrance. Despite the early morning hour, the port was alive. A steady stream of passengers, ship crews, and port personnel moved within.

—Almost home, Jonal, almost home.

He took a deep breath and managed a weak smile. Patting Tem's identification card within his pocket, Cassell strolled into the building. *I hope I look more confident than I feel.*


"The term is wild goose chase." Bron Cadao admonished himself as he settled before the computer monitor.

His shuttle jaunt to New Druka had been nothing more than a wild goose chase, neatly arranged by one Jonal Cassell. While he tracked phantom decoys, Cassell quietly slipped away in another direction. All of which pointed to the fact that Cassell was aware that his movements were monitored.

For a moment, Cadao considered informing his superiors of the latest development, then dismissed the migrant thought. A catalog of errors in this case would not look good in his personnel file. He was too close to retirement to blow everything now. He would make contact again, when he had something positive to report.

Under his command, the computer retrieved passenger lists for every Earth-bound ship for the past ten hours and those departing in the next two days. Like an accountant lost in a column of doctored figures, he studied each list that flashed on the screen. He found nothing, but then he had not expected to discover Cassell's name. New identities were not easy to come by on Tula, but Jonál Cassell was a hunted man. His movements were now ruled by survival logic.

Cadao next summoned a planetwide credit check keyed to Cassell's identification card. He frowned when a single entry luminated the terminal—a bubble cab now enroute from Epai to Farrisberg. Why would Cassell travel by cab when a shuttle offered a faster, more direct route? And why did he use his identification card?

Irritated by mounting suspicions, he shoved away from the computer. The cab had decoy written on it in letters two meters high. He cursed Tula's lack of a police force and the agency's constant secrecy. He needed help and there was no one he could trust. The cab, red herring or not, was all he had to proceed on. When it arrived at Cassell's home, he would be there waiting.

Cassell stepped from the med-unit. A middle-aged attendant, her eyes never leaving the unit's monitor board, handed him his clothes. Cassell placed them over the back of a chair and began to dress. A bell rang. He jerked around.

—Easy. It's only the med-unit.

He smiled meekly with chagrin. The floor beneath his feet felt like a tautly stretched wire on which he balanced precariously. Only one person had to recognize him and everything would fall through. By now "they" knew he had used the crusier out of New Druka as a decoy. They would be searching...

"Mr. Tem," the attendant's voice startled him. He stifled a nervous gasp and turned to the woman. She tossed him a pair of pale blue coveralls. "I think you'll be more comfortable in those."

"What?" Cassell stared blankly at the coveralls.

110

"Most passengers prefer them, more comfortable on board," she said. "Of course, there are no regulations about attire. You may wear your own clothes if you wish."

Cassell looked at her, still missing the point.

"You're a certified nonmedical risk, Mr. Tem." She tore a printout sheet from the med-unit and handed it to him. "Take this and give it to the attendant beyond that green door. Preflight briefing begins in ten minutes. Though you might want to dress before attending the briefing."

Her eyes traveled up and down his nakedness; she winked, then swiveled from her chair and walked out of the small examination room. Pulling on the coveralls, Cassell packed his suit into a travel case atop a second suit purchased in Epai. Through the green door was a small auditorium filled with rows of portable chairs. His fellow travelers sat and talked among themselves, or huddled on the cushionless plastic in a vain attempt to nap. He handed the medical report to the waiting attendant for it to become a permanent part of the freight line's official records. Traceable, he realized, but hopefully, the *Tommy John* would be well underway to Lanatia by the time "they" uncovered it.

"Mr. Tem, a list of berth assignments is posted across the room," the attendant said. "If you require other accommodations, you may arrange them after the *Tommy John* has completed tachyon transition."

Nodding, Cassell walked to the board. He found Doron Tem's name aside a berth in room P-25. All cabins aboard the freighter were designed for double occupancy, yet he could not find room P-25 beside another passenger on the list. The tightness in his gut unknotted a bit. The voyage's complications lessened without the prospect of facing a cabinmate and a barrage of unwanted personal questions.

The knots abruptly doubled, yanking tautly. Everything had gone so smoothly, without a snag. What if all his precautions were useless? He had no guarantee

111

"they" had not seen through the false trails he had laid for them. Anyone in the room could be . . .

—Easy, Jonal. One step at a time. In a few minutes you'll be on the shuttle heading for the *Tommy John.* Within two hours the freighter will be in tachyon space. If they've planted someone aboard, you can handle him later.

*In an hour,* Cassell looked down at his watch, *Doron Tem will be arriving at my front door.*

—Cutting it close, but it's the risk you had to take.

*Easy for you to say!*

"May I have your attention?" A woman who introduced herself as one of the freighter's officers strode behind a podium at the front of the small auditorium.

Cassell took a seat while the officer explained the *Tommy John* was not a luxury cruiser, but a space freighter.

"Our accommodations are more than adequate for the voyage, but planned activities to relieve the tedium of spaceflight will not be available," she continued. "However, we do have a variety of facilities open to our passengers and crew. The *Tommy John* carries an extensive tape library, a full-gee gymnasium, and a weightless gym. Also available is . . ."

Cassell turned her off and let his gaze wander over his fellow passengers. Later, when the freighter was safely underway, he would worry about relief from the flight's monotony. He glanced at his watch again, wondering how close the bubble cab was to Farrisberg. Had Doron Tem awakened yet? Seconds flicked by in digital array. What if "they" were waiting for the cab? Would Tem be killed by mistake?

—Better him than you. This is no time to feel guilty. It won't help Tem, and it won't help you one damn bit. You did what you had to, that's all there is to it.

The shuffle of feet brought Cassell from his thoughts. A tunnel ramp now stood open at the far side of the room. Down the cylindrical corridor he saw the shuttle's open hatch. Noisily the passengers formed a disjointed line that fed into the tunnel. His pulse booming in his ear, Cassell rose and walked to the end of the line.

DORON TEM.

Bron Cadao punched the name into the computer. The screen flashed to reveal Tem's stolen identification card had not been used. Yet, Cassell had stolen it for some purpose.

"Son of a bitch!" It hit him like a solid blow to the seventh vertebra.

His fingers slammed the keys, recalling the passenger lists he had studied last night. The sixth entry produced Tem's name.

"The bastard . . . the bastard," Cadao muttered when he noted the *Tommy John* departed in five minutes. There was no way to halt the giant freighter.

Shoving from the console, he walked across the room and opened a cabinet. Pulling out a bottle of Terran bourbon, he poured three fingers and slugged it down. He filled the glass again and gulped it down with equal vengeance. Then he turned back to glare at the computer. Like it or not, the matter was out of his hands. Cassell was off-planet. He had to notify his superiors and face the consequences.

Jonal Cassell placed his travel case into a compartment beneath the berth. He sat down on the bed's edge and examined his home for the next three months. Having never been on a luxury cruiser, he had no ground to compare the accommodations, but suspected the officer's term "adequate" was generous.

The room was a four-meter square with a connected and very cramped-appearing combination head and shower. Operating instructions for the commode and shower jet were neatly stenciled on a flat, gray wall, along with an explanation of personal hygiene water rationing.

The cabin was equipped with a single built-in desk

113

and tape library console. A single chair was bolted to the floor in front of the console. There were no closets; all personal items were to be placed in the storage compartment under the berths.

The two berths were located on opposite walls of the cabin. Both were equipped with a privacy shield that effectively enveloped the bed and a small area about the berth in an opaque energy screen, the only consideration given to privacy within the small cabin. Once again, he felt relieved that he had not been thrown together with an utter stranger under such confined conditions. It would be bad enough as it was.

—It could have been a lot worse. Be thankful you haven't been stuffed into four-tier bunks.

Before he could reply, a man's voice blurted over the cabin's intercom to announce the ship's approaching tachyon transition. Cassell followed the voice's instructions, lay atop his berth, and strapped himself in. Across the room, he heard the cabin's door automatically bolt. That the lock was a mere safety precaution did nothing to ease his sudden distrust of his position. Accidents still occurred during the transition to tachyon space. Theoretically, each of the cabins would serve as a lifeboat should such an accident happen. In reality little had ever been found of a ship that sent half its atoms into the tachyon universe while the other half remained in normal space.

A buzzer blared from the intercom . . . the ten-second C-plus jump warning. Cassell suddenly recalled his only other experience with tachyon transition, his voyage from Earth to Tula ten years ago.

It was too late. There was a slight sensation of imagined acceleration, then a tidal wave of nausea deluged his stomach. Cassell groaned, working his jaw, popping his ears, and swallowing to relieve the desperate feeling that he was about to vomit out his insides. The nausea passed, leaving his head swimming in a dizzy sea of disorientation. His fingers dug into the berth, searching for solidarity in a universe gone liquid. Then

114

it passed. A buzzer sounded again, and the man's voice announced successful transition into tachyon space. The *Tommy John* now traveled well in excess of the speed of light.

A long breath that Cassell was unaware he had been holding escaped from his lungs in a loud sign of relief. He had done it. He had evaded them. The tension of the past days flowed from his muscles, leaving them with a hollow aching of total relaxation. He smiled.

# TEN

Jonal Cassell stood alone in the observation bay of the *Tommy John*. He locked his hands around the rail in front of him, knuckles a strained white from the intensity of his grasp. Despite the solid deck underfoot and the secure static grip of his shoe soles, he could not shake the falling sensation. Weightlessness and the giant cyclopean eye of the observation window overwhelmed logic. Sensation ruled.

He smiled, savoring the feel. He had discovered it when the freighter first orbited Lanatia. Now, prepared as he was for it, the intensity of the sensation still took him by surprise. It was similar to the thrill of a carnival ride. The senses warned danger while the mind remained rational... almost. The conflicting combination enthralled him like a junkie snorting Skydust.

For the past three days, he had spent the majority of his time in front of the immense circular window. The rest of the ship's passengers and most of the crew took advantage of the Javol freight exchange by shuttling down for on-planet leave. He enjoyed the solitude,

116

but safety was his main reason for staying aboard the giant freighter. In the two months since leaving Tula, he found no evidence that he had been followed. Still, he did not underestimate those attempting to kill him. For the casual tourist, an alien world offered too many opportunities for fatal accidents.

While the ship's human cargo sampled Javol's exotic water cities, he spent hour on hour clinging to the handrail and gazing on the void beyond the crystal eye. Earlier he watched the comings and goings of shuttles as the freighter's cargo holds were emptied and refilled with materials destined for Earth. More interesting were the men in their individual suits, crawling the outer shell of the *Tommy John* to make minor repairs. Though dwarfed by the freighter's immensity, the space-clad workers gave the metallic behemoth a touch of humanity, placing it in a proper perspective—a machine that served man rather than a gleaming god that rode the streams of faster-than-light space.

No shuttles ran from the planet's surface now. Javol filled the center of the observation window, a giant orb marbled in blue, green, red, and orange. Blue-white polar caps and thick cloud banks stood in sharp contrast to the world's mottled surface.

However, Cassell's eyes were drawn to the magnificent display that hung suspended behind Javol. The crew dubbed it the Devil's Maw, the remnants of an exploded star, cosmic clouds of expanding gas and matter. With little difficulty, he saw the formation responsible for the ominous name. The clouds enclosed a dark void, giving the appearance of gaping jaws stretched wide to swallow the planet.

The beauty of the star's ashes was too delicate for such hard nomenclature. The clouds glowed like iridescent, gossamer wings, running with fairy fire. Weblike wisps networked through the clouds to form a fine lattice of veins. The wings of a dragonfly, but never the mouth of a demon, he thought. Nor was there any dan-

117

ger of the clouds swallowing Javol. The nova's remnants swirled away from the planet, outward toward the galactic rim.

A man before the throne of heaven, Cassell stood in silent awe, bathed in the radiant beauty. Once the *Tommy John* was underway again, there would be little to see, except the fireworks of tachyon reality and light twisted and contorted by the freighter's speed. Early in the voyage, he found the open view of another universe exciting, but faster-than-light space grew monotonous, a random display of exploding fire. This was *real* space, where planets and stars existed, the vast void that could *almost* be accepted by eye and mind.

A wistful smile curved the corners of his mouth. The *Tommy John* was so different from his first space journey. Ailsa and he had been virtually locked away on an inner-level deck of a freighter converted into a colonial vessel. They shared a cabin, smaller than the one he now occupied alone, with another couple. Like sardines packed into the claustrophobic confines of a tin can, they endured the six-week flight from Earth to Tula, never glimpsing the magnificence that lay beyond the plated hulls.

Easing from the rail, Cassell shuffle-walked to one of the bay's seats. Time closed opened wounds. His two months aboard the giant freighter were like a soothing balm that allowed him to accept Ailsa's death. The emptiness remained, but the pain was a dull, distant ache, like the longing for a time that could never be regained. Ailsa no longer haunted his every waking moment. Life continued; the dead were a part of the past, and he was among the living.

*A lifetime away,* he thought, *so distant, as though it all belonged to another man.* Here, bathed in the majesty of the Devil's Maw, Tula became an estranged, flickering moment. The only reminder of the world behind him was the shadowman. Though, since the ship broke orbit around Lanatia, the shadowman no longer was a constant companion. The faceless voice had left him. Even his dreams went undisturbed.

*An indication of my returning sanity,* he thought, and immediately regretted it, expecting the shadow-man to make some sarcastic remark to prove he still existed. No voice crept into his brain. Cassell pushed fate a bit further, allowing himself a satisfied smile.

The blare of a bullhorn blasted through the ceiling speakers. Cassell jumped, rocked from his thoughts. His arms shot down, grasping the arms of the chair before his startled reaction sent him rocketing, weightlessly, to the ceiling. The horn signaled the pending arrival of the passenger shuttle. A second blast would sound when the ship docked, and a third fifteen standard minutes before the *Tommy John* broke orbit and moved outward to make the tachyon transition.

Cassell's gaze returned to Javol, searching for the arriving shuttle. Minutes passed before he sighted a flyspeck moving across a white background formed by the planet's clouds. From a point of darkness, it grew to a dot, a blot, then a fully outlined silhouette of a shuttle. He watched the winged craft gracefully approach the *Tommy John*, dwarfed by the freighter's gargantuan proportions, then disappear behind the curvature of the hull. He sensed the vibration that ran through the deck rather than heard the shuttle nose into its docking berth. The warning horn blared again.

With a last gaze at Javol and the starry wings of the Devil's Maw, Cassell left the observation bay through a corridor tube. Already crew members, fresh from on-planet leave, scurried by him toward their various stations. The same haste filled the passenger level as those disembarking the shuttle sought their numbered berths to secure for the coming C-plus jump.

Weaving through the chaotic confusion, Cassell made his way to his cabin. As the door slid back, he stepped inside and stopped. The opaque gray of a privacy screen shielded the bed opposite his. It took a moment for the fact to penetrate. He had a cabinmate.

His head jerked around in search of any other sign of the intruder. He found none.

Suspicion, paranoia, caution, all those disquieting feelings he had shed during the flight crept back, gnawing at him. For two months he had enjoyed the security of the room's privacy. Why a cabinmate now?

The third warning horn jarred him alive again. He crossed the room and lay atop his berth to strap in for the tachyon transition. He looked back to the privacy screen, liking even less the thought of his private world being invaded. He tried to push away the speculations, the suspicions, but they refused to stop eating at him. Had "they" finally found him? Why had it taken so long? His charade on Tula had been thin.

*No*, he told himself. It was a matter of passenger space; there were no other accommodations available. After all, this was the last leg of the freighter's voyage. All routes to Earth were heavily traveled. Earth, in a month he would stand on Earth for the first time in ten years.

His attempt to excite himself with the prospect of feeling his homeworld beneath his feet once again failed. Yerik Belen waited for him somewhere on Earth. Belen, who held the answers he needed.

Tula, so distant but minutes ago, again seemed very real and very close. The security he found on the *Tommy John* suddenly proved false, a tissue-thin veneer meant to lull him into complacency.

He glanced across the room, unable to penetrate the gray barrier field with his gaze. He then reached to the side of the bed, found a switch, and flipped it. His own privacy screen rose to envelop the berth. He closed his eyes preparing for the gut-twisting tachyon jump. All his doubts pressed down atop him, fear constricting through his chest, tighter, tighter.

Cassell did not realize he dreamed until the dinner bell sounded over the intercom, wrenching him from sleep. He yawned, stretched, and smiled. A hungry

120

warmth glowed deep within him. The voyage was better for him than he thought. He had just experienced another indication of his stabilizing mental state—a very erotic dream. After months of nothingness, he believed all carnal needs dead within him. To find the stirrings of something he believed lost was like a rebirth, a new life to replace the tattered remnants left on Tula.

Sitting, he swung his legs over the bed. The privacy screen stood but half a meter away. Thoughts of rebirth evaporated. Angrily, he reached down and switched off the field. Across the small cabin, the other screen was also down. The bed was empty. The sound of running water drew his attention to the cabin's head. He hesitated a moment, uncertain whether to confront his unwelcomed cabinmate or not. Deciding to postpone the meeting as long as possible, he rose from the bed and left the room.

Outside, the second dinner bell sounded. Cassell joined the other passengers who moved down the tunnel corridor toward the dining room. Dining room was too gracious a term for what was no more than an expanded mess hall with a few frills added here and there to make the surroundings a bit more pleasant for the ship's passengers. While there were tables designated for the freighter's crew, the *Tommy John* had no regulations that segregated crew members from their human cargo. For the most part, crew and passengers mingled.

Walking to a table designated for cabins P-20 through P-25, Cassell took one of the two vacant seats remaining. There was only one familiar face at the table, a spice merchant from Lanatia. The others were a motley assortment, an elderly couple returning to Earth to visit relatives unseen for thirty standard years, a younger couple oblivious to all but each other, a short-timing Space Corps private transferred to Terra to receive his official walking papers, a xenobiologist, and a Javolian mining representative who laughed too

121

loudly and flashed too much porcelain when he smiled
Hastily, Cassell went through the required introductions and polite small talk, then touched a button on the servo-unit at the center of the circular table. Inwardly, he sighed with relief when his tray slid from the machine. Turning his attention to the meal, he drifted from the conversation around him.

"Tem, Doron Tem?" a woman's voice asked.

Cassell glanced up to see a coverall-clad woman take the vacant seat beside him.

"I'm Nari Hullen." She introduced herself with a smile and brushed a stray strand of auburn hair from her forehead. "Apparently, you and I are cabinmates for the remainder of the voyage."

The plastic fork slipped from Cassell's fingers and fell to the dinner tray. In spite of himself, his mouth dropped open, and he stared at the woman, unable to find his voice.

"I hope you haven't any religious convictions about sharing a cabin with a member of the opposite sex." Nari Hullen punched the servo-unit for her own meal. "Or worse, a jealous bond-mate or wife waiting for you on Earth."

"Neither," Cassell managed to say while he fumbled to retrieve the fork from a half-congealed bowl of pudding.

"Good. Then as long as we use the cabin's privacy screen, there should be no inconvenience for either of us."

Cassell could not describe the slim woman as beautiful, and pretty was too weak. Attractive seemed to be the right adjective. He estimated her height at a bit over a meter and a half, and doubted if she weighed more than fifty-eight kilos. Her loose-fitting green coveralls concealed even a hint of her figure. Yet, there was something in her face that held his gaze for an embarrassing long moment.

At first glance, her eyes, large and brown with an almost Eurasian cast, imprinted on his mind. They radiated an indefinable mixture of strength, intelligence, and vulnerability. A second glance erased the unprepossessing image of her other features. Her full mouth, slightly upturned nose, and strong cheeks complimented those compelling eyes.

Nari Hullen smiled at him again, apparently not minding his rude stare.

Cassell stirred, ill at ease. Something about his self-proclaimed cabinmate made him uncomfortable. He pulled his eyes away, then glanced back, as though seeing her from a different angle would allow him to pinpoint the reason for his sudden discomfort. It did not work. He shook his head, then caught himself before she noticed. His uneasy stirrings could be attributed to abruptly discovering a stranger assigned to his cabin, then topping it off with the fact she was a woman, he told himself.

"I've been berthed in P-18 since Tula," she said, between bites of her meal. "However, when a couple booked passage on Javol, the purser assigned me to P-25. It was either move me, or break up a twenty-five-year-old marriage. He decided moving me was easier."

Tula, a red light flashed in his brain. Suspicion crept back to nag him. "I'm surprised I wasn't informed of the change."

Before Nari Hullen could reply, a crew member approached the table and leaned to Cassell. "Mr. Tem, Lieutenant Ildre asked me to inform you that she is presently assembling a game in the recreation room. Someone has requested your usual chair this evening, if you are not planning to play."

"Tell Ildre I'll be there in a moment," Cassell told the man. "Also tell her, I would not miss the chance of taking her for every standard she has."

The crewman winked and nodded, then turned and left the dining room. Cassell returned to his meal and Nari Hullen.

"You're not leaving so soon, are you?" she asked.

"Sorry," Cassell replied. "Lieutenant Ildre's card

123

games are one of the few luxuries I've allowed myself during the voyage."

"I understand." He noted no concern in her voice. "Lieutenant Ildre's games have become a bit notorious. I've heard several fellow passengers complain of the difficulty in getting a chair at her table. Perhaps we can talk later."

"Perhaps." He swiveled away from the table and walked from the dining room, leaving Nari Hullen staring after him.

Poker, a recently rediscovered card game from Earth's past. Over the two months aboard the freighter, Jonal Cassell found he had an affinity for the game and derived an indefinable pleasure from gambling. Perhaps not that indefinable. He maintained a reputation as a winner. Lieutenant Ildre's games provided the means by which he added a tidy sum to the standards tucked away within the travel case beneath his berth.

However, the cards held little interest for him this evening. Despite the fact he won two out of the ten hands played, he begged off further rounds with a hastily made excuse about an upset stomach. He cashed in the small piles of chips that had accumulated in front of him. As usual he kept the standards with him rather than placing them in the purser's safe. A precaution suggested by the shadowman should a hasty escape become necessary, or should the need arise to grease a few palms. So far, the precaution had proven unnecessary.

Tonight, his thoughts would not leave his new cabinmate. The woman's mention of Tula bothered him, but there was more to it than that. He still was unable to put a finger on it.

Bidding those at the table a good evening, Cassell left the recreation room. He found himself walking to the observation bay, force of habit from the past three days in Javol orbit. It was dark inside, the only illumination coming from the giant observation port and the flashing tachyon universe beyond the window.

Cassell considered returning to his cabin. He dismissed the migrant thought and took a seat before the glass eye. Nari Hullen could be in the cabin. The bay offered more privacy. He tried to edge the woman and his suspicions from his mind by gazing at the fireworks outside. The myriad of exploding patterns was lost on him. It was beautiful, colors that defied description, but it was not the Devil's Maw. What happened beyond the ship's hull was unreal. His brain could not grasp its true significance. It was one thing to accept the fact he rode aboard a ship whose atoms had been transformed into tachyons and now traveled several times the speed of light. To actually grasp and understand that fact was another matter.

A soft hiss floated in the air behind him. He glanced around. A pale orange glow illuminated the shadows hanging at the back of the bay. He was not alone. Someone sat behind him.

"Sorry to disturb you," a woman said. Cassell heard the rustle of clothing, the sound of moving feet. "You have your evening poker, and me, my cosmic light-show."

Nari Hullen stepped from the shadows, a little twisted smile on her lips. She walked to Cassell while inhaling deeply from an unfiltered cigarette. She held the smoke in her lungs.

"Care to share this?" she asked in a cramped voice while holding her breath. "I'm not sure what the regulations onboard are, but it's legal, and most definitely *good.*"

She exhaled and offered the stick to Cassell. He shook his head. "I'll pass. Always makes me drowsy."

"Too bad, this really is good." She stared at the emberlike tip of the cigarette as though it held some cosmic key to the universe. The quirky little smile returned to her lips and she took another deep drag. "Besides, it breaks up the long hours."

125

Cassell repressed the urge to tap his fingers, rub the back of his neck, or squirm in his chair. The woman's presence brought back his earlier discomfort. He vainly dredged for a spur of the moment reason to excuse himself and once again retreat from her. But the last refuge of privacy onboard the freighter, the cabin, was gone. Nari Hullen could intrude there. Circumstances trapped him. "Are you bored with the flight?"

She exhaled. Her lips remained parted several seconds before she spoke. He was not sure whether she searched for the right words, or was lost in the drug's time-dilation effect. "No, not bored, just disappointed."

"Disappointed?" He watched her stare intently at the flashing display outside the window. Her piqued interest came from the drug's heightened sensual awareness, of that he was sure.

"My one and only space voyage." She took another deep hit from the stick and paused until she exhaled again. "Sure you wouldn't care for some of this? They grow potent weed on Javol."

Cassell waved away the proffered joint. "I really don't care for any, Ms. Hullen."

"Nari, please call me Nari. After all, we're to be cabinmates for the next few weeks." Her attention drifted from the window long enough for her to smile at him, then languidly returned to the exploding colors. "I don't know how many times I've come to the observation bay and spent hours watching the universe we travel. It never ceases to fascinate me. Did you know that scientists argued for decades over the existence of tachyon space? Theoretically the tachyon was there, but no one could prove it really existed. Then Nils Rosmer came along, said to hell with all the arguments, and created his drive. Mankind suddenly had the stars at their fingertips. Did you know Rosmer was a dentist? Taught himself the physics he needed, ignored everything that said faster-than-light travel was impossible. Once an interviewer asked him 'why?' Rosmer answered that he read speculative fiction in his youth and always dreamed of standing under an alien sun. Can you believe that? What is considered junk literature instilling such a dream in a man?"

"Perhaps the purpose of literature, or any art, is to instill dreams." He felt ridiculous continuing the conversation. Nari Hullen was stoned, or well on her way to it. She rambled, apparently enjoying the sound of her own voice.

"Perhaps," she said as though his comment had no place in her disjointed verbal meanderings. "Old Rosmer never had the chance to realize his dream. He was accidently killed ... run over by a truck, one of those internal combustion engine vehicles."

"An ignominious end for one who opened the stars for mankind." Cassell found no purpose in her commentary on Nils Rosmer. His discomfort grew. He wanted to get away from her. "And now you stand here on the deck of a starship and are disappointed."

"Exactly." That strange little smile played over her lips again. "All my life, I've wanted what I'm doing at this very moment, sailing through space. Yet, it isn't what I thought it would be."

She sat silent for a few seconds, her gaze still focused on the observation window. "Mr. Tem, I'm thirty-two, have a doctorate, and teach sociology at a small university in the midlands of Earth's North American continent. Not what one could describe as an exciting existence. I pulled every string I could to swing a Combine grant that would take me to the stars. After five years, it was finally approved."

Nari paused to suck the last hit from her stick. The orange ember burned all the way to the built-in mouthpiece and died. She locked the fumes in her lungs for what seemed like a full ten minutes before finally exhaling loudly.

"You really should have tried some of this. It softens everything." She tossed the butt at a disposal unit in the wall. To Cassell's surprise, she hit it. "Where was I?"

127

"The Combine grant," he said.

"There really wasn't much money. But enough for a round trip freighter passage and enough to keep me alive while doing a preliminary study of the cultural structure of Zivon's colony on Tula. Nothing that would shake the foundations of academe or establish me within the scientific hall of fame ... but enough to give me the stars for a few months." She reached into a pocket to pull out another stick. She stared at it a moment, pursed her lips in disapproval, and dropped it back into the pocket. "I don't know what I expected. Adventure perhaps ... whatever, it didn't happen. Now it's over. In a few weeks, I'll be back on Earth."

"A poet's soul searching for romance," Cassell said, politely quelling the sarcasm he felt.

She turned from the window, a distant expression on her face, as though sensing the ambiguity in his casual remark. She smiled, apparently having sifted through whatever drug fog floated within her brain. "Perhaps you're right ... more than I would like to admit to myself."

She looked back to the window. The brilliant explosions of color flashed across her fading, sad little smile in kaleidoscopic beauty.

*Loneliness.* Cassell studied her in the ever-changing light of the C-plus universe. The frightening uncertainty of this woman remained within him, yet it mixed with a compelling attraction. *Loneliness seeks loneliness.* Nari Hullen needed another human being to listen to her much more than she needed adventure. His own loneliness and needs echoed in her words, reflected on her face. They were two strings vibrating in sympathy. He found himself wanting to reach out and touch her hand, to whisper some assurance.

"Are you Tulan?" she abruptly asked. "I saw you on the boarding shuttle in Epai."

"Yes," he replied brusquely. He withdrew as quickly as he had wanted to flow out to this woman. Tula again. Caution dominated openness.

'I thought most Tulans held an unnatural love for the planet," she said, "and wouldn't leave it on threat of death."

Polite conversation, or probing? Offering no further information, Cassell replied, "Vacation."

Neither spoke. The soundless fireworks beyond the observation window only emphasized the uneasy silence. Seconds stretched to awkward minutes.

Nari suddenly pushed from her chair and glanced down at him. "I'm afraid I've worn out my welcome, Mr. Tem."

She leaned down and lightly kissed his lips. An action that took him completely off guard. Yet there were no sexual overtones to the kiss. Its gentleness held a simple "thank you," gratitude for his listening.

"I won't bore you any longer. Besides, this stuff *is* making me drowsy." She walked to the bay's exit and looked back at him over her shoulder. "Thank you, Mr. Tem."

Silently, Cassell watched her leave, then sank back into the cushioned seat, listening to the voiceless cries of exploding light outside the ship.

Quietly, he entered the cabin. Nari's privacy screen stood shielding her bed. He smiled. Nari Hullen might be searching for adventure, but a shipboard affair apparently did not fit into her category of adventures to be undertaken.

That made things easier, he thought. Ailsa's memory was still too vivid, their love too real. It would be a long time before he could give that much, or feel that much with another woman—if he ever could.

Crossing the room, he climbed atop his berth. Nari Hullen needed more than he could give. He glanced at the privacy screen, then reached and flicked the switch on the side of the bed. His own screen crackled and hissed, then solidified. He closed his eyes, the fires of tachyon space still burning on the insides of his eyelids.

# ELEVEN

Nari tucked into a tight ball. Gracefully, she performed a combination somersault and slight twist in midair. She unfolded and threw herself spread eagle. The action halted her tumble; she floated a meter from the ceiling of the court. With perfect timing, her wrist flicked. Her palm slapped soundly against the ball.

Cassell grimaced. Even with a week of daily free-fall handball games under his belt, he still lacked the agility needed to successfully control the oversized sphere. Nari, who had been playing with various crew members since the *Tommy John* left Tula, outstripped him every time they entered the court. Although he doubted he would ever be a match for the woman even with a year of practice.

Nari's shot bounced off the ceiling and sailed toward the far wall. Mentally plotting the ball's trajectory, Cassell pushed lightly from the floor with his toes. In the same instant, he realized he had not put enough force behind the movement to intercept the sphere before its fourth bank. The ball careened off the wall, hit the floor, and bounded upward. It shot by Cassell's fingertips by mere centimeters.

Groaning aloud, he slowly rolled so that he landed feet first on the ceiling. He clung there, held by the static soles of his shoes. A blur moved at the corner of his eye. Nari sailed through the air, snatched up the ball, flipped over and landed defty beside the court's exit. She grinned up at him and winked.

He toed from the ceiling, floated downward to somersault and alight beside her as she opened the door. "That's another one you can chalk up. I guess I can be thankful we'll be in Earth orbit in another week. I don't think my ego can stand being trounced so readily each day."

"It wasn't that bad, was it?" Nari laughed, stepping outside the court. "You've really improved. Managed to score three times the last two games. You just need more practice."

"Right! In another month or ten, I might be able to give you a half-decent game," he answered with a useless shake of his head. "Hungry?"

"A light snack before bed would be nice," she said, shuffle-walking toward a dropchute.

"Good, I'm starved."

They entered the chute together. The ship's slowly increasing gravitational pull sucked them down five levels into a cushioning force field that floated them to the one-gee passenger deck.

No day or night existed aboard the freighter, but the ship's chronometers and routine were based on Earth's standard twenty-four-hour day. When they entered the ever-open dining room, the wall clock read 1 a.m. GMT. Except for three crew members huddled around one table, the room's vacancy reflected the hour. It was too late for most passengers and too early for those gambling in the recreation room.

Selecting a table away from the crewmen, Cassell and Nari seated themselves and punched out their orders on the servo-unit. A few seconds later, two trays slid out. Cassell started to peel the covering from his when Nari reached out and touched his hand.

"I'd like to eat in the observation bay," she said. "Care to join me?"

Cassell nodded. A few minutes later they entered the bay and settled before the big window. The bay was dark and empty as usual. Only the tachyon light from outside illuminated the room.

"I thought you'd given this up?" he asked.

"It's the first time I've been here in the past week." Nari pulled the wrapper from her tray. "Just felt like watching it for a while. Care for some fruit?"

She held out the tray. Cassell waved it away and offered his own sandwich made from some soya synthetic that approximated the taste of Tulan beef. Nari shook her head, then took a slice of fruit he could not identify and idly munched it while she gazed at the window.

Cassell suddenly felt ill at ease. He took a bite of the sandwich, finding himself no longer hungry. He watched his cabinmate with uncertainty. Was it her, or him? Not since their first meeting had he felt like this around her. He wished they had remained in the dining room.

"I've enjoyed this week, Doron." Her eyes never left the gigantic window.

Cassell found what bothered him. Her expression! For a week, he had only seen her smile, eyes alive with an inward light. Now that quirky, little, twisted smile of irony played on her lips. And her voice seemed dull and flat. Not since that first night had he noticed this mood.

"I've enjoyed it, too." He tried to sound as sincere as he felt. "It's beat the hell out of Lieutenant Ildre's poker games."

"Do you remember what you said about me being . . ." She abruptly shook her head, placed the tray at the floor and stood. "Doron, I'm sorry. I don't mean to be

132

maudlin. Things that seemed so clear a moment ago are suddenly very confused. I think I need to walk a bit, to sort everything out."

"All right," Cassell said as he stood.

"No." Nari looked at him with that strange sad smile. "I think it would be best if I were alone for a while."

Cassell nodded, wanting to say something, to do something, to comfort her. Yet, at the same time, he felt relief that she was leaving. His own uneasiness increased with each passing second.

Nari walked to the exit. She paused to glance back at him. "Doron Tem, if I had any sense, I'd take you back to our cabin and seduce you ... or perhaps leave my privacy screen down and allow you to seduce me. But ... but ... dammit, I don't seem to have that much sense ... and that makes less sense than anything."

Before her meaning penetrated, she moved through the portal and hastened down a tunnel corridor. Cassell stepped toward the exit, then stopped, fighting the urge to follow her. He sank into one of the observation chairs and stared blankly at the window.

Uncertain what had happened, or what he felt, he cursed aloud. For the past weeks, he had forgotten Jonal Cassell and lost himself in Doron Tem's identity. Nari had been the reason. She was his first human contact since Ailsa's murder. Loneliness drew them together, need, the want to share the sound of another's voice.

*Damn, damn!* He should have seen it. But it was so easy to ignore the obvious signs, the brush of fingertips over the back of a hand, closeness that went beyond the bounds of friendship. So easy to ignore it while he filled his own needs, the comfort of human contact, letting events take their own course, never heeding Nari and her emptiness.

Nari was attractive, he admitted, and were he Doron Tem, or were circumstances different ... yet now ...

Ailsa filled his mind, standing closer than she had

133

since boarding the *Tommy John*. The past remained too strong for the present. In time, Nari Hullen, or someone like her, might be able to fill the void within him. But not now, not now.

He stared out the window. His life was akin to the contorted light. Despite the relative surcease found aboard the freighter, his mind never wandered far from the real purpose of his flight—Yerik Belen and the answers the man could provide. He did not need a Nari Hullen intruding to muddle his thoughts even more.

He glanced at the chronometer above the window. The digital display read 2:30 a.m. GMT. Rising, he slowly walked down the connecting tunnel corridors to the passenger deck. Outside the cabin, his palm hovered over the pressure plate for several indecisive seconds. Then he pressed it. If Nari were inside, nothing could be gained by avoiding her. He stepped into the cabin.

Nari's privacy screen rose like a solid gray wall enclosing her berth. He nodded silent approval. It made things less complicated. Perhaps, she somehow sensed his inner conflict. He slipped atop his bed and flicked on its screen. This was the way it should be, clean, clear, no commitments to further entangle the knotted strands of his life.

He rolled to his side. The gray force field barricaded his view of the room. It *was* better this way. Yet, why did he wish that both screens were down?

—I don't like it, Jonal.
*Who gives a damn!* Awareness crept through the clouds of sleep. He moaned; the shadowman had returned. *Go away, let me sleep in peace.*
—In pieces, if I left you alone.
*Get lost.*
—What do you know about her?
*Who?*
—This Nari Hullen, your cabinmate.
*What do you care? Let me sleep.*

134

—Dammit, Jonal! You don't need rest. You should be wide awake. Why is this bitch in your cabin? Seems rather convenient doesn't it?

*The passenger berths are all booked. It's the only place the purser could place her.*

—Still seems rather convenient.

More than a month had passed since the shadowman had spoken to him. He thought he had rid himself of the faceless voice. Why had he returned? Why was he bothering him again?

—Because you refuse to think for yourself, Jonal. This isn't a pleasure cruise. You're here because someone on Tula was trying to blow your brains out.

*What does that have to do with Nari?*

—What do you know about her?

*She teaches at a small Terran university. She's returning from Tula where she studied our cultural development. She's bored and lonely.*

—And you like her.

He disliked the sarcasm in the shadowman's voice. *I've enjoyed having someone to talk with.*

—Start thinking, Jonal.

*I am,* he replied. *I haven't told her anything. She doesn't suspect I'm Jonal Cassell.*

—You're thinking with your crotch! Use your brain for a moment or two. She's a woman. You haven't had a woman in months. Companionship isn't what you're after!

He retreated from the shadowman's accusation. The discomfort he experienced with Nari in the observation bay returned. *What the hell do you know anyway?*

—That you're acting like a fool. Think! Put two and two together. You know absolutely nothing about the woman, except what she's told you. You can't see that because you're after her like a mink in rut!

He did not answer. He had never made a move toward Nari. Until tonight there had never been a hint of sexual overtures in their relationship. A flush of

135

guilt coursed through him that he could not understand.

—Jonal, the game is too dangerous. She boarded at Tula. What makes you think she's not here to kill you, to finish a job they couldn't do on Tula?

He had considered the possibility Nari's first day in the cabin. Since then, he had gotten to know the woman. He did not doubt her reason for being on the *Tommy John.*

—Hell no, you don't. You've been so busy trying to knock off a little piece that you've stopped thinking.

*But,* he mentally stammered, unable to arrange his thoughts, *if she were here to kill me, she's had ample opportunity. You've got to be wrong.*

—Damn right she has. You couldn't have made it easier for her, except maybe to put a gun in her hand and tell her when to pull the trigger.

*She hasn't tried to kill me!*

—You heard the reason tonight. Don't you understand what she tried to tell you? The woman is falling in love. A professional can't become personally involved...but she has. And, if she is a professional, Jonal, it won't matter, at least not for very long. She's confused now, but she'll do what she has to. She's trained that way.

He rejected the shadowman's arguments. Still, a seed of doubt planted itself in his mind, germinating.

—It's an old trick. Lull the target with false security, get close to him. Then, when the right time comes, a very tidy but deadly accident occurs. No one is the wiser.

He attempted to stem the budding doubts of paranoia opening within him.

—Forget her, Jonal. There will be time enough for women after you've finished what you've started. But, you have to stay alive to enjoy them.

A smug, pleased smile curving the corners of his mouth, Cassell strolled from the purser's office. He felt relieved and savored a touch of victory. The freighter's passenger log was indeed filled. As best he could discern, Nari was in the cabin for one reason—there was no other place for her to berth.

He felt good, damn good. For the first time since his appearance, the shadowman's suspicions proved wrong. His mental companion was not infallible.

—You haven't proven a thing. I say, it's too convenient an arrangement to be coincidence.

*Sour grapes.* Cassell chuckled. Reaching a "Y" junction in the tunnel corridor, he turned toward the dining room.

—I don't understand this suicidal tendency you persist in nursing. When she pulls the trigger, I'll be there to say I told you so.

He entered the dining room and glanced over the breakfast crowd. Nari sat at the table designated for their cabin. She looked up from the tray before her, saw him, and smiled widely. He returned the smile, attempting to ignore a quaver of guilt that rushed through him. He told himself the visit with the purser was a matter of simple precaution. It brought no ease to the feeling he had somehow betrayed the woman. His smile suddenly felt too big, too friendly, a transparent mask that could never conceal his lack of faith.

"Your usual?" Nari asked when he took a seat beside her at the table. When he nodded, her fingers deftly danced over the servo-unit's control panel, punching out his breakfast order.

"You look unusually bright and cheerful this morning." He accepted the tray she handed him and peeled its cover away. "Have a good night's sleep?"

"Marvelous," she answered. "We can talk about last night later. Right now, eat your breakfast. Afterwards, I want you to teach me to play poker."

"Poker?" He frowned, uncertain whether he heard correctly.

"Mmmmmm-hmmmmm," she replied around the last mouthful of her meal. "I was watching Lieutenant

137

Ildre's game last night. It looked exciting. I saw the Lieutenant win a thousand standards in one hand. Think you can teach me?"

"I've also seen Lieutenant Ildre lose twice that amount in a single hand," Cassell said. "Are you prepared to be on that side of the table?"

Nari's forehead wrinkled as though it had never occurred to her that she might lose. "Yes . . . yes, though not that high an amount. Will you teach me?"

He raised a disapproving eyebrow that dropped the instant a hint of disappointment appeared on her face. He nodded tentatively. "Yes, I will. But first, I want to finish breakfast. Then we'll go to the recreation room. No one should bother us until late in the afternoon. By then you should be ready for Lieutenant Ildre this evening. She's always glad to find another easy mark."

Nari's pleased smile returned. She nudged the tray closer to him. "Eat up."

Cassell stood to one side of the table, not wanting to watch, but unable to drag his attention from the seven players. Earlier he had stood close to Nari. When she lost five consecutive hands, his nerves got to him. Unwilling to stand and watch her lose everything in front of her, he went for a walk. An hour later, he returned to see her take three small pots. After that she proved to be a cautious player, losing small amounts, usually folding before the action got too heavy, or betting equally small amounts on hands that most would describe as sure things.

But now—for the first time in months, he wanted a drink to steady himself.

At the center of the circular table lay a pile of chips and credit slips amounting to ten thousand standards. A Javolian dressed in a flowing caftan and with a fire gem stud in his left nostril pushed five hundred standards into the pot. Cassell felt a sickening sinking in his stomach. Nari only had two hundred standards safely stashed away in the purser's safe. The man was boosting the pot to frighten the others off.

One by one the betting moved around the table with all the players folding, except for Nari. The Javolian looked at her. "You're bet, Ms. Hullen."

"I'll see your five hundred," she said without hesitation. She reached into a pocket and pulled out a purser's receipt. "And raise you another thousand."

The hollowness in Cassell's stomach churned violently. She did not have the thousand. Yet, he saw the figures on the receipt as the Javolian lifted and examined it. The man looked at Nari, trying to hide a scowl that forced its way across his face.

Nari sat there, five cards tidily fanned in her hand as though she were unaware of the man's eyes. Not the slightest twinge of doubt creased her brow, nor did her lips tremble with uncontainable excitement. Cassell could not read her, which only aggravated his stomach's panicked rumbling. If Nari had learned only one thing from his lessons, it was the meaning of a poker face.

"It's up to you, Mr. Adet." Nari lifted a glass of water and sipped at it.

"I know," the Javolian mumbled. He sucked in a noisy breath and stared at the cards in his hand for a long, silent moment. With a disgusted shake of his head, he closed the cards and dropped them to the table. "I'm afraid it's too rich for me."

Nari calmly closed her hand and placed the cards face down on the table. She reached out and raked the pot to her. "Citizens, thank you for a most enjoyable evening. I'm afraid I must bid you good night. Perhaps some other evening."

"Your hand," the Javolian asked, "might I see what you were holding?"

Nari smiled, but shook her head. "As I understand this game, one must pay for that privilege. Sorry, Mr. Adet."

He smiled, a bit chagrined, but made no further attempt to see the cards. Nari stuffed her winnings into a waist pouch buckled to her coveralls. She handed the hand to Lieutenant Ildre, who placed the cards back into the deck.

"Again, thank you for an enjoyable evening." She rose to walk to Cassell's side. "Care for a stroll?"

He stared at her, still not believing what he had seen. He nodded.

"Good," she replied in a whisper. She slipped an arm through his and leaned against him. "Very slowly. My legs feel as though they are going to give way. I don't want them to see how nervous I am."

Tilting his head in a "good night" to the remaining players at the table, Cassell locked his arm about her for support and did as she requested, walked slowly from the recreation room. Outside, he glanced at her, questioning.

"In a moment." Her voice quavered a bit. "I need to sit down and gather my strength. Somewhere we can be alone."

"The cabin?"

"No, it's too far," she said. "I don't think I'd make it. The observation bay is closer, if you don't mind."

Doing his best to ignore the uneasy apprehension that licked at his mind, Cassell escorted her to the bay. After a double check to assure their privacy, Nari melted into a chair with a long, relieved sigh. She looked up and grinned with impish delight.

"Can you believe it?" She patted the overstuffed pouch.

"Saw it with my own eyes." Her obvious delight nudged back his apprehension. He laughed. "Still can't believe it."

"I can't either." She shook her head in disbelief. "I don't remember having so many standards at one time. This is a whole year's salary for a university instructor. It feels good."

"A tidy sum." He sat beside her. "A fine showing for your first night. Some would call it beginner's luck."

"They would be wrong. I had a good teacher." She winked. "Aren't you going to ask what I was holding?"

"No," Cassell said. "I might be across the table from you tomorrow night. Wouldn't want to take unfair advantage."

"I'm going to tell you anyway." She gave him a disappointed pout, then laughed. "I didn't have a thing. Not even a pair!"

"*What?*" It took a few seconds for what she said to sink in. "Nothing?"

"Not a thing." She looked at him, amused.

"I don't believe it." He didn't. "I didn't teach you to play that way."

"But you did!" She threw her arms around his neck, hugged him tightly, and loudly kissed his cheek. Leaning back, she grinned, a mischievous light flashing in her eyes. "You said poker was a game of chance . . . that risks had to be taken occasionally. You also said never take wild chances, make sure there's a foundation for the risk."

"Having nothing in your hand isn't what I would describe as a solid foundation," he said.

"No, but the way I played was," she replied. "I established myself as a very, very cautious player, refusing to bet on anything but an exceptionally good hand. When I bet, I won. The others noticed that too. I made my betting pattern quite obvious. It was worth the risk."

"And if the Javolian had called your bluff?" Cassell asked. "How did you intend to pay the debt? You've only got two hundred standards in the purser's safe. Where did you get that thousand standard credit voucher?"

"Visited the purser's office after our lessons," she replied. "I borrowed one of the receipts."

"Forged!" He suddenly realized Nari's big killing had been carefully planned, step by step. Instead of being shocked, the touch of larceny that surfaced in

141

the woman appealed to him for some indefinable reason. "What if you had lost?"

She winked again and shrugged her shoulders. "Adet might have found himself with a new berth partner for the remainder of the voyage."

He shook his head, unable to accept everything she had done.

Nari grinned and looked to the tachyon fireworks outside. "That's what it's all about, isn't it? The risk, I mean. It's not the winning or losing, but reaching for something."

He stared at her when she turned back to him. "I might have lost tonight, and it wouldn't have mattered. I admit it's more enjoyable to win. But what *was* important was that I was willing to take the chance."

"Be damn grateful you won," he said.

"Oh, I am, believe me," she replied. "But it's really not the money. I'm not sure I understand what it is I've gained, or if I can hold onto it. But here and now, it feels so real and right."

"Try reckless," he said. Couldn't she see how irresponsible her actions had been?

"I'm not being very clear. But I wasn't reckless. On the surface it looks that way, but I knew exactly what I was doing." She paused, searching his face. "I'm still not explaining it well. That's because I still feel uncertain about what's happening inside me. Doron, I've spent my life chasing security, shoring up the walls around me so they can withstand whatever is waiting outside."

She glanced back to the window. Cassell caught his breath, expecting to see that ironic smile curl her lips. Instead, she grinned.

"This room is me, my life," she said. "Safe and secure, I sit and watch the raging beauty outside. I want to be part of it. Yet, I'm too frightened to reach out and touch it. I've got a nice, secure position at a university. Once I had a nice, secure bond-contract with a nice, secure man. When he chose not to renew after three years, it

142

hurt. Instead of finding another lover, I retreated behind nice, secure walls. All my life, I yearned to travel to other planets. When the opportunity presented itself, I retreated again. I've been a tourist, maintaining a very nice, secure schedule. I've been too frightened to reach out and touch the beauty I've seen. Afraid it would touch me . . . or worse, terrified it wouldn't. Now, there's you . . ."

Her eyes rose to him, lingering. "You scare me, Doron Tem. Last night you frightened me so much I ran away. I'm not certain what I feel . . . but I do feel, and that's a beginning. I don't want to lose that."

Her hands rose, fingertips brushing his cheeks, palms cradling. Nari leaned forward. Her lips lightly touched his with uncertain expectations, as though he might shy from her. She eased back, her gaze exploring his face. Something, he should say something before . . . This was not what he wanted from her. The shadowman was wrong.

Nari's head tilted forward. Her lips, warm, yielding, pressed firmly to his mouth, opening. Her tongue flicked moistly at his lips and reached inward. His arms surrounded her, pulling her to him. The contours of her body molded snugly into his. Her warmth suffused through the fabric of their coveralls. So close, so close.

Abruptly, he pulled away, needles of guilt pricking hotly at his flesh. Nari stared, hurt and confusion in her eyes.

"I'm sorry." He tenderly touched her cheek. "For a moment . . . Nari . . ."

"I'm not asking that you love me," she said softly. "I want you, Doron. It might end with the morning bell, or when we arrive on Earth. I don't care. I accept the risk."

He glanced away, uncomfortable beneath her probing gaze. Ailsa's image burned in his mind—the completeness of their love. Nari wasn't Ailsa, could never replace her, even for a night.

"Is it me, Doron?" she asked.

"I was married," he said, unable to look at her. "My wife died in an accident shortly before I left Tula. She's still with me, Nari. It's not you. Another time . . . but now, it's all too close to push aside. It wouldn't be fair to you, or me."

"It's the chance I'm willing to take," she replied.

"I'm not." He turned from her. "There's more . . ." He caught himself before he told her everything. "It's just *too close.*"

She nodded silently. He expected rejection in her expression, but only found understanding. She kissed him tenderly, then rose. "I think I understand. Doron, the privacy screen around my berth will be down from now on. If you . . ."

She stopped and smiled, then turned to walk from the room. Cassell closed his eyes, listening to her footsteps echo down the tunnel corridor. The shadowman was wrong, he told himself, again and again.

"First your cabinmate, and now you." Lieutenant Ildre tossed her cards to the table. "Too much in one night for me to handle. I'm calling it quits."

The other players nodded and voiced their agreement. Pocketing a stack of standards, Cassell watched the others rise to return to their cabins, leaving him alone in the recreation room.

He swiveled from the table and walked to a wall servo-unit. He selected a cup of fruit juice and pulled it from the dispenser. Sipping at the thick sweetness, his gaze moved around the room, noting every minute detail as though he were an artist studying the compartment for a future painting. By far the most colorful room aboard the freighter, he had always found it pleasing. Now, it seemed to be a mishmash of gaudy colors randomly paneled to hide the ship's metallic skeleton. The remnants of the night's gaming lay strewn over the table tops, spilling onto the floor, crushed beverage cups, ashes, half-smoked sticks of consciousness-altering drugs.

He took another sip from the cup. The *Tommy John* loomed about him. He shrank to a dwarf before its immensity. He stood alone, abandoned.

*Wasting time*, he thought in an effort to dredge himself up from the muck of self-pity. The compartment's chronometer read 3 a.m. GMT. The poker game had lasted three hours, and he still needed something to occupy his time. He glanced at the remaining mouthfuls of the juice in the cup. He sloshed them around, watching the red liquid lap up the sides. *Wasting time.*

He lifted the cup and drained it. Crushing the disposable plastic in a clenched fist, he tossed it aside and walked from the recreation room. Guilt, confused frustration, writhed within him. But he could not postpone returning to the cabin any longer. Nàri could never understand what he had shared with Ailsa. It *was* too close. Nari did not belong. She was an intruder.

Nari's face flickered in his mind's eye. It tore at him, the hurt in her eyes.

He paused at the cabin door. Hesitantly his hand rose to the pressure plate. With abrupt resignation, he pushed it. A slight hiss and the hatch opened. Cassell stepped in; the door closed behind him.

Relief suffused through him. Nari's privacy screen was down, but she lay asleep in her bed. His gaze coursed over her. The light sheet draped across her rose and fell in the soft rhythm of her breathing.

Crossing to his berth, he switched on its privacy screen, undressed, and climbed atop the bed. He closed his eyes; they opened seemingly of their own volition. He stared blankly into the darkness above him.

Ailsa—Nari, Nari—Ailsa. He shoved them away by concentrating on the night's poker hands, his winnings. They wiggled back to demand his attention. Could Nari understand? Did he understand?

Ailsa's and his life together was more than a simple bond-contract. It had been a full commitment of two persons desiring a lifetime at one another's side—a marriage of mind, body, and soul. Could another ever

145

understand the full measure of their love and passion? For him, it remained vivid—the texture of Ailsa's body as they met, smooth and yielding, slickening to a sleek tautness as she gave herself totally. He could taste her, smell the sweetness of her perfume mingling with the musk of passion.

So real. No room for Nari. Yet...

He tossed to his side and closed his eyes. Sleep balked, shied away, refusing to provide a shelter from the conflicting emotions, desires. He flopped to his back. Nari just did not fit, did not belong. There was no love, no feeling...

He lied to himself. He did feel. The shadowman had been right. He wanted Nari, desired her. The guilt, the squirming discomfort, stemmed from the desire that frightened him so to admit. He could not accept his needs, the very thought was infidelity to the ghost that still dwelled in his mind, a memory that guarded against all intruders.

A knocking sound outside the privacy screen, a dull, metallic rap. Startled, he jerked around, unsure he had not imagined the sound. He listened. Nothing came. Closing his eyes, he lay back and tried to sleep.

Once more the knock came. "Doron?"

"Nari?" Cassell hit the switch on the side of the bed. The privacy screen melted in a crackling hiss. The gray wall faded; light stabbed into his eyes.

He blinked, accustoming himself to the brightly shining globe overhead. Nari stood beside his bed, a bed sheet draped about her. Her gaze moved over him. He was suddenly aware he lay naked on the bed.

Without a word, she seated herself on the edge of the berth. Her eyes rose to his, her breath came soft and steady. The sheet about her parted slightly, and a hand slipped out from the folds. Gently her fingertips traced over his lips. He felt their trembling. Or was it his own?

Nari leaned forward; her mouth covered his, a tender caress that increased in passion. When they parted, a

146

slight smile upturned the covers of her mouth. Her left hand released its crumpling grasp on the sheet. She cradled his face with both hands. The sheet fell away, dropping to the floor.

For a moment, he resisted looking at her, as though the act would give unspoken validity to her presence. He could not contain the compelling attraction. His gaze drifted over the feminine curves of her nakedness. Her breasts rose and fell in a heavy rhythm as her breathing deepened.

"Nari . . ." He denied himself in an effort to retain loyalty to the ghost floating through his brain.

"Shhhhh." She pressed a finger against his lips and slightly shook her head.

The words forming in his mind faded. Again she leaned down to him, her mouth meeting his. Warm and smooth, flesh on flesh, she eased onto the bed beside him, her length pressed to his.

He felt her nervousness, her uncertainty, swirling out to mingle with his. Her breath fluttered, and his hands calmed her, gently stroking away the tremblings. Warmly, their bodies caressed, neither moving nor seeking more.

Their lips parted; they inched back, each searching the other's face for seconds that convoluted into a ponderous eternity, a weighty moment that hung forever. Decision. Time to deny and scurry away in shameless retreat. He felt it around him. She gave him time once again to reject the offering of her body, to escape into past memories.

His palms edged from her side to stroke her back. His fingertips read the tension strung taut along her spine. She carried the same weight. Her eyes questioned. Her brow creased slightly; the corners of her mouth trembled. She sensed the balance of the moment. Time remained to slip away from their mutual warmth and return to her own berth. They both would find the lies to shelter them in the morning. It would be no more than a moment's indiscretion that could be forgotten. Time enough to choose once again the nice, secure life she had so carefully programmed for Nari Hullen. Nothing risked . . . but nothing lost.

He sensed the pocket of eternity that held them dwindle; exterior time prevailed. He saw the same awareness in her face and read unspoken acceptance. Her head rolled on the pillow. She touched his shoulder, her lips slipping up his neck until their mouths met once more.

Afraid words would conceal hollow promises and lies, their hands spoke, stroking, soothing, tasting the feel of one another. Neither moved in urgency nor a frenzy of fevered desire. Man, woman, friends, responded to the mutual need of intimacy; the touch of another human being.

The graceful fluidity of erotic holocasts, the unhampered ease of first union glorified in novels and dramas found no meaning between them. They lay in the palm of reality. Awkwardly, with the clumsiness of two bodies ignorant of each other, he entered the yielding liquid warmth of her body. They clung to each other, kissing deeply, desperately struggling to breach the walls of loneliness surrounding them.

Doubt, tension, unvoiced fear, anxiety faded. Nor did their artless joining have any weight. They rocked together in a gentle, sleepy rhythm. Expectations of a consuming nova of passion melted with acceptance of the moment and contentment in their lullaby of comfort. His release or the need to fulfill her did not exist. They were not engaged in a writhing contest of sexual agility, but quenched the inner hunger to touch and be touched by another.

He felt the roar, the blood pounding in his ears, and when it passed, the embracing satisfaction of being alive. He demanded nothing more of that moment than to be where he was, harbored in the shelter of her arms. He snuggled against the honest nakedness of her body, trying to retain the rightness of that instant until his body's strength ebbed.

148

Beside her again, they clung tightly to one another, refusing to dissolve the security of their union. The shared awkwardness, the embarrassing uncertainty had passed to bring more than fictional promises.

"Thank you," she whispered, almost in afterthought, or beset by some social need to finalize commitment with words.

He kissed her tenderly in gratitude, then drew her closer, reveling in the feel of her.

"It was me, wasn't it?" Her voice was hesitant, doubtful. "I wasn't your wife?"

"Yes," he whispered and kissed her again, understanding her need to be reassured that their sharing had been real. "It was you."

She sighed, contented, and nestled against him. Her breath trickled warmly over his bare chest, shallowing to the deep, steady rhythm of sleep. He brushed the softness of her hair with his lips, a last gentle kiss. Then he lay there, holding her pressed to him, protecting her from her fears, at least for the night.

Guilt twinged within him in a brief spasm, not rooted in their love-making, but in the realization Ailsa had never entered his mind.

# TWELVE

"I don't like this." Nari frowned from across the cabin while she strapped into her berth to prepare for the transition back to normal space. "I've grown accustomed to having you beside me in bed."

Cassell tightened the straps across his chest. "I don't think you'd find me very satisfactory right now. The jump always leaves me nauseous."

Nari pursed her lips and kissed in his direction. She winked and grinned, eyes flashing impish mischief. "Get 'em while their resistance is low, I always say."

The last warning horn resounded within the cabin. Cassell gave her a weak smile. He lay flat on his back and stared at the ceiling, attempting not to anticipate the instant of transition. It did not help. Every muscle in his body knotted and reknotted itself. His stomach turned flip-flops, unwilling to wait for any real cause of distress. He breathed deeply and closed his eyes, trying to force calmness.

—Playtime's over, Jonal. It's been a fun few weeks, but it's time to get back to your real purpose for being here.

Cassell's spirits sank. *Won't I ever be rid of you?*

—Since you ignored my warning about the woman . . . *You were wrong about Nari!*

— . . . and since she appeared harmless enough, I decided you needed a bit of uninterrupted recreation. But, enough is enough! You'll be on Earth in a few hours.

*As soon as I get to Nari's home, I'll use her computer to find Yerik Belen. I haven't forgotten.*

—And get yourself killed in the process. Tula was easy, Jonal. Earth isn't. If you don't stay on your toes, they'll eat you alive before you take two steps. The woman is nothing but a piece of fluff. She's been fun in bed, but she's extra baggage. If you're not careful, she'll get you killed. Get rid of her, Jonal. Dump her before it's too late.

Cassell tried to ignore the shadowman. But truth was truth. He wanted to feel more for Nari, but he didn't. He knew she felt more, had watched it grow since their first night and had done nothing to stop it. They both had needed someone; now that time had ended for him.

—Landing is going to be dangerous. If they've traced you, they'll be waiting. You've got to get the woman out of the way.

The image of Ailsa stretched atop a hospital table invaded his thoughts. She was dead, killed by accident. Her only fault was standing too close to him when the assassin's finger tightened on the trigger. Ailsa's face wavered, replaced by Nari's. She stood too close now. It could happen again; another innocent murdered because of him.

—If you have to be gallant about it, then be gallant Your reasons don't matter, as long as you ditch her.

He gave a mental nod of agreement. *And when I arrive on Earth?*

—First, you need to get out of the port. After that, it should be relatively easy, if you keep alert. Until then, you've got to play it by ear. Be ready for anything. If you blow it, they won't give you a second chance.

*This is Earth, not Tula,* Cassell replied with thick sarcasm.

—Don't forget it, Jonal. Don't you forget it for one second. You have to find Yerik Belen.

*Where do I start?*

Cassell's thoughts disintegrated in a rushing tidal wave of nausea. The *Tommy John* slid back into normal space. He worked his jaws and swallowed. He fought back his upheaving stomach as it sought to empty itself. A fine sweat prickled over his face. Each cell of his body radiated an interior inferno that sought to explode.

As suddenly as it started, it ended. Drained, Cassell found himself still atop his berth, filled with the realization that he still lived. He trembled a bit and his stomach continued to churn in queasy protest, but once more he survived the jump no worse for the wear.

He remembered the observation bay and wished he stood before its giant window. The Earth approach would be magnificent to view, but there was not enough time. The schedule from here out was tight. A half-hour remained to gather personal items and board the shuttle that would return him to Earth.

"Doron?" Nari's concerned voice wedged into his thoughts. "Are you okay?"

Cassell opened his eyes, his head rolling on the pillow. He nodded and managed a less than enthusiastic, but reassuring smile. "My stomach is trying to digest itself. Every muscle in my body is vibrating like a plucked harp string . . . but other than that, I'll live."

The "all clear" buzzer blared over the intercom. Nari deftly flipped open her retaining straps, then bounded across the room in a single stride. Cassell did a double take. It took a moment for him to realize the transition had returned them to weightlessness.

"Hold on, fumble fingers." Nari deposited herself on

the side of his bed. "I'll have you out of these in a moment."

Cassell grinned sheepishly while she extracted him from the harness straps. He pushed to his elbows and gave her a grateful kiss.

"Better get to it," she said. "We haven't that much time to get to the shuttle bay."

Cassell swung his legs over the edge of the bed, paused a second to assure the static soles of his shoes gripped, then rose. When Nari moved back to her bed, he opened the compartment beneath the berth and pulled out his single suitcase. He glanced at Nari who stuffed things into two small pieces of luggage.

Turning back to his own case, he withdrew an unopened suit package he had purchased in Epai. Tearing it open, he stripped away the flight coveralls he wore and dressed in the suit. While he once again looked the part of a man come to Earth on business instead of a space tramp, he felt surprisingly uncomfortable. The suit was stiff and harshly coarse to his skin, accustomed to months in soft, yielding coverall fabric.

From the travel bag, he lifted a thick bundle of standards. He placed half the bills in a pocket of the suit. The remainder he returned to the case and carefully locked away. He did not know how long it would take to locate Yerik Belen, but his poker winnings over the past months gave him a bit more security. He had enough money to last a year, maybe two, if he were frugal. Money should not be a problem.

Nari would.

The image of her stretched out on a hospital table flashed before his eyes again. He winced—dead meat. Once was enough. Nari was not Ailsa, but he could not allow her to become more entangled in his life than she was.

It would be easier if he could slip away from her while they were still aboard the *Tommy John*. However, he saw no way to manage that. There was only one passenger shuttle. He would have to make his move in the spaceport. After they filed through customs, while they mingled with the port's crowds, would offer the best opportunity to separate. He would simply fade back, lose himself, then flee in a bubble cab.

That was, if "they" allowed him to get that far, if they weren't waiting for him the moment the shuttle landed.

"Damn!" Nari's voice rose, irritated.

Cassell carefully turned in the low gravity. Nari stood holding a handful of credit slips, exasperation on her face. "I forgot about these ... winnings from my first night at Lieutenant Ildre's table." She looked up at the cabin's chronometer. "Doron, wait for me here. I think there's enough time to make it to the purser and get these cashed."

"You can do it when we land," he suggested. "There's no need to rush."

"No " She shook her head. "I want these credit slips cashed before the others have a chance to withdraw their money. Wait for me?"

He nodded as she left. "Nowhere else for me to go."

Placing his case on the floor beside the bed, Cassell lay down. Twenty minutes remained until shuttle boarding. Nari had ample time to visit the purser and make the flight down.

Idly, his gaze moved over the cabin. He would miss the *Tommy John* and the three months of relative quiet security it had provided him. The shadowman's warnings for renewed caution would not leave his thoughts. He did not want to believe "they" had followed him from Tula to Earth, but the possibility existed.

And Yerik Belen? Earth was a big, overpopulated planet. On Tula, the journey to Earth seemed rational. Now the task ahead appeared impossible. Could he really expect to find one man among the teeming billions? He had no idea where to begin the search.

The cabin door opened with a soft hiss.

154

"That was quick." Cassell sat up. "I thought you might have some . . ."

Words lodged in his throat. A numbing finger of fear tapped at the base of his spine and ran upward. Lieutenant Ildre and a crewman stood just inside the cabin. Both held pistols, barrels leveled at him.

"Easy, Mr. Tem." Lieutenant Ildre's voice was unsteady. "I don't like this, but I have a warrant from planetside authorities to hold you until they take you into custody."

"A warrant?" Panic gripped him. He repressed the urge to break and run. "Lieutenant, what is this?"

"I'm not sure. There are no specifics," she replied. "I'm only following orders. If you'll come with us?"

"I don't understand what's going on." His brain raced, grasping for anything that could get him out of this situation.

—Easy, Jonal. They're about a kilometer ahead of you. Don't do anything to excite these two. They're so nervous they might accidentally pull the trigger.

"Lieutenant, there's been a mistake," Cassell said. If he could convince them to let him leave on the shuttle, he had a chance. "I suggest you recheck whatever information you've been given. If you continue to play this ridiculous game, I assure you that this freight line, and yourself, will be on the wrong end of a most embarrassing lawsuit."

"Mr. Tem." The pistol's needle muzzle jerked about in twitchy movements that did nothing to lessen his anxiety. "I've no say in this matter. I don't want trouble, but I have my orders. Come with us, and we can get everything cleared up a lot sooner."

The lieutenant signaled him off the bed with a wave of her pistol.

—Best do as she says. Play it by ear.

Cassell rose, lifted his travel case, and slowly crossed the room. He did his best to maintain an indignant attitude that was completely lost on the two. With

155

Lieutenant Ildre before him and the crewman behind, they marched him to the shuttle bay. The lieutenant opened a hatch beside what appeared to be a mechanic's table. She motioned for him to enter. He complied without protest. The door closed behind him; its lock resounded like the grinding of giant gears.

The smell of grease and oil permeated the cramped confines of the small compartment. Cassell glanced around. Under the bright light of a single overhead globe, he found no stains or smears to match the overpowering odors. The walls, floor, and ceiling appeared to be painted in a fresh coat of flat gray. Had the compartment been especially prepared for him? He did not like the thought. It meant the freighter's crew had known about him for some time.

Cassell turned back to the door and tested it. The hatch was locked as securely as it sounded. Like it or not, he was a prisoner. Upending the suitcase, he placed it on the floor. He sat on top of it, staring at the hatch. There was nothing else to do but wait.

—You should have disembarked at Javol and taken another flight to Earth. They've had you pegged since you boarded the *Tommy John*.

*Hindsight is terrific, isn't it! Even makes a bad dream a genius.*

—They knew you might elude them once the shuttle touched down, so they eliminated the risk.

*Lieutenant Ildre mentioned planetside authorities. How did the police get involved in this?*

—Yerik Belen has all the answers.

*Belen isn't here; I am! What do I do now?*

—Just what you're doing, wait. They'll slip up somewhere. When they do, move.

*Great, just great.*

He heard the passengers shuffle by outside to board the docked shuttle. He imagined Nari's confusion, hurt abandonment. He had wanted to lose her, but this was not exactly what he had in mind. He shrugged his

156

shoulders and attempted to ignore the twinges of guilt that pricked his conscience. Nari had taken her chance and lost. If life were a poker game, she would find the cards fell that way most of the time.

He smiled wistfully, recalling their plans for him to return with her. Within an hour or two, she would be back in her nice, secure home. It was better that way, though she would never know that—better than ending up as a cold piece of dead meat on some hospital table.

He felt-heard the clanging release of the shuttle locks, the rasp of metal grating metal when the craft slid free of the freighter to nose downward to Earth. Then there was silence.

For a half-hour he watched the seconds flash by on his wristwatch. It only made the situation worse; each second moved like cold syrup. Unable to keep his gaze from the digital display, he slipped the watch from his wrist and stuffed it into a pocket.

Footsteps sounded beyond the hatch. Opening locks hissed and clanged. Vibrations rumbled deep within the metallic walls about him. Another shuttle nosed into the vacant bay. More footsteps came, and he imagined the crew scuttling about to load the craft's hold with freight brought home from distant stars.

He resisted the urge to pull the watch from his pocket, afraid only a few more minutes had passed. Occasionally, he rose and tested the compartment's hatch. No matter how many times he threw his weight against the metal, it refused to budge.

Eventually, the footsteps outside approached the compartment. The lock ground again, and the hatch opened. Lieutenant Ildre poked her head inside and ordered him out.

Two black-uniformed men with sidearms strapped about their waists stood beyond his temporary cell. The lieutenant tilted her head to the pair. "These men will escort you planetside. If there has been a mistake, they will help you clear things up."

Before Cassell could reply or manage an indignant

157

scowl, the two police officers grabbed his arms and led him through the open nose of the waiting shuttle.

He fell, starchild recalled to the womb. Clouds, dense and ominous in appearance, floated like mountains in the sky. He tried to discern familiar topography, but a large, lazy ocean offered no hint as to the shuttle's glide path. Turbulence buffeted the metal pterodactyl; wind screamed.

He strained to see beyond the limits of the circular porthole beside him. The shuttle fell faster toward blanketing darkness as it moved around the planet's curvature. Diamonds sparkled up from the velvet blackness, lights from the metroplex network that laced Earth's surface.

Sledgehammers hailed against the craft's outer skin. Cassell was thrown forward, restraining straps biting into chest, waist, and crotch. Retro rockets fired. The shuttle's plummet slowed. It no longer hurled itself into the clinging atmosphere, but rode the wind currents, a monstrous soaring bird. The diamonds below expanded to reveal a myriad of lights that bred more. They rushed by outside, blurring as the craft descended.

The landing was easier than he anticipated. There was a sense of speed, a heavy thud, another, then the wail of rubber against concrete. He glanced at the two officers; neither had spoken during the descent, nor had he offered anything.

The shuttle taxied to a halt. Cassell disentangled himself from the restraining harness when the guards flipped their straps open. With the same eloquent speech they had used on the *Tommy John,* they took his arms and escorted him from the craft.

Outside they stepped onto a slidewalk network that webbed the expansive spaceport. Cassell searched for a familiar landmark but found none. Ahead of them rose what appeared to be the port's main terminal complex. A brightly luminous sign on the left end of the

complex marked the entrance to the local police headquarters.

—Do something. If they get you in there, you won't
have a chance.

Cassell agreed, but before he could contemplate a
course of action, his silent guards tugged him onto a
slidewalk angling away from the terminal building. A
high-rising building loomed ahead. Spotlights illuminated metal letters on the side of the structure—AG-
RICULTURE EXPORT COMMISSION.

*What?*

—I don't know?

*Terrific!*

—Count your blessings. Anything is better than
being in the hands of the police. Stay sharp. You might
get only one chance to make a break.

Cassell doubted he would recognize that chance, if
and when it occurred. The guards tightened their hold
on his arms as though reading his thoughts. He glanced
at them. They were not that big. He might . . .

The migrant thought dissolved. His gaze dropped tu
the two overly large pistols holstered to their sides.
With luck he might be able to take both men, but he
could never outrun their firepower. He cautiously re-
solved that the shadowman's mentioned chance had
yet to come.

They entered the building so brightly marked as the
Agriculture Export Commission. Light glared from
overhead glowpanels and harshly reflected off what
appeared to be highly polished marble walls. The building's interior disturbed Cassell. Solid and expansive,
it appeared official and very governmental. The archi-
tecture was meticulously designed to intimidate those
outside the circle of civil servants who had the audacity
to enter the hallowed halls. The anonymous architect
who masterminded the design had achieved his purpose. Cassell felt intimidated.

His ever-silent escort hussled him down a corridor
toward a series of drop and liftshaft openings. They

moved him into a liftshaft before he realized it was not just the oppressive design of the building that bothered him.

The Agriculture Export Commission was empty. Despite the well-lit hall, he had not seen another soul in the corridor, nor in the offices he had passed. The building had either been evacuated for his arrival, or it was later in the night than he realized.

—It doesn't matter. The place is deserted. You're still in the running, Jonal. Just stay on your toes.

Fifteen floors up, his guards shoved him from the shaft. Briskly, they led him down another brightly lit and equally empty hallway. They stopped before an unmarked metal door that wore a worn coat of institutional green paint.

—You can take these two.

The opportunity did not look tremendous to him. The officers still had pistols strapped about their waists. He elected to wait awhile longer.

—Damn you!

One of the guards opened the door. Inside was what appeared to be a simple office for a low-ranking bureaucrat. A metal desk and two chairs were the room's only furnishings. Three men standing by the room's single window turned toward him. The man in the middle smiled when his eyes lighted on Cassell.

"Thank you, officers," the man said. He nodded to his companions, who replaced the guards at Cassell's sides. "We'll handle everything from here. I'll see that your superiors receive a report of your efficiency and cooperation."

The officers smiled and left without a word. The man still at the window pointed to the wall. "Search him."

Abruptly his companions shoved Cassell against the wall, spread his arms and legs, then patted him down. He could not determine if the two were armed, but each one was bigger than both the officers put together.

"He's clean," one of the men announced. "Only this bundle and a watch."

160

"Return the money and check the watch for explosives," the man at the window said. "Wait outside. I'd like a moment alone with Mr. Tem."

The two gorillas in business suits released Cassell and left the room, shutting the door behind them. The man at the window pointed to a chair in front of the desk.

—Move! You can take him and be out of here and past those two in the hall before they know what's happening. Once in the dropshaft there's no way they can stop you.

Perhaps he tensed, or maybe the man at the window sensed the thoughts running through his head. Either way, the man was two steps ahead of him:

"It would be foolish, Mr. Tem. I've got men on every level of the building. All are armed. It took us a long time to get you, and we don't intend to let you slip away that easily. Now, please be seated."

Cassell did as he was told. The man sat behind the desk and smiled, a pleased and smug smile. "For a while, we were afraid we misread you. If you decided to jump ship at any of the *Tommy John*'s ports it would have complicated matters. And you've managed quite enough as it is."

—Jonal, don't sit there listening to him. You've got to get out of here.

"Why am I being held?" Cassell wanted to sound firm, indignant, angry, but a slight tremble crept into his voice. "What is going on?"

The man's right eyebrow arched, and he stared at Cassell for a long, heavy moment. He smiled again, as though they shared some secret. He reached over the desk and tapped the buttons of a phone. Cassell heard a crackle when the screen came to life. He craned his neck, unable to see the face on the receiver.

"Mazour here," the man behind the desk said. "Put me through to Director Santis. This is a Red-A priority."

A buzz-like whisper answered. Cassell could not

make out the reply. The man who called himself Mazour bit his lip and frowned.

"Dammit! I don't care," he said. "Hurry it up. I'll be here until she contacts me."

There was another buzz and a crackle. Mazour looked up at Cassell, still frowning.

"Mazour, or whatever your name is, I demand to know why I'm being held against my will." His voice sounded more steady now.

Mazour laughed. "Who the hell do you think you're kidding, Mr. Tem? Or should I say Cassell?"

"What?"

"Playing dumb won't help." Mazour grinned widely, obviously enjoying Cassell's discomfort. "You've no weight to throw around here. This is Earth. If we're all lucky, we just might be able to save your life. At the moment, the agency is the only friend you've got. I suggest you do as I say. It'll make it easier for everybody concerned."

Cassell stared at him. He felt like a fool, anger growing with each passing second. "What in hell are you talking about? I've got the right to know why I'm being detained. I've got the right . . ."

"You don't have the right to scratch your own ass here. This isn't Tula!" Mazour leaned forward. His voice rose, belying his smile. "Play ignorant. It won't help. Remember that! If I had my way, I'd eliminate you and be done with it. But the agency has other ideas. I just follow orders. You can be damn thankful for that."

Mazour paused to gather a breath. Before he could continue, the desk phone chimed. He leaned back and calmed himself before he reached to answer the call.

—Jonal, you're playing a dangerous game. Don't trust him. You have to get out of here.

Mazour's fingers stabbed the receiver bar. The screen flicked to life. "Yes, Director Santis. Yes, it came off without a hitch."

Cassell found himself straining to hear the buzzing voice on the other end of the line, or to glimpse the face on the receiver screen. He could discern neither, and found himself once more listening to a one-sided conversation.

—Jonal, it's time to move. Take him now, while he's occupied.

"Rest assured of that, Director," Mazour said. "Yes, I am positive this is Jonal Cassell. Ragah Tvar was right."

*Ragah? Ragah was involved in this?*

—You have to escape!

*Ragah?* Something deep within Cassell churned, dark and writhing. Something he refused to acknowledge, was afraid to even consider.

—Jonal, it will be too late, if you don't act now!

Cassell tried to close off the voice hammering in his head. He wanted to hear Mazour, needed to know how this man and the "agency" fit into the confused jumble of his life.

Mazour sat quietly now, his attention held by the soft buzzing voice. He visibly paled, shaken by whatever the unseen Director Santis said. His eyes shifted from the screen to Cassell. He pursed his lips and sucked at his teeth.

"Yes, I've enough men for adequate protection," Mazour finally answered. "We'll use six vehicles, three as a decoy unit. I'll have him in your office within an hour. Don't worry, nothing will go wrong."

He switched off the phone and stared at Cassell before he stood and walked to the door and opened it. Mazour's two gorillas stood outside. Pistols were tucked tidily in their hands.

"Just talked with Santis," Mazour said. "Word is out that our man is on-planet. The World Combine Liberation Front has got wind of us. Santis suspects an agency plant."

"Those bastards again," one of the gorillas said with contempt.

"Yeah," Mazour replied. "One of our agents has infiltrated their organization. Seems they want Cassell

163

to expose the agency. Santis needs Cassell as quickly as we can deliver him. Santis wants him processed and off-planet before the WCLF makes a move."

"The Director overestimates those sons of bitches," the gorilla said.

"She's still the director," Mazour cut the man short. "Hil, you assemble the men in the basement. Ord and I will take Cassell down."

Cassell heard everything, but made no sense out of it. What value could he be to the World Combine Liberation Front, whoever they were? There was no way he could expose the "agency" when he didn't know who in hell they were either.

Mazour and his remaining gorilla, Ord, came back into the room. Both carried guns now, and both muzzles were aimed directly at Cassell's chest. He repressed the urge to say something about being tired of staring down gun barrels. Instead he stood without protest when Mazour ordered him on his feet.

"It's yours, you carry it." Mazour tossed his travel case at him. "Let's go. If we're lucky, we just might be able to save your miserable life."

Under the directing muzzles, Cassell marched docilely from the room and down the hall to a dropshaft. They floated down fifteen floors to ground level, then three below to exit in a sub-basement. A ground shuttle hummed out of the dimly lit parking area to halt before them. The canopy swung open and Ord stepped in, motioning for Cassell to join them. He did.

—This might be even better. Take the goon and you've got a weapon and transportation.

Cassell did not get the opportunity to consider overpowering the armed man. A small army of business-suit attired men filed from the dropshafts. Five other ground cars pulled behind him.

"Clapton, Bes, and Adams, you'll decoy." Mazour stood beside the open cab shouting directions. "You leave first. Take the direct route, and be careful. The WCLF is on to this."

Nine men, three to each cab, separated and climbed into the waiting vehicles. Cassell watched the decoy unit swing around the shuttle and trundle toward the exit ramp. Rounding a corner, they disappeared, their chorusing hums fading behind the solid wall of the sub-basement.

"Hil," Mazour ordered, "five of you take the lead vehicle. Kra and the rest, cover our tail."

The men hastened to their positions. Mazour surveyed the scene one last time, then slid into the seat beside Cassell.

"Now, keep your fingers crossed," he said, then signaled the lead ground shuttle to move out.

# THIRTEEN

Hil's vehicle swung out, taking the point. Immediately, Cassell's ground shuttle jolted forward, following five lengths behind. At the rear, the remaining escort trundled along at a five-length distance. Like three cars joined by some invisible line, the shuttles moved through the sub-basement, then up the exit ramp.

—Jonal, there're only two of them. You can handle them.

*You handle them!* Ord still held his pistol, but the barrel no longer aimed at his chest. Cassell relaxed a bit. The prospect of finishing his journey dead on the floor of a ground shuttle with a hole burned in his chest by men professing to be his saviors was not the way he envisioned his search concluding.

"Over there." Ord directed him to the shuttle's opposite seat. "I want to keep an eye on you."

—Take his gun. You can scorch Mazour before the goon realizes what you're doing.

Cassell scooted into the vacant seat opposite Ord. He found himself once more staring down the barrel

166

f the man's gun. The gorilla in human form smiled and leaned back in his seat, his eyes never leaving Cassell.

Mazour sat beside Ord, pistol balanced across his knees, within reach. The man's attention, however, was on the night beyond the plastic canopy. The ground shuttle shot from the exit ramp and onto a feeder line that joined the spaceport's main concourse. The man's gaze constantly surveyed their surroundings. His hands rested on a manual override console. With a flick of a switch, the vehicle controls would be at his fingertips.

Ten years on Tula and Cassell had forgotten about the manual controls Terrans demanded on their ground transportation and the regulations that allowed privately-owned vehicles. For either to exist on a planet as overpopulated as Earth seemed to be a form of social Russian roulette.

—Jonal, you can't just sit there. You have to do something!

The shadowman's voice was a piercing scream; he jumped in spite of himself. He glanced at Ord. The man had not noticed. Ord now also stared beyond the bubble canopy, cautiously searching the night. Cassell's pulse quickened; he turned to the pistol on Mazour's knees. If he acted quickly ...

"Forget it," Mazour said casually. Cassell's gaze rose to find the man staring at him. "You'd never pull it off. Relax and enjoy the ride. That way you won't get hurt."

Cassell did his best to do just that.

—Belen, Jonal, remember Belen.

Cassell tried to block out the shadowman's pleas. They echoed his own mounting anxiety. He told himself he was better off sitting there helplessly than attempting anything foolish. Mazour had said "the agency" could save his life. The thought brought no comfort. Both men retained their firearms and had given every indication they would use them on him if the opportunity arose.

167

—Jonal, you can't give up. You've got to get away from them. You've got to find Belen!

*How?* He gave in to the shadowman's persistence and answered. Outside, the blur of buildings and city lights offered no hint as to his location. *How am I going to find Belen? I don't know where I am.*

The irrational obsession that dominated him, forced him to flee Tula in search of Yerik Belen, settled heavily on him, pushing him deeper into the seat's cushioning. For three months he had traversed the light centuries of half a galaxy seeking a man contrived by his own mental aberration. He had no proof Yerik Belen existed. If there were a Belen, how could he ever expect to find him among Earth's billions?

—Kansas City, Jonal. You're in Kansas City. Belen does exist. I thought you'd gotten all that crap out of your system.

He shook his head, unwilling to accept anything the shadowman told him. He looked at Mazour and Ord. "Where are we?"

Never pausing in his constant surveillance of the city, Mazour said, "KCplex. Thought you'd recognize your hometown. Guess it's changed since the last time you were here."

Incredulous, Cassell stared at the man. "I was born in the EasTex Metroplex."

Ord chuckled and Mazour grinned smugly. Neither volunteered further information.

"What is going on here?" Cassell's frustration boiled up and overflowed. He felt like a blind man being led through a maze of razors. He was tired of being the butt of some private joke that held no meaning for him, tired of guns poised and ready to sear away his gut. "Why are you holding me? Where are you taking me?"

Mazour clicked his teeth and looked disgusted. Ord chuckled some more and shook his head. Both returned to their surveillance, denying him another glance.

"Bastards! Can't you get it through those moronic minds that I don't know what's happening?" Cassell

168

refused to let the matter drop. They had no right to treat him this way. "What do you intend to do with me?"

"Look, Cassell," Mazour said sharply, "no one asked you to come. My orders are to take you to Director Santis. She didn't say anything about my having to hold polite conversation with you."

"Dammit! You don't just kidnap a man without reason," Cassell persisted. "Who is this Director Santis? What could she want with me? I haven't done anything!"

A yellow light flashed on the override console. Mazour waved him away, then thumbed a stud.

"We've picked up a tail," a man's voice crackled over the intercom. "A single bubble cab off about a hundred meters. Been with us for five kilometers."

"Occupants?"

"One as best as we can make it," the voice answered. "Want us to drop back and take a look?"

"No," Mazour replied firmly. "That would leave our flank open. Maintain your present position, but stay alert. We could have an eagle trying to eyeball our pigeon."

"Will maintain present position," the voice affirmed, then the intercom clicked off.

Cassell glanced behind the ground shuttle to locate the suspect vehicle. His view was blocked by the rear escort.

"Don't get your hopes up. Your only shot of getting out of this alive is with us," Mazour said. "It's hard to believe you were stupid enough to come back here."

"Where else was I supposed to go?" Cassell asked, contempt in his voice. "Someone was trying to kill me on Tula. Earth is my homeworld."

Cassell still could not find the cab trailing them.

"The World Combine Liberation Front isn't out to help you, Cassell," Mazour said. "They want you for cannon fodder."

"And you and your agency?" Cassell looked at him.

"The agency has played hell keeping everything under wraps." Mazour's gaze drifted back to the night outside. "Zivon's directorship has been the biggest headache."

A chord snapped within Cassell. "Then Zivon *is* involved! They killed my wife, have been trying to kill me!"

Both men chuckled, dry, mirthless. Mazour stared at Cassell and sucked at his teeth. "Still playing dumb, huh? Have it your way. But like I said, it won't do you any good."

He could not tell what Mazour's sarcasm meant. He was the fool, a straight man for Mazour's perverted sense of humor. "Dammit, man, is Zivon behind everything?"

Mazour returned to his search, refusing even to glance at him. The ground shuttle sped over an arching interchange ramp and moved onto a three-slotted concourse. Traffic was virtually nonexistent. Cassell started for his pocketed watch to confirm the apparent late hour, then remembered it had been confiscated.

"It had to be Zivon." Cassell stared at the floor, trying a new approach. "Who else on Tula would gain from my murder?"

Mazour sighed. "Cassell, I can't decide if you're serious, or if you've got the act down nice and pat."

"Serious," he answered. "Wouldn't you be if you had been taken off a freighter by armed officers and then turned over to kidnappers?"

The intercom crackled to life again. "Mazour, we've got a cab coming in behind us at high speed."

"The same one?" Mazour questioned.

"No, this one's got at least six passengers."

"Damn!" Mazour flipped another switch that connected him with the lead shuttle. "Looks like the WCLF has made us. Get us out of here!"

The shuttle lurched with sudden speed, throwing Cassell forward. Ord's arm shot out and threw him

170

back into his seat. From behind, a single running light was visible now. It quickly gained on the rear escort.

"Ahead of us, to the right," Ord snapped, "two cabs coming off the feeder line."

Mazour's head jerked around. His fingers did a frantic dance over the console buttons, stealing the shuttle's control from its auto-driver. "They're trying to cut us off!"

The cab braked. Cassell grabbed the armrests to the seat as the vehicle cut sharply into the concourse's inner slot. Metal screamed; plastic shattered. Cassell twisted around. The lead shuttle plowed into one of the two cabs that had shot from the feeder. Fire and smoke billowed from the tangled wreckage barricading the concourse's outer and middle slots. The second cab slowed, dropping back toward them.

"We're under fire!" The intercom blared the warning from the rear escort.

Mazour did not answer. Again the shuttle jerked. In a maniacal maneuver, he fed full power into its motors, shooting in front of the breaking cab's nose. The ground shuttle jumped into the middle slot, then back to the inner one. A piece of fire-blackened metal gouged at the transparent canopy as they shot by the smoldering remains of the wrecked vehicles. Cassell glimpsed movement, survivors struggling to free themselves.

"They're still on our tail," Ord said when the cab managed to dodge the wreckage. "Coming up on the left."

Mazour's fingers stabbed the override console. The cab responded, shooting in front of the pursuing vehicle.

"Kra?" Mazour snapped.

"Haven't come from behind the wreck. Looks like they've been cut off. We're on our own," Ord answered.

Cassell sat frozen in his seat. He saw the bubble cab closing on the shuttle's rear, saw the silhouetted heads enclosed in its transparent canopy, but could not accept it. This was not happening. He lived some surrealistic nightmare that his brain rejected. Earth held the promise of answers, not his death at the hands of two groups battling over him for unknown reasons.

The cab behind jerked toward the left.

"They're trying the inner slot," Ord shouted.

The ground shuttle swung to the left under Mazour's deft guidance. Immediately the pursuing cab reeled back into the center slot and raced forward, maneuvering alongside the shuttle.

His mind numb, refusing all that happened, Cassell stared. The cab's canopy swung up, then ripped away in the wind. A young man with a shaven head grinned at him. In his arms nestled a rifle. It rose.

Mazour's palm slapped the console. The shuttle screamed, braking sharply. Light exploded from the rifle's muzzle. An energy beam shot harmlessly before the shuttle's nose. Ord's pistol jerked up. His finger squeezed the trigger stud.

An actinic glare flashed. The discharged energy bolt melted the shuttle's canopy, sliced the night, then lanced the shaven skull of their attacker. The bald youth went rigid, his face a mask of total surprise.

Two flaring beams shot from the cab in reply. Cassell paid them no heed. He only saw the five other young faces within and the crumpled, dead youth stretched grotesquely at their feet.

Ord's pistol fired again, again. Its beams cut new holes in the canopy and licked over the cab. The bubble cab shot forward wildly, then disjointedly skipped into the outer lane out of control. There was no explosion. The cab tipped on its side, skidded down the concourse, then rolled over and over to slam into a retaining wall.

"Damn!" Mazour's fingers jabbed the console. "The shuttle took a hit!"

The vehicle slowed of its own accord. Cassell heard the sputtering of short-circuited units within the shuttle's heart.

"Behind us," Ord said. "It's Kra . . . and he's got company."

"Kra," Mazour shouted at the intercom, "get up here and cover us. We took a hit. Stuck here like sitting ducks!"

Blankly, Cassell watched the approaching shuttle draw near. Beyond the rear escort, he saw the running light of the cab pursuing it. The escort shuttle swung into the center slot and braked beside them. The canopy doors popped open, and Mazour's reinforcement troops piled out.

Hands grabbed his arms, pulled, pushed, shoved, jerked. He came out of the cab, unable to find a sure footing and fell face down on the concourse's grassy median. Cassell lifted his head to see the pursuit cab shoot by on the outer slot, halting twenty meters up the concourse. Mazour and his men, fanned out to each side of him, opened fire. Energy beams lanced the cab while its occupants scrambled out to take refuge behind the base of the vehicle. Beams sizzled back from the bubble cab in a determined answer.

Over the searing din of exchanging fire, Cassell heard the hum of a bubble cab. Down the concourse came a single vehicle. Inside he discerned the dark outline of its solitary passenger.

The cab shifted to the outer slot to avoid the shuttles in the two inner lanes. It blurred past him, came around the shuttles, then shot into the center slot to avoid colliding with the halted WCLF cab. The shadow within threw itself to the floor as the vehicle entered the flaring beams of crossfire. Cassell closed his eyes, unwilling to watch the senseless massacre. When he looked again, the cab continued to speed down the concourse. He saw a shadowy head rise within the bubble. Somehow the passenger survived the onslaught. Cassell slumped, hugging the ground, finding himself drained.

"Ord, Kra," Mazour shouted. "You've got to get him

out of here. Dead or alive, the WCLF can use him to smear the agency."

A man rolled to Cassell's left side. Ord took a position on his right. Both clutched pistols while they stared at Mazour.

"Make a break for it on the count of three," Mazour said. "We'll give you cover. Get him to the opposite concourse. We can hold these punks long enough for you to get to the Director."

Ord opened his mouth as if to question the order. Mazour glared at him. "I don't care how you do it. Just get him to Santis... if not alive, then dead."

The men nodded. Mazour's attention turned to Cassell. "I meant that. Cooperate, or we won't give you a chance to cause trouble. Understand?"

Cassell understood; he nodded.

"All right." Mazour turned back to the WCLF cab and started counting.

Cassell's two guards jerked him into a crouch. Mazour shouted out his count of three. A sizzling chorus of flashing energy beams exploded from the men's pistols, providing the promised cover.

"Run!" Ord urged, pulling his ward forward.

Crouched, hugging close to the ground, they ran, a three-sectioned insect scurrying over the grassy median. Light and heat traced the air around them. Energy bolts ripped the turf, throwing sod into the air like confetti. Cassell ran, tugged along by his guards while he clutched his travel case to his chest.

A scream, then another, came from behind him. He resisted the temptation to glance back. Mazour and his men, or the WCLF members, it did not matter now. He could do nothing for them.

Another scream tore into his head, threatening to shatter his eardrums. Kra danced in midair beside him. Grotesquely, like a disjointed marionette, the man's arms and legs flailed. His head rolled liquidly on his shoulders. A hole, the size of a child's fist, gaped in his chest. No blood flowed from the black-charred, cauter-

174

ized wound. A spineless rag doll, the man crumpled to the ground, no longer twitching, no longer wrenched by jerky spasms—*dead*.

"Down!" Ord shouted.

The warning went unheeded. Cassell ran; he stood and ran. His legs pumped, his lungs ached, burning with dry fire. He fled before the night-rending beams could find him and tear life from his chest. No longer was he estranged from the battle raging about him. Death drove home reality. Kra's nightmarish death dance replayed in his mind like a loop of holotape. He would not die, not this way, not at the hands of men he did not know, not for reasons that remained beyond his grasp.

Cassell's feet flew from under him. He fell forward, slamming solidly to the ground beneath a full body tackle. Ord collapsed on top of him. Overhead, energy beams hissed.

"Crawl!" Ord ordered.

Cassell glanced ahead. The opposite concourse lay but ten meters away—beyond, the security of an embankment that sloped downward.

"Crawl!"

Rough hands shoved him forward. Flat to the ground, he crawled. His fingers clawed at grass tufts; his shoes plowed deep craters in the soft soil. Centimeter by centimeter, like a human lizard, he slithered to the edge of the three-lane concourse.

"Got to run for it," Ord said. "For God's sake, don't hit a slot. I don't want you accidentally electrocuted after getting this far."

Cassell peered over the edge of the concourse. The concrete seemed to stretch a full kilometer before him. Fear, cold and gripping, knotted tightly in his chest. His breath came fast and shallow. He could never make it across that man-made wasteland before the searing beams found his body.

"Move!" Ord shouted. "Run, damn you!"

The man's voice jarred him to life. Cassell clutched

175

his travel case and leaped forward. In long strides, his legs flew over the concrete, clearing the deadly electric slots that would have taken his life as surely as the force beams that laced around him. He hit the embankment in a roll, tumbling toward a drainage ditch, down into safety.

Ord rolled beside him, pistol still clenched in a ham-sized hand. The man's head jerked from side to side as he surveyed their position. He rose in a crouch.

"Over there," he said pointing with the muzzle of his gun. "It's a warehouse district, but we should be able to find a cab ramp."

Ord reached down to haul Cassell to his feet.

—Now!

Cassell was ahead of his mental companion.

Grasping Ord's outstretched hand, he jerked the man downward. Simultaneously, he swung the case up in a wide arc. The suitcase, Cassell's full strength behind the blow, hammered into Ord's temple. Without a groan, a cry of alarm, the man went down like a felled oak, sprawling on the embankment.

—The pistol!

Cassell scrambled over the unconscious man and retrieved the gun. Then he stood up and ran along the embankment toward the warehouses Ord had located.

The hum of a bubble cab came from behind him. He glanced over his shoulder. The vehicle was braking; its single light swung out toward him.

Dropping to the ground, Cassell rolled into the drainage ditch. He hefted the pistol, leveling at the cab halted above him. His finger squeezed the trigger stud. Then again.

Nothing happened.

Before he could toss the useless weapon at his pursuer, the cab's door rose. A head poked out.

"You?" he gasped, uncertain of his eyes.

Nari grinned down at him. "Get in. Hurry!"

He scrambled up the embankment and crawled into

the cab. His feet still dangled outside the canopy when Nari sped away from the war erupting the night around them.

# FOURTEEN

Unable to find his legs, Cassell managed to climb-crawl
on all fours into the seat beside Nari. He stared behind
the bubble cab. Green energy beams raked the air between Mazour's men and the WCLF. With any luck,
they would kill each other. Somehow he did not think
his luck would be that good.

Moist, warm lips pressed firmly against his cheeks,
followed by a loud, wet smack. He turned. Nari gave
him a broad, self-pleased smile. He blinked and lifted
shaking fingers to touch her shoulder, assuring himself
that she was real and not some fear-conceived hallucination. Her smile widened to a grin.

"I don't understand . . . how did you get here?" His
fingertips fed on the security of her warmth. His hand
slid down her arm, then moved to the small of her back.

Artfully, she dodged the intended embrace, then offered a cheek for a kiss. "I've got this on manual control.
About the third time I've ever tried it, and I'm not at
all sure I know what I'm doing."

He kissed the proffered cheek gratefully, then gazed

at her, his brain unsure it fully accepted her presence. His eyes were once more pulled behind them. The glare of city lights swallowed the battle's glow. He sank back into the seat, shaking. He sat there, staring blankly ahead, telling himself it was over, that he still lived. It did not help. The impact of what had happened hit him head-on. He sat motionless, afraid to move, to breathe; afraid his bladder would suddenly, uncontrollably relieve its inward pressure of its own volition.

"Are you all right?" Concern tautened Nari's face when she gave him a quick glance.

"Yes," he forced a single word over dry lips. He breathed deeply to steady himself and looked at her. "How did you get here?"

"Lieutenant Ildre told me about the police." Her fingers tapped a series of buttons on the control console. "When the shuttle landed, I inquired with the police. They didn't know anything about your arrest."

That did not surprise him. Had they told her he was an assassin wanted on a hundred worlds that would not have surprised him either. Secrecy seemed to be the password when it came to Jonal Cassell.

"I finally forced my way into the chief's office. He also claimed never to have heard of you," Nari continued. "Something was wrong. I decided to stay at the port awhile and see if you turned up in police custody. You did. When they took you into that agriculture building instead of police headquarters, I got a bubble cab and waited for you outside. I saw you leaving with those men and followed."

"You could have gotten yourself killed." Cassell felt a sudden rush of anger that she had endangered herself. "You had no business involving yourself. Nari, they could have killed you."

She glanced at him. Hurt and confusion mingled in her eyes.

The anger was illogical, irrational, and stupid; its source evaded him. The fact remained that he might

179

now be dead had she not followed him . . . if not dead, then Mazour's captive, or in the hands of the WCLF. "I don't know what possessed you to come after me, but thank you."

She smiled with obvious pride, then frowned. "Doron, what was all that about back there?"

He shook his head, unable to piece the fragments together and make any sense out of what had occurred. "I don't know."

A doubtful expression moved across her face.

"Honestly, I don't know," he repeated. "After they brought me down from the *Tommy John,* it all happened too fast."

Doubt remained on her face, but she did not press him further. He understood the disbelief. He still did not believe everything that had happened. She deserved a better explanation.

—It will be a mistake, Jonal. She knows too much now. They can trace you through her. They can make her talk.

The shadowman was right. He pushed aside the idea of providing her with even a censored version of Mazour and the WCLF attack. The thought of Nari in either of their hands sent chills up his spine. The sooner they parted company again, the better it would be for her. She still did not know anything.

"Where are we going?" he asked.

"My home," she said.

"No good." Cassell emphatically shook his head. "Drop me off somewhere. I can get another cab. You're in too much danger with me."

"Am I?"

"You might not have noticed, but those men were trying to kill me back there," he said. "It wouldn't be hard for them to put two and two together and discover we were lovers."

"Are lovers," she corrected, then looked at him questioningly. "That is, unless things have changed."

"Yes, dammit, things have changed." He attempted

180

to suppress the irrational anger that surged within him again. He was not prepared to argue with her. "The police, or whoever those men were back there, will be looking for you, trying to get to me. I don't want you involved."

"I *am* involved." She tilted her head to the numerous holes in the cab's canopy, each melted by a force beam. "It will be easy enough for them to find out who rescued you. I used my identification card to pay for the cab."

"Damn, damn, damn!" Cassell vented his disgust and frustration. She was purposely being difficult, ignoring the danger to her life. "It's not too late. If I vanish in another cab, there's the possibility they'll believe that . . ."

"That I'm a woman looking for her lover, who ran out on her again?" she asked.

"Exactly," he said. "You'll be interrogated, but it won't take them long to find out that you don't know anything."

"But, I want to know, Doron," she persisted. "I want to know why someone is trying to kill you. I want to help."

"I don't need your help . . . I don't want it!" He hammered a fist into the arm of the seat.

She sat silent, eyes glued to the concourse ahead of them.

"Nari, it's better my way," he said in a softer tone. "Just drop me off at a ramp where I can get another cab. When I have this thing straightened out, I'll . . ."

He did not finish. He had not lied to her until now. It made no sense to start now.

"If that's the way you want it." She bit her lower lip, still not looking at him.

Nari's fingers moved over the driver console. The cab slowed, then scooted down an exit ramp onto a feeder line. A kilometer later, she pulled the cab before a loading ramp. Another cab sat vacant before them. Cassell opened the canopy, grabbed his case, and started out. Nari trapped his arm. He looked back at her.

"Doron, you can't go off like this," she pleaded. "You need someone to help you. Who do you know in KCplex?"

—Gore Enfor.

"Gore Enfor," Cassell mechanically repeated the name the shadowman fed him.

Nari appeared less than convinced. "Who is this Gore Enfor?"

Cassell waited for the shadowman to supply the necessary information. Nothing came, not a single word. He turned from her to hide the blank expression on his face.

"See! You need someone," she said. "And you don't know anyone but me. Let me help you, Doron. Please."

"No," Cassell wrenched his arm from her clutching hand. "You'd be in the way . . . end up getting us both killed."

"Go on," she said when he climbed from the cab "But that won't stop me from following you."

He pivoted back. Determination was set firmly on her delicate features. He took a deep breath and started in, pulling forth every verbal abuse, derogatory name and term he could summon in a hope of jarring some sense into her head. She sat there, her expression unchanged, resolution ingrained in her face.

"I still am going to follow you," she said simply when he ran out of breath.

Cassell gave in and waved her after him. Nari lifted her two bags and scrambled from the cab and slid into the new vehicle beside him. Without glancing at her, he punched coordinates for the Tulsaplex into the console. The cab jolted forward and eased from the ramp onto a feeder line.

"You know, Doron Tem," she said, leaning close and kissing his cheek, "I love you."

Cassell stared straight ahead, unable to repeat those

182

ree words. The KCplex melted in a blur of passing
ghts outside the plastic canopy.

Four shuttle flights, ten ground shuttles, a myriad
'bubble cabs, countless slidewalks, two sleepless days
d nights, and Cassell and Nari returned to the
Cplex satisfied they had left enough false trails across
vo continents that would keep Mazour and the WCLF
isy for a week. Using the name Raine, they checked
to a local hotel, stayed there long enough for Nari
› confirm that one of her friends was out of town on
two-week vacation, and then moved into the woman's
partment.

"I'm not sure this is a good idea," Cassell said after
cursory inspection of the apartment's four rooms. "We
in be traced through your friends."

"You worry too much." Nari's face was drawn and
aggard. Her voice thinly veiled niggling irritation.
My friends at the university don't know Kara, and she
iesn't know them. There's no way for anyone to find
s here."

"Still, it might be wiser..."

"I'm not going to argue." Nari's patience snapped,
er voice sharpened to a keen edge. "For two days, I
aven't slept longer than ten minutes at a time. If the
olice come here, they are going to find me passed out
n that bed!"

His own temper simmering, he glared as Nari
alked into the bedroom and collapsed atop the bed.
I didn't ask you to come with me! You're the one who
uck her nose into my problems!"

Nari lay motionless; she did not answer, bat an eye,
r even turn to glance at him. He walked to the bed-
oom and stared down at her, and found himself smiling
1 spite of his anger. She was sound asleep.

—Now's the time to dump her.

Too tired to argue, he ignored the shadowman. Qui-
:ly, he slipped atop the bed beside Nari to nestle

against her warmth. His leadened eyelids closed their own accord. Without a second thought to the sha owman's screaming protests, he sank into the dee comfort of sleep.


It took hours to push away the thick blankets, wiggle upward shedding their heavy weight, and fir the persistent tickling sensation. With a Herculea effort, he forced his eyes open, focusing after three u successful attempts. He stared around blankly, unsu of how long he had slept or exactly where he was. Th only thing he was certain of was Nari's lips playfull taunting his exposed earlobe.

"Awake?" she whispered.

"Mmmmmm," he answered tentatively.

"You look like a little boy when you're sleeping Her lips still busied his ear. "Did you know that?"

"I feel distinctly like a man who just crossed th century mark." He rubbed a hand roughly over his fa to wipe away the sleep. Thick stubble pricked his fi gertips like a forest of tiny needles. "My face feels li a bramble patch."

He rolled to face a grinning, auburn-haired im Nari ran a testing finger across his chin and frowne a bit. With a toss of her head, she leaned forward an kissed him, apparently not minding the beard's harsl ness. Then she came to him with a passion and hung he had not experienced during their time aboard th *Tommy John.*

"I love you," she said softly when he entered her.

The three words drove deep, double-edged knive that twisted within him.


Cassell leaned away from the small table. The rem nants of a satisfying breakfast cluttered its surfac Nari glanced at him over the rim of her third cup coffee. She wore a translucent robe found in one of th bedroom closets. The vaguely veiling material did littl to hide her nakedness beneath.

He smiled, remembering the first time he had seen her aboard the freighter. First impressions often proved wrong. Nari was more than just attractive; she was beautiful. At that instant, radiant and alive, she was perhaps the most beautiful woman he had ever seen.

Ailsa's image floated in his mind for a moment, then faded. His smile widened. There was no guilt, no apprehension. Time and Nari had exorcised his mental ghosts. The past belonged to the past, and memories.

'Feel better?" Nari lowered her cup to the table.

"Better tnan I should." Cassell nodded. "I can almost forget that somewhere out there are two groups of madmen trying to find me . . . almost."

Nari's face hardened a bit, but she did not comment. Pushing from the table, she rose and cleared away her share of the breakfast mess. Sipping at what remained of his own third cup of coffee, he watched her. Rested and well-fed, he found his thoughts returning to the arguments he had avoided for two days. He tried to push them aside, to savor the luxury of the moment. It was not the time or place. Yet, they persisted, demanding attention. He gulped down the last of the coffee.

"Well," Nari asked when he cleared his plate from the table, "what do we do now?"

"I'd rather there wasn't a 'we.'" He could no longer dodge the issue. It had to be dragged back into the open. "You can't afford to get involved in this any deeper."

"I don't see how I can afford not to," she replied.

"Nari, you've got to be sensible," he said. "This isn't a game you're playing. Those men out there probably have every intention of killing me."

"We've had this conversation before." An icy determination flowed into her voice. "We'll be wasting time to go through it again. Nothing has changed."

Cassell paused, studying her, hoping she would rescind and pull out. She glared back at him with the

185

same stubbornness she had exhibited the night of the WCLF attack. He pursed his lips and shook his head.

"Perhaps it will, when I tell you the truth." She deserved that, he convinced himself. She had the right to know everything.

—Jonal, don't! You can't afford to trust her. You've got to dump her and find Yerik Belen!

"Like the fact that you're not Doron Tem?" Her gaze froze on him.

A jolt of electricity sizzled along Cassell's spine. The shadowman howled within his skull.

"Doron Tem, Jonal Cassell, the name doesn't matter," Nari said. "It's the man I love."

"You know?" Cassell muttered in disbelief.

"Since I saw you board the *Tommy John*," she answered with a slight nod. "I told you I'd been on Tula. I don't think even a casual visitor could have missed you on the holocasts. I was hoping to interview you as part of my study until your wife was..."

Her voice trailed off and she glanced down, nervously staring at the table.

He reached out and took her hand in his, squeezing it tightly. "Why didn't you tell me?"

"Damn you! Why didn't you tell *me?*" Tears welled in her eyes. "Don't you understand? I knew I was competing with memories. I didn't ask to fall in love with you. I tried not to. The first night I was so afraid you were making love to her, that I was..."

He hugged her to him, holding her close. Her words came in jumbled spurts, disoriented and random. When she finished, she clung to him, trembling.

"I loved Ailsa." He lifted her chin with a finger and kissed her. "She was very much alive when I met you, Nari Hullen. You helped me accept everything that has happened. It's never been Ailsa with you—always you."

Her eyes rolled up to meet his. Tears still welled, threatening to overflow and roll down her cheeks. "Are you sure?"

He nodded and lightly kissed her lips.

"I love you, Jonal Cassell," she said. "I love you."

Words and feelings he had refused to acknowledge wedged their way through his carefully constructed defenses, shattered solid walls of restraint, and burst to the surface. Before he could stop himself, he said, "I love you."

—Stupid, Jonal, damn stupid!

"I know." Nari took his hand and pressed its palm to her lips. "That's why I've hung on, waiting for you to admit it to yourself."

He smiled. "Now, you can understand why I want you to get out of this."

"I'm not even sure what I'm in," she said.

Cassell led her into the living room. Sitting together on the divan, he told her everything, starting with Ailsa's murder. He watched her face. Horror, confusion, disbelief, bewilderment, doubt, they were all there, changing her expression with each new detail. Nari listened, never once interrupting.

". . . and that's where you entered the picture," Cassell concluded.

Without comment, Nari rose, walked into the kitchen, and returned with two fresh cups of coffee. Seating herself beside him once again, she sipped thoughtfully at the steaming cup, still without uttering a word.

Finally, she turned to Cassell. "This shadowman, is he still around?"

"Right now, he's telling me I'm a fool for explaining everything," he said with a sheepish grin.

"He bothers me more than anything. It's like having an invisible third person standing around spying on us," she said.

Mirthlessly, he chuckled. "I won't say he's exactly a joy for me to have around."

Nari took a few more sips of coffee. "You're probably right. Somehow, while you were first in the hospital, someone attempted to tamper with your personality. The shadowman is all that is left of their failure."

"To me, he seems a bit more successful," he replied "You have to admit having a voice constantly in your head is enough to make anyone believe they're insane."

"If I hadn't seen those 'agency men' and the WCLF blowing each other to hell," she said, "I would have to admit *I* thought you were crazy."

"I'm not at all sure I'm not," he said.

"But there's something substantial about this shad owman," she went on, ignoring his remark. "He seems to be the only friend you've had until now. I think we should try to find this Yerik Belen."

"*I* should find Belen," he corrected.

"Chances, remember?" she asked. "The risk and de cision is mine, not yours. You've no choice in the mat ter. I do. And *I* think it's worth the chance."

She smiled sweetly up at him, an expression that could not conceal the cold determination he had come to recognize in this woman over the past few days. He shrugged his shoulders, giving in to her for the moment.

"Good!" she said. "Now that we've got that settled where do we go from here?"

"A computer," he replied. "I need access to all the publicly available reference systems I can tie into. I want to run checks on everything from Belen to Zivon What system in the city would come closest to filling the bill?"

"Depends." She pondered for a moment. "Overall the university would be your best bet. It's available for faculty use. I could get you access."

"It's completely off limits," Cassell said firmly. "Ma zour probably has men planted all over the campus waiting for either one of us to show up."

"Then," she said after thinking for another minute, "the city's own system would be next on the list. Kara has a terminal here."

Nari pointed to a closed cabinet amid a tape shelf. Cassell caught himself rising and stopped. It had been

oo easy to trace his activities on Tula via his private
erminal. He was not willing to risk it again.

"What about public access?"

"Most hotels are equipped with private terminal
ooths," Nari said. "Governmental buildings, the li-
rary..."

"The library!" he said. There were risks venturing
nto the public, but he would lay odds Mazour also kept
abs on the local hotels. "I think the library would be
afer."

"It's about a half-hour by slidewalk from here," Nari
aid. "Soon as we dress, we can go there."

She stood and walked into the bedroom, waving him
fter her. Cassell pushed from the couch and followed
er, watching for a moment while she laid out a change
f clothes borrowed from her friend's closet.

"Nari, isn't there anything I can say that will make
ou change your mind?" he asked.

"No," she said, pulling the robe over her head and
lipping into Kara's clothing.

Cassell felt more than a touch of pride at having this
voman at his side. At the same time, he wished she
vere safely hidden in another city thousands of kilo-
neters away.


He waited outside Nari's booth. Inside, she jotted
lown several more lines to a voluminous column of
notes. The terminal blinked off, fading to a flat gray
green. Nari swiveled toward the door, saw him, and
miled. The booth opened and she stepped out.

"Well," she asked, "how did it go?"

"Outside," Cassell said. He took her arm and ushered
er toward the library exit. "We've been in here too
ong. If anyone is monitoring computer use, they've
ad time to pinpoint us."

Their footsteps echoing from the library's lofty ceil-
ng, they moved down a line of terminal booths and
ushed through the exit. As inconspicuously as possi-

ble, to avoid alarming Nari, Cassell surveyed the pas
ing pedestrians when they stepped onto the slidewal
Despite his niggling paranoia, he found nothing to i
dicate they were being followed, although he doubte
his ability to detect Mazour's men if they wished
remain hidden.

"Have any luck?" Nari pressed close to his side.

"Little or none," he said. "Nothing on Yerik Bele
Mazour, or Jonal Cassell for that matter. The info
mation on Zivon was sketchy. Nothing we didn't kno
already."

"The same on my end. The Agriculture Export Con
mission was formed when the Combine Governme
began planetary colonization," Nari said. "Rather tha
scrap the agency when Earth began importing mo
than it exported, the commission's regulatory jurisdi
tion was enlarged. Its title is a misnomer. The con
mission is responsible for regulating all of Earth's e
ports and imports."

"Zivon obviously has to work through the agency
he said, trying to imagine the scope of such an organ
zation's intelligence network. It would be immens
capable of monitoring the actions of an individual wh
aroused their interest. "But what would they want wit
me? I was never involved in Tula's exports. Loc
administration was as high as I ever rose within Z
von."

"Perhaps Zivon is exporting something . . . somethir
important that the commission is afraid will be cut o
if Tula goes independent," Nari suggested. "Your lea
ership of the Autonomy Party might have threatene
that something."

"I don't know." Cassell shook his head dubiousl
"Timber is Tula's major export. That and various foo
stuffs."

"But it's something we shouldn't discard withou
first checking into it." Nari attempted to sound enthu
siastic, but Cassell detected an undercurrent of unce
tainty in her words.

"We're no closer to any answers than I was on Tula."
He no longer cared whether he hid his disheartened
spirits. "It could be a Tulan export. It could be something as simple as graft, Zivon paying kickbacks to
commission officials. It could be anything. The only
way to confirm any suspicions is to have access to Zivon's and the commission's records. On the assumption
we could get those records, it would take a lifetime or
ten to go through them. If interior irregularities are
at the bottom of this, we'd never be able to find them."

"Which leaves you," Nari said. "And Yerik Belen...if
he exists."

"And if I'm not completely insane," Cassell said as
they moved onto another slidewalk that took them toward Kara's apartment complex.

Nari gazed at her feet a long moment. "Someone is
trying to kill you, that is real. Mazour and the WCLF
are hunting you, that is real. Jonal, you're not insane."

"Yes," Cassell answered, finding no comfort in Nari's
line of reasoning.

"I also checked the list of assassination victims the
shadowman gave you," Nari continued. "Everyone was
in the reference banks."

"However, it doesn't tie the shadowman and my
dreams into Zivon, or the Agriculture Export Comission." Cassell did not mention that he had also reaf-
firmed the victim list. "Did you locate anything on the
World Combine Liberation Front? They might be a key
to all of this."

"A minor, radical group that spun off an anti-Com-
bine movement ten years ago." Nari recounted briefly
the various political issues the WCLF had been involved with, from cloning body parts for medical treatment to Terran planetary colonization.

"Despite rhetoric concerning individual rights and
an official 'radical' label, the WCLF seems to be a hard-
core reactionary group devoted to the abolition of the
World Combine and a return to separate nation-states,"
Nari said. "To achieve that end, the WCLF has used

191

violence on several occasions. Police authorities hav
publicly announced shattering the organization thre
separate times. They've resurfaced a few months aft
each of those announcements."

"But why are they after me?" Cassell looked at Na
hoping she could conjure answers from thin air. "The
involvement makes no more sense than anything else

"Mazour said they could use you to expose th
agency," she replied.

"What agency? The Agriculture Export Comission'
Cassell asked impatiently, frustrated by the ceasele
questions that had no answers. "Or was Mazour talkir
about another agency?"

"My guess is the Agriculture Export Commissio
though it makes no more sense to me than you," sh
said, pausing a second. "There was something else. Th
commission is headed by a Pao Santis."

"Santis! Mazour spoke on the phone to a Direct
Santis!" Cassell sensed something flit across his brai
shadowy, evasive. It eluded him like a memory tha
refused to be dredged from the subconscious. "Did yo
find anything on him?"

"Her," Nari corrected. "Sixty standard years..."

Cassell mentally filed the notes Nari provided. Pa
Santis was a lifetime civil servant who had worked h
way through the ranks of several governmental age
cies. For the past twenty years she had been with th
Agriculture Export Commission. The last ten year
she had spent at the commission's helm.

"...she has to know what's happening," Nari sai
a pleased smile brightening her face. "I'm sorry I didn
think of her sooner. If we get to her, we could find th
answers you need."

"Want to lay odds on getting within a kilometer
Director Pao Santis?"

"Any better suggestions?"

"Gore Enfor," Cassell replied. "The name the sha
owman gave me when you asked if I knew anyone
the KCplex. I checked him on the computer. There

192

a Gore Enfor who is the proprietor of a dream parlor in the city."

"And you want to find him?" She stared at him incredulously.

"He seems safer than phoning for an appointment with Pao Santis." Cassell shrugged his shoulders.

"What could the owner of a dream parlor have to do with you?" Nari's expression remained unchanged. "Do you know him?"

"No." Cassell shook his head. "But the shadowman mentioned the name. This Enfor might lead us to Yerik Belen."

Disbelief still on her face, Nari relented, admitting Gore Enfor was a safer course to explore for the time being than attempting to see Pao Santis.

"Shall we go see him now?" she asked.

"On the way out of town, or at least after we move out of the apartment," Cassell replied. "We've been in one place too long."

"Do we have to?" Nari frowned. "Kara's place is comfortable."

"We'll get our things, then see Enfor," Cassell said, unwilling to argue about it. "After that depends on what Enfor provides."

With a comment on his ancestry, Nari gave in. "Could we get something to eat first? We haven't eaten since breakfast. It's almost six p.m." She pointed to a cafe they approached.

Cassell took her arm and stepped from the slidewalk. Despite the late hour, only two customers sat within the cafe. Selecting a table by the front windows, Cassell fed several standards into a servo-unit. Sandwiches and coffee slipped from the unit's serving slot a few minutes later.

They ate in silence, watching the pedestrians pass outside, occasionally glancing to one another for a reassuring smile or the brushing touch of a hand. Their attention always returned to the growing stream of people on the slidewalk. Without speaking, Cassell sensed Nari shared his apprehension. Anyone on the walk could be with Mazour . . . or the WCLF. A friendly smile could disguise a pistol tucked beneath a jacket.

Nari lifted her cup and washed down the last bite of her sandwich. "If we find Belen, what then?"

"Hope he can give us the answers to clear this up," Cassell said. It was not what she fished for, but he could not offer her anything else. He had not thought beyond the point of finding Belen.

"If we get all this straightened out, will you be returning to Tula?" She pressed with another approach.

"I don't know." Tula seemed more than light years away now. Three months ago, the planet had meant life to him. Now he found he really did not care whether he ever stepped foot on its surface again.

"Stay on Earth?" Nari refused to let it drop.

"It's too distant, Nari." Irritation crept into his voice no matter how hard he tried to conceal it. He loved this woman seated across the table. Just as real as the love he held was the reality that love had no place in his life now. He could never promise the commitments of man to a woman. "I've got to find Yerik Belen. That is if Mazour and the WCLF let me get that far. After that, I just don't know."

Nari glanced away and bit her lower lip. She said nothing, but he saw her hurt. She wanted reassurance he could not provide. Reaching across the table, he took her hands and squeezed. She made an ineffectual attempt at a smile.

Once again the shadowman was right. Nari, his growing love for her, his fear for her life, only complicated an already entangled situation. Whether he wanted it or not, he had to get away from her. Only his selfishness kept him from leaving. In keeping her with him, he had dragged her deeper into something neither of them understood, had placed her neck on the chopping block beside his.

*Before the day is out,* he told himself. He studied the strong, yet somehow delicate features of Nari's face.

Something tugged at him. He ignored it. What he had to do was right. There was still time for her to come out of this alive. It would be simple. While she slept, he could slip quietly out of her life.

Afterward... There was no afterward, only Yerik Belen.

"Rush hour," Nari said, nodding to the mounting pedestrian traffic outside the cafe. "It's growing late. We'd better get back to the apartment."

Neither bothering to clear the waste from the table, they rose and joined the crowds packed on the slidewalk.

Rush hour, Cassell thought while he flowed with the stream of human bodies. Three separate lines of traffic formed on the one-way slidewalk. He had forgotten about Earth's equivalent to Tula's shift change. The outer edges of the conveyor were reserved for persons standing or stepping on or off the walk. The center belonged to the walkers, a frenzied domain for those striving to arrive at their destinations with the saving of a few minutes. They shoved; they pushed. Faces reddened. Anger and frustration howled forth in a ceaseless chorus of obscenities. Occasionally verbal abuse gave way to a striking fist, a groan, a crumpling body lost in the ocean of humanity.

Chaos, social insanity—had he forgotten so much? He remembered his doubts while he watched shift change on Tula. He felt Earth's madness close around him, squeezing with claustrophobic tightness. He wanted to run, flee before he was dragged down by the undertow.

"Here's where we get off." Nari took his arm.

Together, they stepped from the slidewalk. Before them rose three towering columns of concrete and steel. The farthest building in the complex contained Kara's apartment. What had been empty pavement stretching in front of the buildings when they left that morning was now spotted with workers returning home. Cassell's gaze moved over them, searching.

195

They were five meters from the complex entrance when Cassell saw him. Mazour stood inside the building, framed by a sliding glass door. Cassell grabbed Nari's arm and jerked her backwards in mid-stride.

"Mazour!" He tugged her toward the slidewalk. "Quick, before he spots us."

"But our money," she said. "It's in the apartment."

In a long-strided walk that verged on a trot, he pulled her after him. He patted his coat pocket, thankful he had taken the precaution to keep half his money on him.

"Cassell! Stop!" a voice shouted behind them. "Cassell, you can't get away!"

He risked a glance over his shoulder. Mazour stood outside the door. In his right hand, he clutched a needle-nosed pistol. In his left, a small black communicator. Mazour lifted the black box to his lips.

Cassell increased his pace. Heat pounded in his temples. His breath came fast and shallow. From the corners of his eyes, he saw panic and fear trembling across Nari's tightly drawn mouth.

"Faster," he urged her, fingers clamping into her arm.

From the left, a man in a business suit stepped toward them. He reached into his coat, pulling free a gun. On the right, two men with pistols already in hand rushed them.

"Run!" he shouted at Nari. "We've got to make the slidewalk!"

She cried out in a piteous whelp of surprise when he wrenched her forward, but ran at his side.

—Down!

He did not argue with the shadowman's warning. Throwing an arm about Nari's waist, he dropped to the pavement. Pain, like liquid fire, raked across his elbows and knees as they scraped over the concrete. Overhead, he sensed the flash, the blast of heat, before he heard the telltale sizzle of an energy beam.

A woman screamed.

In reflex, Cassell's head twisted to the right. A once-attractive blonde jerked with rigid stiffness. Then, like a puppet whose strings had been severed, she collapsed to the ground. Her head twisted at a grotesque angle, revealing the charred remains of what had once been a neck.

Nari whimpered beside him. Nausea churned in his gut.

"Don't fire, you fools!" Mazour's voice shouted over the roar in his ears. "Stop firing! I want them alive!"

—Run. Get up and make a run for it!

Footsteps reverberated in Cassell's ears. He wasted no time looking back. Locking an arm around Nari's waist, he hauled her to her feet, then forced her to run toward the slidewalk.

Ahead, a group of people stepped from the moving walkway, then scattered. One man remained to block their escape. He stood legs spread in a wide defiant stance. A smile that sought to widen to a pleased smirk twisted over his lips. Cassell cursed—Ord, the man he evaded during the WCLF attack.

"Run!" Cassell shouted and released Nari's arm. "Get to the slidewalk."

—Jonal, don't be stupid. He's ready for you. Dodge him. Give him the girl!

Cassell did not listen. He barreled straight down on the lone man barricading his path. Ord's smirk grew to an anticipating grin. His arms opened as though inviting Cassell into them.

Forcing his legs to pump as hard as they could, Cassell continued on his reckless path. At the last possible moment, he ducked his head and threw his shoulder forward. He groaned when he slammed into the wall of human flesh. Ord's moan of pain and surprise mingled with his. His shoulder drove solidly into the man's solar plexis.

They went down together, a tangle of flying arms and legs. Cassell rolled, writhing free. Nari was there, her panicked arms yanking, dragging him to his feet.

She pulled and shouted something. Disoriented, head spinning from the force of the impact, he stumbled forward under her urging hands.

"The slidewalk," Nari said. "We're at the slidewalk."

He managed to jump-step up and landed on the conveyor in a wobbly stance. Before he could regain his balance, Nari shoved him forward. Running, they moved into the slidewalk's chaotic center lane. They thrust aside those blocking their way and ran . . . ran.

# FIFTEEN

Night cloaked the KCplex. Overhead, the bright glare of carnival lights blotted out the stars. Beyond the gaudy harshness hung the glow of the city. Autumn moved on the slight breeze, giving it a lingering chill that warned of approaching winter.

Cassell and Nari sat on a bench amid the hussle of an amusement park. For three hours they had fled, running long after they had lost Mazour and his men among the throng packing the slidewalk. Like electrons in direct current, they flowed with the crowds and the protection they offered from the sizzling death of energy beams.

The spider web of slidewalks brought them to the park. Surrounded by the carnival glare and the constant river of people, they sensed a moment's refuge from possible pursuers. They found the bench and rested, eyes trained to the passing herd of boisterous thrill-seekers.

"This is for real, isn't it?" Nari mumbled.

Cassell nodded without pausing in his search for Mazour.

"That night at the spaceport and on the concourse . . . it happened too fast for me to really think about it . . . to be afraid." Her words came slow and unsteady. "It has all seemed like a game, an adventure. I knew there was danger. I just never realized what that danger was. Jonal . . . I'm frightened."

He slipped an arm about her and hugged her to him. It was not much comfort to offer, but her closeness, her warmth, helped to calm the fear within him. "I know. On the *Tommy John,* I forgot how terrifying this really is."

"They killed that woman," she said. "I've never seen anyone murdered before. She could have been you . . . or me."

"It was a mistake. I heard Mazour calling his men off." He did not sound convincing to himself. The lack of conviction came with the realization that Mazour would eventually tire of attempting to apprehend them. When that moment arrived there would be no hesitation about using guns. "There's still time for you to get out. Mazour will want to question you. But he'll have to release you after he discovers you don't know anything."

"I think it's too late for that." She sounded hopeless, an innocent cast into hell's own heart for another's sins.

—She involved herself. No one asked her to butt in. Cassell knew better. His own selfishness had delayed his leaving. He tightened his arm around Nari in silent confirmation of his decision earlier that day. Tonight, he would find a way to leave. Better to abandon her to Mazour's inquisition than for her to die at his side.

"What do we do now?" Her eyes rose to him, reflecting the uncertainty in her voice.

"Gore Enfor," Cassell said.

"And if this Gore Enfor isn't the shadowman's Gore Enfor?" A demanding edge found its way into her words.

"We'll deal with that when and if," he replied.

200

Nari glanced away to stare at the crowds milling about them. "Jonal, we're so vulnerable. If we had a weapon, something to fight back with. If we..."

He placed a finger against her lips to quiet her. Inwardly, he said a quiet prayer, grateful he did not have a weapon in hand. Had he possessed one, he realized, he would have used it the night of the WCLF attack and again today. Too many had died already; he did not want to add more to the list.

Shifting his arm around Nari's waist, he helped her from the bench. They stared at one another for a moment, then began to weave their way through the carnival crowd.

Dream parlor, the name conjured images of a sleazy hole dug amid the filth and squalor of Earth's welfare cribs. A grimy, shadowy room populated by fear-bent patrons who huddled in corners muttering to themselves, their eyes constantly in motion, but never meeting the gaze of another.

The Golden Dream was anything but that.

Located in what Nari explained was KCplex's most exclusive residential district, the Golden Dream even smelled of money, crisp, freshly minted standard notes. The entrance was a door of darkly polished mahogany, ornately decorated with floral relief carvings. The door also sported a shiny brass knob that had to be turned by hand for the door to open. It appeared genuine, an antique dating back several centuries. Inside, the faint smell of blossoming flowers hung coyly in the air—real flowers, not some artificial scent given birth within an aerosal cannister.

Cassell and Nari stepped down from a landing of arabesque tiles onto a carpet so thickly piled it crept toward their ankles. Wood paneling, dark and rich, covered a spacious entry lobby. Tapestries and paintings, each placed to be viewed separately rather than objects designed to cover bare space, hung about them. Chairs, sofas, and an assortment of potted plants were

strategically positioned about the room. There wa
enough furniture to seat a small army, but each piec
appeared to stand alone within the immense room.

"May I help you?" A voice floated to them, a whispe
that seemed a kilometer away.

Cassell turned his head to locate a well-dressed ma:
in a silvery gray suit stiffly seated behind a massiv
wooden desk at the far end of the room. The man ros
and motioned them to him. Behind his desk, half hid
den by opulent velvet drapes, stood an entrance to an
other room.

Overwhelmed by the presence of money, Cassell tool
Nari's hand and walked to the man.

"My name is Istory." He smiled at each of them. Hi
voice was soft, reverent. "Have you come for a session
Mr. . . ."

—Throm Hammille.

"Throm Hammille," Cassel said, an involuntary re
flex to the shadowman's voice. Nari glanced at hin
strangely, but said nothing.

"Mr. Hammille," Istory repeated while he examine
a calendar atop the desk. "I'm sorry, Mr. Hammille
but I don't find an appointment for you."

"I didn't make an appointment," Cassell replied. "
would like . . ."

"I'm terribly sorry, sir," Istory interrupted before h
could finish, "but the Golden Dream requires appoint
ments be made at least three days prior to a session
I'm sure you understand the necessity of ample tim
to prepare a program designed to provide maximun
benefit for our clients. I can arrange a visit with on
of our counselors this evening if you are considerin
a future session. Allow me to summon Mr. Portales
He is free at the moment."

"I'm not here to arrange a session." Cassell manage
to wedge in a few words. "I would like to see Gor
Enfor. Would you get him, please?"

"Mr. Enfor is presently engaged in a business con
ference." Istory's polite attitude lost some of its polish

His face hardened with a touch of haughty impatience. "Mr. Enfor was left strict instructions that he is not to be disturbed. However, I will make an appointment with him for tomorrow, if that will be sufficient?"

"No, it won't," Cassell said firmly. "He'll see me tonight. Tell him that Throm Hammille is here."

"I am sorry, Mr. Hammille, but ..."

"Tell him! Or I'll find him and tell him myself. When I do, you'll be looking for another job," Cassell said, his voice straining to contain a growing anger. "Because, *I* am the one man he will *want* to see tonight!"

Dubiously Istory eyed him as though unable to decide how to handle the situation. Apparently the man chose the safest course of action. "One moment, sir."

Istory stepped from behind the desk and disappeared through the velvet drapes.

"Throm Hammille?" Nari raised an eyebrow.

"The shadowman," Cassell answered with a shrug of his shoulders. He surveyed the Golden Dream's lobby again. "Have you ever been in a dream parlor before?"

"Yes and no," she said. "At the university, we have a similar arrangement—the equipment, but not the fancy decor. The principle is the same, chemo-electrical brain stimuli, akin to psycho-reconditioning. This equipment, however, only provides the user with an illusion, or a dream if you prefer. The university uses the equipment as a teaching aid. It's an easy method for keeping abreast of what is happening within a field of research. Various monographs on a given subject are programmed and fed into the subject's brain. A year's reading is absorbed in a night's sleep."

"I don't think any of the Golden Dream's patrons come here for knowledge," he replied. "The learning experience couldn't support a place like this."

"Dream parlors are also psychiatric tools," Nari said. "Subjects are allowed to live their aggressions, fears, and fantasies in a controlled illusion. Earth isn't as progressive as Tula. Regular psycho-reconditioning sessions aren't required. Our population is too big for

203

that ever to become practical now. The cost would b
prohibitive."

"You think the Golden Dream is used for psychiatri
purposes?" he asked.

"Dream parlors vary in quality. There are those sim
ilar to the ones in the amusement park, and there ar
those in hospitals," Nari replied. "Probably the Golde
Dream has patrons who come here under a psychia
trist's supervision. But I'd guess the majority of client
come seeking the same thrills others find at an amuse
ment park parlor. Only here, they pay exorbitant fee
to maintain a degree of discretion and anonymity. Mor
likely than not, many of the patrons are bored wit
existence, junkies preferring illusion to reality."

*Dream junkie—is that what I am?* The thought raile
in Cassell's mind. Did he prefer the horrors the shad
owman led him to over the peaceful sanity he had foun
on Tula? He stared at Nari and smiled. One could fin
sanity even amidst the most disjointed nightmare.

An arm pushed through the drapes to hold then
parted. Istory smiled pleasantly at them. "I'm terribl
sorry about the delay, Mr. Hammille. If you will follov
me, Mr. Enfor will see you now."

Taking Nari's hand again, Cassell led her througl
the drapes into a long wood-paneled and thickly car
peted corridor. They passed several doors on each sid
of the hallway, but Istory entered one at the end of th
hall and motioned them after him. Cassell and Nar
stepped into an office that equaled the opulence of th
Golden Dream's lobby. Books, printed and bound vol
umes, not tapebooks, lined the walls in glass-enclose
shelves. The nutlike aroma of aromatic tobacco, wit
an underbite of latikia blend, tickled its way into Cas
sell's nostrils.

"That will be all, Istory," a deep voice said, drawin
Cassell's attention to a man seated in an overstuffe
chair before a small fireplace.

Cassell had never seen the man who sat half-hidde
in the chair. Over steepled fingers, the man watche

Istory leave. When the office door closed, he turned to Cassell, casually giving him a thorough once-over from head to toe. A nervous tickle scratched at Cassell's suddenly dry throat. The man offered no indication of recognition. But why should he? Cassell did not know the man.

"Throm Hammille!" A broad grin abruptly split the man's face. He pushed from the chair to cross the room and grasp Cassell's shoulders. "How many years has it been? I thought you had given up this corner of the universe."

Cassell returned the grin, feeling awkward, off balance. Gore Enfor obviously knew him. He rummaged through his memories and found nothing. He called the shadowman, receiving no reply. How could Enfor know him? He had never seen Gore Enfor before in his life. Cassell managed a mumble, "A business interest brought me back."

"Anything I can get a cut of?" A knowing expression spread across the thin features of Enfor's face. "After our last little venture, I parlayed the bankroll into ten dream parlors in five cities. Each of them equals this beauty. The clientele is the cream of the crop."

"I don't think you would want a piece of this action." Cassell played it by ear. That this man thought he was someone he once knew named Throm Hammille did not matter, that he might lead them to Yerik Belen did. "I've got trouble."

"Police?" Enfor asked. "What are you wanted for . . . no, don't tell me. It's better if I don't know. How close are they?"

"Close." Cassell saw an apprehensive wrinkle furrow deeply across the man's forehead. "We weren't followed. I made sure of that."

"I wasn't worrying about that. I know you're not sloppy." Enfor waved away Cassell's comment. "It's just that my contacts aren't what they used to be. Except for a few small ventures now and then, I'm legitimate.

I can't do much on short notice. The moon at best. Would that help?"

Cassell was not certain what Enfor meant, but he nodded. "How much?"

Enfor laughed. "Nothing, my friend. After what you did for me, a hundred Luna runs wouldn't be enough to balance the scales. A man doesn't forget someone who saved his life. What about tonight?"

"We need a place to stay." Cassell's confusion multiplied. He had never saved anyone's life. What had they fed into his brain on Tula? How did this man know him?

"No problem," Enfor replied. "That is, if you've no objections to a dream capsule."

Cassell glanced at Nari, who gave her approval. He had doubts, but the man offered more than they had. "None."

"Good," Enfor said. "Food? Money?"

"Okay on both counts," Cassell replied.

"All right," Enfor said. "I don't want to rush you, but I think we should tuck you both away for the night. I've got several calls to make and get things set up. The dream chamber is down the hall."

Without further discussion, Enfor led them back down the hall and opened an unmarked door. The dream chamber held every appearance of some oddball sculpture. Twenty-five silvered-glass eggs sat seventy centimeters from the floor, neatly cradled atop transparent support columns. Various wires and plastic tubing ran from the floor and fed into each of the capsules.

On a wall panel, Enfor flipped two switches. Two eggs parted at their middles, sliding back to reveal contoured couches within. He glanced at Nari and held out a hand toward the first capsule.

"Any preference for your night's dreams?" Enfor asked.

Neither Cassell nor Nari offered any suggestions.

"Then, I'll make them erotic." Enfor chuckled. "Never have any complaints about my sex programs."

Again he directed Nari to take the first egg and Cassell the other. Both complied, stretching out within their separate capsules.

"Pleasant night," Enfor said while he examined their positions within the eggs. "And don't worry. I'll have everything arranged by the time you wake."

Cassell watched Enfor walk back to the wall panel. His fingers ran over a series of switches.

The silvered-egg closed around Cassell. Instead of the expected darkness, a soft, pleasing green glow pulsed about him. The slight smell of flowers wafted in the air. Cassell smiled, experiencing a sudden calm, contentment. He blinked. His eyes opened, wide, wider.

He no longer lay within Enfor's dream capsule, but sat amid a plush pile of cushions scattered over the floor of a palatial room. At his side sat two of the most gorgeous women he had ever seen, very blond and— very naked. His smiled widened to a broad grin.

# SIXTEEN

—Jonal, you're worse than a mink in rut!

The two very willing women shimmered and vanished from the cushions. Cassell cursed the man leaning against the far wall, hands stuffed into his pockets. *You've got a bad habit of popping up when you're not wanted.*

—They were an illusion. Chemical and electrical stimuli, remember?

*They were real enough!* His body still tingled from their taunting fingertips and the moist warmth of their lips running over his bare flesh. Across the room, the shadowman smirked.

—What about the moon?

*I wasn't thinking about it.*

—I have been. And I've decided it would be the best course to take.

*I didn't travel to Earth to leave without finding Belen.*

—I know, but it's too hot here now. You'd have more success if the police weren't on your tail.

*And the WCLF!*

—Go along with Enfor. Take the Lunar jaunt, then book passage somewhere, anywhere.

*I don't want to go anywhere.*

—You won't. Shanghai someone and put him aboard in your place. Drug him so he won't wake until the ship's in tachyon space. Then slip back to Earth.

*More false trails.*

—Always. You've got to keep laying them. The more the better. You stop and you'll find your ass in hot water.

*Nari?*

—You've made that decision. Stick to it.

Cassell suddenly noticed the shadowman had been standing in the light during their conversation.

—It's time you returned to your twins. Have a pleasant night, Jonal.

The man quavered. Cassell leaned forward to discern his facial features. Before his eyes focused on the quivering image, the shadowman dissolved. The twins were at his side again. Within moments the shadowman was completely forgotten.

A soft, green glow rose to wash away the palace. It grew, enveloping Cassell. Gore Enfor's smiling face hovered over him. Cassell blinked, remembering where he was. He pushed up on an elbow. It refused to support him. He collapsed back to the contour cushioning.

"Take it easy," Enfor said. "It takes a couple of minutes to readjust. I interrupted the program before it completed the cycle. Lay there and rest, and I'll wake your woman."

"No," Cassell forced the furry caterpillar that now lived where his tongue had been to work. "Let her dream."

Enfor looked at him with a quizzical expression. Then the man smiled. "Do you want her disposed of?"

"No!" Cassell tried to sound emphatic, but his voice chords had been transformed to steel, inflexible and unresponsive. "Let her sleep. She doesn't belong in this.

Wake her after I've gone. The police don't have a thing on her."

"No problem," Enfor replied. "How are you feeling?"

"Like I've been on a month's binge."

"This should help."

A pinprick of pain bit at his arm. Cassell winced; a warm needle lanced his flesh. The pain faded. Foggy veils cleared from his mind.

"A mild stimulant. No stronger than about three cups of black coffee." Enfor helped him from the dream capsule. "Sorry to rush you, but we have to meet a contact at the spaceport in an hour. You'll eat dinner on the moon tonight."

Cassell nodded. He stood alone, a bit shakily, his knees watery. Cautiously, he took a step, then another. He could walk. "I think I can make it."

"Good." Enfor took his arm and led him from the dream chamber.

Cassell paused a moment at the door to glance back at the egg still wrapping Nari in its false illusions. *It's better this way*, he told himself, repressing the desire to have Enfor wake her. *It's better this way*.

Cassell turned. Enfor patiently waited for him. "We really have to leave. We're operating on a tight schedule. If we miss my contact, I won't be able to get you out of there for another thirty-six hours."

Down the hall and through another of the numerous doors, Enfor directed him to a bubble cab that waited in the alley behind the Golden Dream. Taking their seats, Enfor fed coordinates into the vehicle. Its motor hummed a moment, then the cab jerked forward moving from the alley and onto a feeder line.

"You'll make the hop via a cargo shuttle." Enfor reached into a pocket and took out a small black folder. "Here're your papers and identification. I've also got some for the woman. I'll give them to her when she wakes. It might be best if she went into hiding for a while."

Cassell opened the folder. For a man who claimed

210

a lack of connections, Enfor had performed a remarkable job in the space of a few hours. Cassell found himself now taking the name Boa Palmquist, a native of Tevar Five, thirty-six years old, unmarried. The folder also contained a computer resume of Palmquist's employment for the past five years.

"You'll be a member of the shuttle's crew ... grapper fifth class," Enfor explained. "Which means you push cargo around. The cargo mate is aware of everything. His name's Bansen. He'll look after you."

Cassell nodded while he thumbed through the folder once more.

"When you arrive at Etel Station, you'll be rushed to the hospital ward, an appendectomy case," Enfor continued. "There, you'll be contacted by a Gregory Askell. He'll arrange another identity and passage to wherever you wish to go."

"You've done a thorough job." Cassell slipped the folder into his coat pocket. "Thank you."

"Not that thorough." Enfor shook his head. "Those papers will never hold up under an identification check. Just hope Lunar authorities won't verify the papers due to the emergency nature of your ailment."

"Any other problems?"

"One, but a minor one," Enfor said. "There's a grapper strike at the spaceport. I'm afraid you will be a strikebreaker."

Cassell laughed. "A short-lived scab."

Ahead, Cassell recognized the port entrance. The bubble cab scooted through it, then swerved down a feeder that ran toward the port's transport area.

"One more thing," Enfor said. "No weapons."

"I'm clean," Cassell assured him.

"They were adamant about that. But I don't like the idea. I've got a little something that's easy to conceal." From inside his coat, Enfor eased the butt of a small pistol. "Not that much, but it will come in handy if ..."

Cassell shook his head. The one time in his life he

211

had held a gun had resulted in two men's deaths. Onc was enough.

"You're probably right for this leg of the journey. Enfor pushed the gun back in his coat. "However, As kell can get you whatever you need once you're on th moon."

A bubble cab shot by on their left, then swerved i front of them.

"Fool!" Enfor cursed. "The idiot's on manual in high traffic area!"

Another cab pulled beside them.

"The bastard in front is slowing down!" Enfor's fin gers flew over the console in an attempt to brake.

Too late. They thudded solidly into the cab ahead o them. Cassell tumbled forward, catapulted from hi seat. The two cabs slowed to a full stop. He pushed fron the floor caught in a sense of *déjà vu*. The cab besid them also stopped. Its door swung up. A man with rifle poked out of the opening, leveling the weapon a them.

"What the hell!" Enfor threw himself to the floor "That's not the police."

Cassell had no time to explain. He dropped back t the floor. The man with the rifle squeezed down. Ligh and heat seared through the canopy; the beam sho harmlessly over their heads.

Enfor's pistol crackled in answer. Their assailan jerked back from the line of fire, then swung the rifl toward them for another shot. Again the energy bol sizzled overhead.

"The door," Enfor urged while he fired into the op posite cab. "We've got to get out of here!"

Cassell rolled. His hands groped and found the doo release. Upward the canopy opened. He belly-crawle to the exit and threw himself to the ground below.

Behind him, Enfor, now on his knees, edged towar the open canopy. A force beam exploded from the op posite cab. Like a man hit head-on by a runawa ground shuttle, Enfor hurled through the door, pisto arching high in the air as it was torn from his grasp. The dream parlor proprietor thudded heavily to the ground. A charred crater smoldered in his chest.

Cassell did not need a second glance to tell Enfor was dead. He scrambled to his feet and scurried toward the pistol laying a meter from Enfor's head.

"Another step and you'll join him," a voice shouted behind Cassell. A force beam ripped the ground centimeters from his feet. "I mean it. Don't take another step."

Cassell froze. Stiffly, he turned toward the voice. A black-haired young woman stood beside the cab that had first swerved in front of them. She held a pistol trained on him.

"Lenot wants to see you," she said.

# SEVENTEEN

Two men leaped from the cab behind the black-haired woman. She tilted her head toward Cassell. They ran to his side, seizing his arms to pin him between them.

"Move it," the woman snapped. "We haven't got all day. The police will be here any minute ... or worse, Mazour."

Her two companions jerked Cassell forward, shoving him into the open plastic bubble. Hands within grabbed and pulled at him. Others wrenched his arms behind him. Metal clinked; steel bit into his wrists. He tugged once to confirm what his senses already told him. He was handcuffed. More roughly grasping hands pushed him into a seat.

There were four in all, the woman and three men. All were young. Too young, he thought, to be involved in this. University students, maybe younger.

"Get us out of here," the dark-haired woman ordered a youth seated at the driver console. "If we found him this easily, Mazour can't be far behind."

"Who are you?" Cassell asked. "The WCLF?"

The girl started to nod, then ordered, "Blindfold him."

One of the men grabbed his shoulder and yanked him to one side. A piece of dark cloth was pulled over his eyes. Hands shoved him upright in the seat. The cab lurched forward. High acceleration pushed him into the cushioning.

"He's not bad looking," he heard the girl say. "From what Lenot said, I expected a disease-ridden old man."

Someone chuckled and one of the men spoke. "Don't let the bastard's looks fool you. You saw the psycho-profile. This is one mean son of a bitch."

*Me?* What was he talking about?

—Stay calm, Jonal. Play it by ear. When the opportunity . . .

Cassell tuned the shadowman out. He had heard all of it before.

"I don't know," the young woman replied, a bit hesitant. Cassell felt soft fingertips trace tiny swirls on his cheek. "We might have made a mistake. He wasn't armed."

"Let him be, Estelle!" one of the men said. "He's the one we want."

"I'm not bothering the handsome man," the girl protested in a whining voice. She pressed closer to Cassell and whispered, "You didn't do all those things Lenot said you did, did you?"

"What things?" Cassell asked.

He heard a rustle of clothing. Something thudded against his shoulder. He felt the girl move, then a heavy thump as if something, or someone, had been thrown into the seat beside him.

"Take it easy, Paul!" the girl whined in protest. "I wasn't hurting him."

"Estelle, you're here for one reason," the same man answered. "So keep your eyes open and directed outside."

The young woman did not reply, though Cassell

thought he heard a whispered curse and someone shift
about in the seat beside him.

The bubble cab swerved to the right, its speed increasing. *A right turn? Or a slot change?* He tried to
visualize their course. Not that it mattered. He knew
nothing of the KCplex. The cab jerked to the left. The
hint of light penetrating his blindfold faded. Had they
entered a tunnel? Perhaps tall buildings blocked the
sun. He felt like the fool of fools. He had just witnessed
a man's murder, a man who apparently thought him
a friend. He was being kidnapped by four revolutionaries who would not blink an eye if required to kill
him. And he sat playing mental guessing games, attempting to picture the route they traveled.

"Estelle, Vic," a deeper voice said, "get ready. Drop
point coming up."

Hands clutched his arms again. The cab slowed, then
halted. The slight hiss of the opening canopy came from
his right. Then the yanking, the pushing, the wrenching. His temple banged into the side of the door. Hands
thrust him through the opening. He stumbled from the
cab, somehow managing to keep his feet beneath him.
The hands caught his again and jerked him forward in
a half-run, half-walk. Their footsteps echoed hollowly
around him, as though they moved down what sounded
like a long corridor in an abandoned building. Behind
Cassell caught the whirling motors of the bubble cab
fading in the distance.

His mind rushed in a chaotic attempt to make sense
of their movements. He found himself counting strides,
craning his neck from side to side, seeking anything
that would orient him. His captors shoved him to the
right, raced on a few steps, shoved him to the left, then
back to the right.

The pace slowed. He heard their strained breathing
mingle with his own short-winded gasps. Abruptly the
hands clutched firmly, jerking him to a halt. Something
hissed before him. Metal grated on metal. A hand

lammed between his shoulder blades, catapulting him
orward.

Cassell slipped-stumbled, blindly fighting to main-
ain his balance. The toe of his right shoe collided with
omething solid, unmoving. Equilibrium lost, he tum-
led facedown into what felt and smelled like a pile of
usty rags.

"No need to call for help," a man's voice called to
im. "It's soundproof in here. Besides, they'll never
hink of looking for you here."

The grating metal and hiss returned, and the real-
ation the estranged sounds came from a closing door.
olling to his back, Cassell twisted his head from side
o side. No hint of light penetrated the blindfold. Wher-
ver he was, it was dark. He caught his breath and
stened. He no longer heard his captors' heavy breath-
g.

"Where am I?" he shouted.

His own words echoed back at him. But no one an-
wered.

He cocked his head, unsure he was alone. "Where
m I?"

Again the echo, but no answer.

Cassell sucked in a deep breath and cursed loudly.
n effluvium of confused odors assailed his nostrils.
eneath the thick dust, he caught a trace of grease or
il, then a sharp, pungent scent. The sour smell evaded
is nose; almost familiar, but he was unable to place
. He cursed again in frustration.

His captors, if they remained, made no sound. De-
iding to risk the chance they had left him unguarded,
e drew his knees to his chest and worked his wrists
own below his buttocks. The handcuffs bit at his flesh,
ut he wiggled them over his feet and up his legs. His
ands were still bound, but at least they were in front
f him and not twisted painfully behind.

Reaching up, he tore the blindfold from his eyes.
lackness, unviolated by even a trace of light, sur-

rounded him. Once, he remembered, he had visited cave on Tula. His guide had ordered the lights exti guished for a minute. The darkness had been complet never meant to be touched by natural light. The sam blackness now enveloped him.

Frustrated, frightened, he cursed. His shoutin bounced off unseen walls and echoed back. He four no solace in the fact Nari was safely tucked away her dream capsule. He was alone and afraid, and mi ery loves company.

He strained forward, attempting to pinpoint th sound. It came again. A scraping scurry like tiny claw scratching on concrete. *Rats?* His body tensed, leg ready to lash out should one of the furry visitors deci to wander in his direction.

A minute, an hour, a day, a year? Cassell lost a concept of time. There was only blackness, his curse and the answering rats running across the floor.

Then a hiss and the grate of metal on metal pen trated the darkness. A glaring white rectangle opene in the blackness. A man stood silhouetted in the doo Another man walked behind him. Cassell peered u eyes blinking against the onslaught of light.

"Get him up," one of the intruders said. Cassell di not recognize the voice. "He doesn't look like much o top of all those feed sacks, does he?"

*Feed sacks? Rotten grain!* Cassell now recognize the souring stench within the room. He was inside storage elevator, or perhaps some warehouse. Despit the speed of his kidnappers' escape, he doubted the had come far from the spaceport. This building coul even be within the complex.

"Anonymity is the key to success with scum like th one," the second man replied as he approached. "Whe you're in his line, you don't want to be noticed."

*My line? Scum?* What were they talking about?

The man seized Cassell's shirt collar and hauled hi to his feet. He blinked, unable to distinguish their fe

res in the dim light. The man pushed him toward
e door.

"He's noticeable now," the waiting man said. "He
nells like a crap pile."

The man in the doorway reached out and yanked
assell into the light. He rammed something hard and
d into Cassell's ribs, and said, "Move."

Cassell did, letting the pistol muzzle guide him. Both
e men were as young as those who attacked Enfor
d him at the spaceport. Both dressed in black, from
ghly polished boots covering their feet to tight tur-
necks tucked beneath their chins.

They moved through several empty rooms that had
l the appearance of being abandoned warehouse
ace. Entering a hall that ran past empty offices, they
opped him before a gray metal door. One opened it
hile the other pushed him through.

"In that chair," a youth with shoulder-length blond
air ordered. When Cassell complied, the man turned
a woman who leaned against the wall. "Get rid of
e cuffs. He can't do anything in here."

"Hi, handsome." The young woman smiled when she
alked beside him, a small key in her hands. When
assell last saw Estelle, she held a pistol. She still
peared too young to be tangled up in this. He found
mself wanting to ask her if her parents knew where
e was.

A twist of the key and the cuffs dropped from his
rists. Gratefully he returned the smile, then rubbed
s wrists, restoring circulation to hands tightly con-
ned for too long.

A light glared on overhead. Like a spotlight, it sin-
ed him out. Beyond the harsh fringes of light, he
uld see four people to each side of him. Metallic
ashes exposed several pistols in what seemed to be
ager hands.

"We finally meet." Someone edged from the darkness
adowing the far corner of the room. The youth in
ont of Cassell stepped aside, glancing at the ap-

proaching figure. "I thought we'd lost you a couple o
times. But perseverance does have its rewards."

A man, jet hair chopped close to the skull, leane
down. His face stopped mere centimeters from Cas
sell's. He was young, too, perhaps a year or two senio
to the others Cassell had seen, but no more than in hi
mid-twenties. The young man smiled. There was
sweetness to his breath, as though he had just used a
breath freshener.

"Faham Lenot, Mr. Belen," he said. He waved a
arm to the others. "And these, as I'm sure ycu suspec
are the heart of an organization we call the World Com
bine Liberation Front."

*Belen?*

"Cassell, Jonal Cassell," Cassell replied, uncertai
he had heard Lenot correctly. "I'm searching for a ma
named Yerik Belen."

*Belen?*

Someone snickered. Cassell glanced toward th
mocking sound, but was unable to discern any of th
faces outside the harsh ring of light. *Belen?*

"Yes, yes, we know about Jonal Cassell." Impatien
hung in every one of Lenot's words. He leaned bac
an eyebrow arching. "There's no need for the charac
here. We know everything . . . everything."

"Charade!" Cassell could not disguise his own co
tempt. Lenot looked different, but he had had this co
versation with Mazour before. "Charade! My wife h
been murdered, someone blew half my body away, se
eral attempts have been made on my life, I've bee
arrested for no reason, I've been chased across th
planet, shot at, kidnapped—all to find Yerik Bele
You can take your charade and . . ."

He stopped. Anger would do no good. It did not he
him, and, in all likelihood, it would provoke the
would-be revolutionaries. He sank back into the cha
glaring at Lenot.

The smug smile evaporated from the young ma
thin lips. Lenot studied Cassell for a long, silent m

nent, his eyes lingering on each detail of his face. Abruptly, he pivoted and walked from the light. Cassell heard the shuffle of feet, muted whispers. He leaned to one side, straining to catch the mutterings, but was unable to distinguish any of the words that passed between Lenot and his followers.

"Cassell, I believe a mistake has been made." Lenot walked back to him. "However, we need you to answer a few questions... then, we might be able to aid you in finding Yerik Belen."

The edge was missing from Lenot's voice. Cassell detected a trace of impatience, but it was obvious the young man was making an attempt to control himself. Cassell nodded his willingness to cooperate. Not that he had a choice. Pistols were still drawn and visible.

A half-hour, an hour, Lenot drilled him about Tula, its culture. He asked for and got details of that day in the Supreme Council. Lenot probed into Zivon and Tula's political scene. The promise of locating Yerik Belen dangling before him like a carrot in front of a goat, Cassell answered everything. Nor did he avoid the barrage of questions into his personal life.

He felt like a sponge that had been wrung dry when Lenot finally concluded and once more counseled with his followers in the shadows. Again, Cassell sat listening to the murmurs, the whispers, the nervous shuffle of anxious feet. Eventually Lenot returned. Relief rather than triumph was in the young man's face.

"Cassell," Lenot began, hesitancy in his voice, "you are a victim of history's most blatant disregard of individual civil rights. The World Combine government has perpetrated an atrocity for the past fifty years, and you are but one victim of that injustice... an unknowing victim of a clandestine conspiracy designed to propagate and perpetuate the present economic and social class system imposed by the World Combine. Through you, Cassell, we have the means to shatter the World Combine's foundations and free the world's population from its tyranny."

Cassell refused to listen to the meaningless rhetori It meant nothing to him. That Lenot could lead hi to Belen was all that mattered. "Yerik Belen! You sa you could help me find Yerik Belen."

Lenot looked down at him, his gaze lingering. "Loo to yourself, Cassell. Look to yourself. Jonal Cassell an Yerik Belen are one and the same. *You* are Yerik B len."

—Jonal . . .

"No!" He would not be cheated by some cheap tric "No, you bastard! I want Yerik Belen!"

— . . . find Yerik Belen.

"Belen, you're a fool." Anger furrowed Lenot's for head. "We're here to free you and millions like you wh have been manipulated by the World Combine. Jon Cassell—Yerik Belen is the key. With you we sha expose the atrocity the World Combine has intentio ally cultivated to subvert the individual freedoms every person on this planet!"

—Find Yerik Belen, Jonal. Find Yerik Belen.

"Key! I don't give a damn about your key!" Casse no longer controlled himself. The guns did not matte "Somebody murdered my wife. Somebody totally d stroyed my life. I want to find them. I want them pay for what they've done. I want them to pay!"

—Find Yerik Belen.

"You stupid son of a bitch! It was never your life Lenot glared down at him. "There never was a Jon Cassell. He's no more than a program in a compute You are Yerik Belen."

—Yerik Belen. Yerik Belen. Yerik Belen.

"Psycho-reconditioning," Lenot said, "the erasure an individual's personality and the implanting of a ne one to meet the World Combine's needs."

Personality molding, minor memory erasures—psy cho-reconditioning could provide that. But the creatio of a new personality? More of Lenot's cheap tricks, p litical rhetoric.

"Belen, listen and understand," Lenot continue

As best as we can determine, fifty years ago the World Combine Security Organization implemented an experiment called the Tula Project, the purpose being the establishment of a star colony for the rehabilitation of recalcitrant criminals—a prison planet."

Cassell tried not to listen. He was not Lenot's key to overthrow the World Combine. He was a lone man searching for Yerik Belen.

"Hints, rumors of Tula's true purpose have leaked now and then. But the Combine's cover-up was too good to break," Lenot went on. "The Tula Project was disguised amid a myriad of governmental agencies. Some performed their duties without knowing what they did. Until your wife's assassination we could not uncover the central organization that coordinated the project's activities. When Jonal Cassell escaped, Mazour and his crew were forced to surface..."

Cassell heard and rejected the young man's every word. What Lenot suggested was too immense—too impossible. No government could ever conceal an operation of the scope he described. He was Jonal Cassell, a Zivon immigrant from Earth.

Yet...the shadowman, the dreams.

—Yerik Belen, Jonal. You must find Yerik Belen.

"...infiltrated various agencies. They were able to locate Mazour through his inquiries pertaining to the *Tommy John* and one of the freighter's passengers— Doron Tem, alias Jonal Cassell." Lenot refused to stop. "Via Mazour's activities we found a pipeline to the Agriculture Export Commission, Director Pao Santis, and Yerik Belen."

Lenot paused, staring at Cassell as though to ascertain his reaction.

Cassell shook his head. "What do you take me for? You can't expect me to accept this!"

"You don't have to accept it," Lenot said, that smug smile returning to his lips. "It's easier to ignore the truth. Still, the fact remains that you are Yerik Belen...Yerik Belen responsible for at least fifty murders on thirty different planets . . . Yerik Belen, professional assassin, hired killer . . ."

*Madness!* Lenot's voice became a hurricane within Casseil's head, screaming with the force of a thousand thunderstorms. It rolled, multiplied, churned in on itself, then exploded outward. It assailed his sanity. Threads of reason stretched taut by the unrelenting onslaught. His head pounded, temples roared. His mouth opened to scream, but his lips only mouthed a silent "No . . . no . . . no."

". . . Yerik Belen was apprehended and tried for the murder of Hartael Stinon ten years ago . . . and sentenced to death. The same Yerik Belen whose memory was erased to give birth to Jonal Cassell, mind-slave of the World Combine . . ."

Thinner the strand stretched, elasticity gone. Cassell bent beneath the weight. He rocked in the chair, cradling himself against the relentless assault.

". . . only those under death sentence were selected for the Tula Project. Their lives were forfeited anyway." Lenot was unmerciful, unyielding in his barrage. "Without choice, they were subject to complete personality erasure, then shipped to Tula, mindless robots, men transformed to zombies . . ."

The strands crystallized. *Yerik Belen? Yerik Belen?*

". . . if the Combine condones the use of such personality erasures on criminals, what is there to stop them from eliminating political opposition through similar means? What evidence is there that they aren't already using . . ."

*Belen!* Cassell's brain burned, fire devouring fire. *I am Jonal Cassell.* Something slipped, something he could not define, could not grasp. *I am Doron Tem.* I soared and plummeted, evading the net of reason he cast in its path. *I am Throm Hammille.*

—Jonal, find Yerik Belen. He has all the answers.

". . . freedom of the individual, Belen. Through you the WCLF will rock the very . . ."

Cassell stared beyond Lenot. The shadowman stoo

224

there just outside the light's blinding glare. He stepped toward Cassell.

—Yerik Belen holds all the answers. Have I ever lied to you, Jonal? All you have to do is find Yerik Belen.

The crystal strands vibrated violently. Hairline fractures ran along their cloudy lengths. *I am Gyasi.* The ground buckled beneath Cassell's feet. The door to the room imploded. He catapulted forward, tumbling, twisting. More explosions hammered around him. He heard Mazour shouting. *I am Jonal Cassell.* Screams howled in his ears, drowning the sound of his own horrified wails. *I am the shadowman.*

—Find Yerik Belen.

The shadowman stepped into the light and grinned down as Cassell lifted his head from the floor.

—One and the same, Jonal. I can't say it's been a pleasure.

Cassell jerked his head away. Lenot glared down at him screaming. He could not hear the words. Green light flared, washing over the young man's face. Then there was no face, only a smoldering black ember. The shadowman laughed. *No!* Cassell heard his own voice, laughing. *No!*

Hands seized his shoulder like steel vises. They wrenched upward, jerking him to his feet.

"Move it, Cassell," Mazour shouted into his face. "Get the hell out of here."

Cassell reeled, laughter pealing from his lips. He stood in the center of hell. Demons disguised as Mazour and his army of business-suit attired gorillas swarmed through the room. Each held a pistol, its muzzle spitting forth a ceaseless stream of energy beams. Lenot's followers danced in the air, their bodies skewered time and again by the rain of lancing light.

—I am Yerik Belen.

*That's right, Jonal.* The shadowman stood beside him, hand resting casually on his shoulder. He spoke with Cassell's own voice. *You are Yerik Belen. I am Yerik Belen. We are Yerik Belen.*

Cassell saw him now, the features of his face. The face belonged to Jonal Cassell. The shadowman laughed maniacally.

Hairline fractures cracked across hairline fractures.

Hot coals ignited in Cassell's belly.

Crystal splinters showered the air.

A volcano erupted. Molten lava spilled from Cassell's abdomen. *I am Yerik Belen!*

Cassell clutched his stomach, fingers meeting stone. He stared down. A black hole smoldered in his gut. The stone was cauterized flesh. No blood flowed from the dark wound. *Energy beams are clean,* the migrant thought ran through his head as his knees gave way. He collapsed to the ground. *Death shouldn't be this clean.* Even the pain did not matter once he immersed himself in the lava.

"Get him out of here." He heard Mazour shout. Mazour was always shouting. "He's still alive."

"Ailsa," Cassell mumbled. But Ailsa was dead. He forced his eyes open. Nari's face danced, transposed on the faces of the men who lifted him. "Nari, I didn't have to do this. It didn't have to be this way."

*Damn!* It was so unfair. He could see that now. There had been other ways, things he could have done—ways in which he did not have to die.

"But, you and I would have never met," Nari's image said. He felt her cool, deathlike fingertips caress his brow.

"No," he said managing a wistful smile. "And that would have been wrong . . . so wrong."

Cassell closed his eyes and let the darkness draw him to its core.

# EIGHTEEN

He floated. A steady, reassuring throb surrounded him. Contentment suffused every cell of his body, warm and soothing.

*Are you there?*

He listened. No answer came except the constant thump-a-thump umbilical rhythm. Alone? The possibility was a quietly contained trembling.

*Can you hear me?*

Thump-a-thump, thump-a-thump.

He felt a tentative smile move across his lips. He opened to himself. He trembled, not in fear, but in completeness. He sensed himself, the self, whole, full.

*I am.*

He was. He existed. And he was alone, and sensed it was right.

*I am.*

The loneliness no longer frightened him.

Downward he drifted. Awareness crept back. He flexed arms, wrists, hands, fingers. They responded to his slightest mental command. He flexed, savoring the delicious sensations that coursed through his legs from hip to toe.

Still, he sank. The comforting warmth receded. Unyielding metal pressed into the softness of his back. The soothing rhythm faded, replaced by . . . ?

A voice?

He listened, forcing his ears to locate the source. An indistinguishable buzz sluggishly penetrated the milky clouds about him. It *was* a voice. *No! Voices!*

*I am!* He called to them. *I am!*

"Cassell, Cassell." One of the voices answered him. "Cassell, Cassell."

"He's coming around, but he seems to be fighting it.

*No, I'm coming.*

"Can you blame him?"

"Try Belen. He might respond to that."

"Belen, Yerik Belen," the voices urged him.

Consciousness filtered into the awareness. Jonal Cassell opened his eyes and screamed, a child wailing as air rushed in to fill his lungs. Life recalled him once again.


Nari waited when they wheeled him from the Accelerated Growth Module into the hospital room. With a warning for her not to overtax him, the doctors and attendants left them alone. She came to the side of the bed, lifted one of his hands and kissed its palm. She smiled, tears welling in her eyes.

"Twice in five months," Jonal Cassell returned the smile, his fingers tracing over her lips. "I've got to break this habit of getting pieces of me blown away."

Without warning, she threw herself atop him, arms clutching desperately, lips covering his mouth. Just as abruptly, she pulled back, her eyes wide with fear. "I forgot! Did I hurt you?"

Cassell shook his head and grinned. "Couldn't ask for better medicine."

He opened his arms and she returned. He held her

228

close reveling in the feel of her, the luxury of her near-ness. *I am.* He kissed her hard and long. She was alive, so alive. Together they were a gestalt, the whole greater than the parts. *I am.*

"I thought they had killed you," she whispered, her voice trembling despite an obvious effort to conceal the fear. "I haven't slept since they put you into the AG Module last night."

"Less than a day?" He found it easy to joke about it now. "Last time, they had me in one of those things, I didn't come out for a month."

Nari pushed to her elbows. She hovered over him, love radiating from a face he found so very beautiful.

"Hey?" The Golden Dream crept into his mind. "How did you get here?"

"I told you I wasn't going to be shaken off." She smiled, that impish light flickering in her eyes. "After you and Enfor left me in the dream capsule, Mr. Istory came along and woke me. Seems Gore Enfor forgot to tell his employee about the unscheduled use of the capsule."

Cassell remembered Enfor. Once, in a time that now seemed three or eight lifetimes ago, they had been part-ners in a less than legal smuggling enterprise. The image of Enfor's dead body sprawled on the ground outside the spaceport invaded his mind. It was no way for a friendship to end.

"When I got over being angry, I went back to my home. A news bulletin came over the holo, reporting the WCLF attack and Enfor's murder," Nari explained. "I called Pao Santis."

"From there, Mazour put one and one together and came up with the fact that the WCLF was holding me." Cassell pieced the rest of it together.

"Hmmmmmmmm." Nari nestled against him. "However, Mazour didn't say he intended to almost kill you in the process of rescuing you."

"For which you have my most sincere apology." A

229

woman's voice came from behind Nari. "But accident
will happen."

Nari shifted to one side. At the door stood a short
stocky woman with short, thinning hair. Behind her
Mazour and two of his ever-present gorillas entered
Ord was one of the two. He grinned at Cassell.

"However, it appears no real damage was done." The
woman gave Cassell the once-over. "A bit of an incon
venience, but the medical staff says your new stomach
is twice as good as the old one."

"Pao Santis," Cassell said in a statement rather than
a question.

"Mr. Cassell," the woman replied. "Or is it Yerik
Belen?"

"Cassell," he answered. "I'm still Jonal Cassell."

"Which may be in your favor," Director Santis said
Cassell detected skepticism in her attitude. "How much
do you remember about Yerik Belen?"

Cassell caught Nari's perplexed expression. Appar
ently Santis had elected to keep her in the dark about
the Belen-Cassell personality. Why was the woman
bringing it into the open now? Cassell squeezed Nari's
hand. "Everything."

"That is not so good." Santis rubbed at her neck
"Ms. Hullen has told us everything she knew. This
shadowman?"

"He's gone," Cassell replied. "The shadowman was
Belen's personality re-exerting itself. I didn't realize
what was causing my schizophrenic condition until
Lenot confronted me with the truth. The shadowman
vanished then, assimilated into Jonal Cassell."

Yerik Belen, the shadowman, had never fully re
exerted himself, Cassell realized. Thus his mental com
panion's inability to reveal himself, to provide the an
swers he had sought. The Yerik Belen personality only
managed to poke itself through occasionally, never
having the strength to take control.

Santis's hand moved over her neck some more. "And
now, you have all of Belen's memories."

"Yes." And the horror, the guilt, and shame. Cassell would never be able to remove them.

Abruptly, he bolted upright in bed. A man entered the room and smiled at him. "Ragah?"

Ragah Tvar glanced at Director Santis. The woman waved away any comment and turned back to Cassell. "Bron Cadao, one of my agency's top field agents. Bron was assigned to you when you started to rise within the Autonomy Party."

Cassell did not need to hear more. Answers fell into neat little niches. Ragah...Bron Cadao had been responsible for all that had happened to him on Tula. Angrily, he thrust Tula from his thoughts. It did no good to replay the events again and again. Ragah had been loyal; Cassell just had not realized where his loyalties had lain. Perhaps one day...again he avoided the flood of thoughts deluging his mind. Revenge would prove nothing, nor right all the wrongs.

"And Tula?" Santis questioned. "What do you know about Tula?"

"The Tula Project," Cassell corrected. "A clandestine governmental venture based on the premise that criminal personalities can be erased and socially acceptable personalities can be implanted in a subject. Your subjects are shipped off to colonize a new planet."

"Non-rehabilitatable criminals, those whose aberrant behavior cannot be corrected by normal methods," Santis added. "And only those under a sentence of death."

"Yerik Belen?" Nari stared at Cassell as though everything sorted itself in her mind.

"Your Jonal Cassell is in reality Yerik Belen," Santis replied. "Yerik Belen, hired assassin, murderer of at least fifty individuals throughout the inhabited planets."

"Was," Cassell said. *I am.* "I remain Jonal Cassell, whose brain also contains the memories of Yerik Belen."

Nari's eyes never left him. An uncertain furrow

wrinkled her forehead. She did not pull from him. Instead her hand squeezed tighter around his.

"I'm sure," he told her. "I found Yerik Belen, and now he's gone."

Nari nodded. Her expression told him she understood, but was having trouble accepting all she heard. She slowly turned to Director Santis.

"You erased a man's personality, then implanted a totally new one within his brain?" Cassell noted a hint of disbelief and disgust in Nari's voice.

"It's not that distasteful, Ms. Hullen," Santis replied with a shake of her head. "Each subject undergoes personality erasure of their own free will. We offer them a new life in the face of certain death."

"With the condition that should the new personality prove unstable or threatening to the Tula Project, that death sentence will be executed," Cassell added.

"A reasonable condition," Santis said. "Yerik Belen, like the thousands who accepted the terms, entered the Tula Project with the self-delusion he could beat the system, that he could undergo reconditioning and emerge unchanged. In Tula's fifty-year history, no subject has ever done that."

"But Yerik Belen did," Nari said.

"We're not exactly sure how that happened," Santis answered. "My staff psychiatrists speculate that the violent shock of the assassination attempt, the near-death state sustained for an abnormal period in the AG Module, weakened the conditioning. Somehow, Yerik Belen found a way to step into the conscious again."

"Or at least get one foot in the door," Cassell said.

"But the assassination attempt?" Nari asked.

"I'm afraid that was a mistake on our part," Santis said. "We weren't ready to reveal the Tula Project . . ."

"And it was easier to eliminate one man than expose Tula to public scrutiny before you were fully prepared," Cassell said. "In the process, you killed my wife."

"We aren't gods. We make mistakes," Santis said,

though Cassell could not detect a defensive stance in her voice. "You endangered fifty years of agency work."

"Ailsa?" Cassell asked, suddenly aware that his Ailsa was also a programmed personality. "Who was she?"

"Ammar Cil, murdered two contract-mates and two children," Santis replied. "Your lives were programmed together, as are most couples' when the opportunity arises."

"Must have breeders to populate the colony," Cassell said, realizing Ailsa and he had cheated them on that point. His cutting comments did not ease the fact that nothing in his life for ten years had been real, only part of a predetermined program. Or was it?

"The other attempts on Jonal's life?" Nari asked.

"Bron arranged those when it became apparent Yerik Belen was re-exerting himself," Santis explained. "Belen was the real threat to the project."

"Justice," Cassell said. "Tula means justice—warped and twisted."

"Tula means Zivon," Santis said, irritated by his accusation. "Tula is a chance for a second life. Despite what the WCLF would like to make of the project, Tula stands as one of the few truly humanitarian ventures of the past century. It is the first successful alternative to capital punishment mankind has ever devised. You and all of Tula's colonists were given the choice, life or death. You chose life, no matter what the conditions."

"And Ailsa?" Cassell pressed.

"We gave no guarantees, just a second chance," the woman replied. "There are inequities in the system. All systems have faults. But Tula's benefits far outweigh the few rough edges that have appeared since autonomy became an issue."

"Then why keep it hidden?" Nari asked.

"Tula's scope is too broad, too new," Santis answered. 'It needs time to prove itself to Earth and all the inhabited planets. Mankind holds the stars in its hands, yet still butchers those who transgress society's boundaries. Kill them or lock them in prisons. We scream for humane treatment of pets, but we imprison men without an attempt to rehabilitate. If by some miracle an individual does rehabilitate himself while incarcerated, we turn him back into the environment that shaped him to begin with. The cycle begins anew. Despite the occasional public surges for prison reform and the abolition of capital punishment, the old system remains. A viable alternative was never given the chance to prove itself until the Tula Project."

She paused looking at Nari, then Cassell. "On Tula we hope to show mankind there is another way, a method to use society's transgressors in a productive manner. The criminal is given the opportunity to truly repay his debts, to extend mankind throughout the galaxy."

Again she paused. "To a lesser degree, Zivon proved reconditioning is effective for minor criminals."

"Zivon?" Cassell asked.

"The agency's first venture," the director said. "Minor offenders elected to undergo psycho-reconditioning and enter a new productive life free of their old environment."

"A self-perpetuating system," Nari said. "Zivon exists to funnel colonists to Tula."

"Not in the beginning," Santis replied. "When the Tula Project was conceived, Zivon presented a natural vehicle to serve as a facade for the operation."

"Any planet can create an army of slaves, then reap the rewards of colonization," Nari said, contempt lacing her words.

"That's the way we intend to sell the Tula Project to this world and the other inhabited planets. It's a matter of economics, pure and simple. Criminal colonization has had a long history on Earth, but has not yet been used for the stars. We've made that feasible," Santis said. "I admit it will take time to gather acceptance for Tula, but we will. Tula offers an answer to the disposal of society's criminal element. In return, society receives needed material resources. Most people will listen; it affects their pocketbooks."

Despite his personal hell, Cassell could not deny the basic reasoning in Santis's arguments. Yet there were kinks in the Tula Project Santis did not see. Things Cassell had not viewed until the shadowman had intruded into his life. "You're not creating new men—only half-men."

Santis's head turned to him, her gaze freezing on his face.

"Tulans are nothing more than zombies," Cassell said. He had to get through to her. Despite everything that had happened to him, Tula remained significant; it had meaning. It could be all Santis and her agency envisioned. And he was the key to achieving that end. "Tula isn't peaceful, it's passive. There's no real life in the hearts of its inhabitants, no striving, no ambition, only mindless existence. If Tula were ever confronted by a crisis, it would collapse. Tulans are incapable of thinking for themselves, of making decisions. They're organic automatons controlled by Zivon."

"You are proof that your premise is wrong," Santis replied. "You seem quite capable of handling a crisis. Something several of my agents will regret when this matter is finally settled."

"No," Cassell protested. It was so clear now. Would Director Santis be able to see it? If she did not? He tried not to think about the consequences, attempting to repress the urgent desperation that crept through him. "Jonal Cassell was incapable of dealing with any crisis he faced. Jonal Cassell lacked Yerik Belen's survival instinct."

Santis stared at him, her face an expressionless stone.

"Yerik Belen was wrong. He was an embodiment of evil, an incomplete man. But the Jonal Cassell you created was just as incomplete, just as wrong. Cassell was a program of everything society considered good. Cassell lived without spirit, no reason for existing. He accepted without question."

"You said you were still Jonal Cassell." Santis's face remained unmoved, betraying no hint of what her mind concealed.

"I am, but not the Cassell you created for the Tula Project." He struggled for words. It was happening too fast. The urgency, the desperation, mounted for no apparent reason. He needed time to gather his thoughts. "I am a blending of your psycho-reconditioning program and Yerik Belen. The two personalities have merged to create a third, a more complete personality. Both good and evil exist within me. Neither can exist independent of the other. An individual must conceive evil to know good. Good must be understood to grasp the meaning of evil. One concept defines the other. The choice between good and evil must be present for free will to exist. I faced that choice—Yerik Belen or Jonal Cassell. I chose Cassell."

"Nonsense. Philosophical rhetoric!" Santis's stone mask broke. No trace of sympathy was in her face. "Belen's memories exist, thus Yerik Belen still exists."

"I'm the only true success you've achieved in the Tula Project's fifty years. I'm not a psycho-reconditioning program. I'm not a mindless zombie. *I am.* I am a man who can think and reason. A man capable of making a correct decision without that decision being fed to him from a computer."

"You are also the only case of a re-emerging personality we've experienced," Santis replied. Cassell realized she had not heard a word he said. It meant nothing to her. "I wish there was further time to study your case. I'm sure my psychiatrists would find a complete analysis valuable. However, there isn't enough time."

"Not enough time?" Cassell sensed time twisting away from him. Reason had failed. He needed another avenue. "Why?"

"The re-emergence of Yerik Belen is a blot on the

236

Tula Project that we can't allow. It's a minor mistake in the scope of a fifty-year success. But minor mistakes have a way of being blown out of proportion by the media. We are faced with remolding public opinion, altering the concept that demands social revenge on criminals. I'm sure you understand our position."

Cassell understood her sense of desperation. Santis had not come here to listen to him. He glanced about the room. Mazour, his gorillas, and Bron Cadao stood by the door. Outside? He would worry about outside when he got that far.

"Jonal, what is she talking about?" Nari squeezed his hand like a vise, cutting off circulation to his fingers.

"About eliminating Jonal Cassell," he said glaring at Santis.

"Killing you?" Nari's head jerked around to the woman.

"Oh, no, Ms. Hullen." Santis shook her head. "There are those who would prefer this situation concluded in that manner. However, I think we have a viable alternative."

Inwardly, Cassell breathed a relieved sigh. She didn't intend to kill him. His gaze moved to the door again. Yet, Santis had something up her sleeve.

"I'm afraid, Ms. Hullen," the woman continued, "arrangements will also have to be made for you. You pose a threat potentially greater than Belen."

"Threat?" Nari twisted to Cassell, eyes wide, uncomprehending.

"You know too much," Cassell said. "You could spill everything. They can't leave loose ends."

"We intend to leave the loose ends," Santis said, raising a hand to Mazour. "Just tuck them away where they can't be found."

Mazour handed the woman a manila folder. The director opened it and flipped through a few loose sheets of paper within. Cassell barely made out the index tab—Yerik Belen.

237

"Ten days from now, Zivon will launch its first co-lonial ship to the terra-formed world of Anizi. We've arranged passage for two additional colonists aboard that ship. It won't be easy. Life is never easy for those colonizing a new world. But you will be alive."

"She hasn't done anything!" Cassell fought the urge to glance at the door again. He could not risk the slight-est suspicion. Surprise was his only advantage—a slim one. "What happened to your freedom of choice?"

"Ms. Hullen is one of those inequities that occur in any system," Santis replied.

"And me?" Cassell demanded. He sat straight in bed.

"A new personality . . . one for Ms. Hullen as well," Santis said. "Yerik Belen and Jonal Cassell will be replaced by the most important colonist on a new world—a farmer."

"What if I re-emerge again?" He stalled, waiting for the right moment. Every muscle in his body tensed, ready.

"The imprint will be total this time," Santis said with finality. "I will personally supervise your recon-ditioning."

Like it or not, it was the door, Cassell realized. There was no other way out of the room.

"Ms. Hullen, I've arranged a personality for you more in line with your present abilities." Santis glanced to Nari. "You will be a Zivon director oversee-ing the sociological development of a new world."

"But Jonal and me." Nari's voice pleaded. "I can accept everything else as long as we remain together."

"Romantic, but not very practical," Santis replied with a shake of her head. "My psychiatrists fear a sus-tained relationship between you and Belen could be a stimulus to another re-emergence of the Belen person-ality. I'm sorry . . ."

Cassell leaped from the bed in a single, fluid motion. Seizing Nari's arm, he rushed the door. Bron Cadao reacted first. The short man stepped in front of them to block their exit.

238

Cassell grinned with relish. Enough of Belen remained within him to savor a moment's revenge. He lashed out, fist driving into the man's gut. Groaning painfully, Cadao doubled over and clutched his belly. Cassell's right knee jerked up. He tumbled through the door to sprawl on his back in the corridor outside.

"Run!" Cassell shoved Nari through the door. "Get the hell out of here."

A hand clamped to his shoulder. He did not need the shadowman's advice. Belen's survival instincts burned within him. He pivoted, flowing with the force of the commanding grip. His fist shot out, smashing into Mazour's face before the man could strike.

He swirled, feeling the heat of the berserker blood burning in his veins. Mazour's unnamed gorilla rushed him. Easily he deflected a blow meant for his face and answered with a fist hammered to the Adam's apple. As the man fell away clutching his throat, he turned to face Mazour again. The man was unprepared for a renewed attack. Cassell's fist struck his upper lip, full body weight behind the blow. Mazour reeled back howling. Blood ran from the split lip.

Something dropped about Cassell's neck. An arm! It clamped tight, cutting off his windpipe. He struggled, trying to twist free, to jerk away from the strangling hold. His hands tore at the arm. He clawed at the man behind him, fingers ripping empty air, unable to reach him. The arm tightened, squeezing his esophagus closed.

Across the room, Cassell saw Pao Santis staring at his futile struggle. She nodded silent approval while his lungs screamed for air.

*Wrong!* He vainly tried to force words up his closed throat. *I am your only success . . . your only success.*

Jonal Cassell regained consciousness in the same windowless room. Nari sat beside his bed. He moaned.

"Are you all right?" She pushed from a chair and came to him.

"They choked me down," he said. "Not a pleasant experience, but far from fatal." He gazed at her and shook his head. "Your luck seems to have been as bad as mine."

"Mazour had more men outside," she said. "I didn't get two meters."

Cassell closed his eyes, trying to avoid facing the futility of their situation. He could not. They were alive, but existence ceased to contain meaning. *The damned thing is, I agree with Santis!* The Tula Project was worth saving. He realized were he in the woman's position he would do anything he could to protect the project. However, the view from the opposite side of the coin left a lot to be desired. *Inequities!*

"Jonal," Nari said softly, "hold me. Please."

He opened his arms and she slid into the bed beside him. He held her close, tightly against him.

"Tomorrow morning," she whispered. "Santis said they would come for us in the morning. Then . . ."

"We won't be anymore." He said the words she could not. He felt a trace of moisture as she pressed her cheek to his. Tears. Nari cried silently.

"We should have stayed aboard the *Tommy John*," she said, her voice trembling. "It was good then."

"Even if I didn't love you."

"Didn't know you loved me."

"Didn't know I loved you," he acquiesced.

Ailsa hung in his mind. Even with Nari so close, even with all the love he held for her, he felt the hollowness within him that would always belong to Ailsa, an emptiness that would never be filled. The knowledge Ailsa had killed four people, or even the realization that their love had been nothing more than a reconditioning program, did not tarnish the love that remained. For those years, what he had felt was reality to Jonal Cassell. And he remained very much Jonal Cassell.

"What was it like?" Nari asked, her words holding uncertainty. "Do you remember the reconditioning?"

"Painless." He recalled Yerik Belen's rage when the infant Jonal Cassell was born within his mind, a personality chemically and electrically nurtured until it dominated their shared brain. "It's complete from birth to the present. Every detail of your new personality is carefully impressed into your mind. Each artificially conjured memory is designed to sustain the creation they mold."

"I don't want Nari Hullen erased," she said. "But it would be bearable if I knew we would be together. Why couldn't they give us that? It doesn't seem too much. Why couldn't they leave us something?"

He held her tightly, hugging her closer to him. He had no answers. Nothing made sense. Stupidity never did.

"How did Yerik Belen survive?" Nari asked. "If he did it, we can."

"Sheer stubbornness," Cassell answered. "He pulled within himself. Belen's a natural survivor. He raged and fought Jonal Cassell. When he recognized the futility of his struggle, he blended. He mingled his personality with each bit of information they fed into his brain. He implanted himself on their implant. They never truly erased Belen, just subjugated his personality to Jonal Cassell's."

"Mingle," she repeated. "Mingle."

"He slipped in beside everything they planted in his brain," Cassell said.

"Yet, Jonal Cassell had to almost die before Belen emerged again," Nari said. Cassell detected the hopelessness in her voice. "For a moment, I thought there might be a chance... something we could do."

He offered no answer. He wanted the same thing, some hope on which to cling, to anchor himself to. Hope was not there. Yerik Belen might survive, but never Jonal Cassell. There had not been enough time for Jonal Cassell. He was still learning from Belen.

"Perhaps if we had... something that we could hold on to so that we'll know each other..." Her words trailed away. "I don't know, Jonal. Something only we would know . . . like the *Tommy John.* Something . . ."

"I love you," he whispered. "Nari Hullen, I love you."

He rolled over to her and kissed her, attempting to express everything he felt that words could never say.

"I'm being foolish," she said when they parted. "It wouldn't work, would it? Nari Hullen won't exist; they will erase her."

"It's possible. Yerik Belen did it." He tried to sound as convincing as he could in an effort to instill in her the hope he could not find.

"I love you, Jonal Cassell." A weak smile moved over her lips. "You're nice to try . . ."

"Belen did it. He survived. They couldn't erase him." He encouraged her. Hope would make it easier, though it was false hope.

"Shhhhhh." She placed a finger to his lips. "I don't want lies. My life has been nothing but self-delusions. It took you to end that. I don't want to go back to the lies now."

She kissed him. Soft and tender, her lips lingered against his.

"I don't want anything but Jonal Cassell and Nari Hullen." Her lips brushed his as she spoke. "I want a lifetime together. Do you understand? Anything else would be a delusion."

He nodded, aching for the same thing. He held the answers that had obsessed him. They meant nothing. Tula, Earth, the shadowman, Mazour, the WCLF, Santis, Yerik Belen—nothing. Only Nari mattered, offered any meaning.

"But we won't have that lifetime," she whispered. "All we have is one night."

Feeling the universe in his arms, he held her, knowing it would be torn from him in the morning.

"Make love with me, Jonal," she said. "We've one night to take the place of a lifetime."

He did; they did. Years of love forced into minutes, a life of caring and need crammed into hours. He im

242

mersed himself in her desire, her love. Desperately, they strove with mind and body to hold back the morning.

Mazour and two of his gorillas found them still clinging to one another. If Nari felt embarrassment or shame to be discovered in their intimate embrace, she did not display it, but glared coldly at the men. Sentimentality seemed out of place, meaningless, yet a warm pride filled Cassell's chest. In a world suddenly filled with wrongness, Nari remained right. She pulled him to her nakedness once again, her mouth covering his. They clung to one another, desperately attempting to extend one moment into an eternity, to define all of space and time. The impossible was impossible. They parted.

Silently, they slipped from opposite sides of the bed and dressed while Mazour and his men stood watching. Neither spoke as they surrendered themselves to the inevitable and crossed to Mazour.

Outside the room, Nari reached out and squeezed his hand. Director Pao Santis stood waiting for them at the end of a long corridor. Behind her stood two green doors labeled PSYCHO-RECONDITIONING.

"Mingle," Nari said softly when they entered the doors. "Mingle."

# NINETEEN

Daulo Neith crawled atop his third-level bunk and la
on his back. He glanced around the cabin, unable t
contain the disgust that churned deep within his stom
ach.

Cabin was too generous a term for his berth aboar
the colonial ship *Dovewing*. Human storage compart
ment offered a more accurate approximation of the liv
ing conditions the Zivon Development Conglomerat
provided their Anizi colonists. Four-tier bunks line
two walls of the four-meter-square cabin. At the foo
of the berths, a single combination head and showe
module stood attached to the wall, the cabin's only fur
nishing. Rust streaks, etched by seeping water an
urine, ran from beneath the module staining the floo
in ever-widening fingers, testimony to the makeshif
workmanship employed in converting the old freighte
to accommodate human cargo. The wall opposite th
module held the cabin's hatch, manual not pressure
plate actuated. The remainder of the cabin was bare
flat-gray painted walls.

Eight men were packed together for the two-month voyage, their only refuge of privacy—the bunks.

For Daulo Neith, a man born to the land who thrived in open skies overhead and the caress of the breeze on his face, a month aboard the *Dovewing* had transformed the cabin into a prison cell. He ached to feel soil beneath his feet rather than the unyielding hardness of the ship's deck.

Daulo Neith closed his eyes to block out the claustrophobic confines of the cabin's walls. Even within his bunk, his seven cabinmates intruded into his privacy. Their smell hung in the air like a thick blanket that invaded his nostrils, suffocating him.

Others had endured similar conditions for longer periods, he tried to rationalize away his distress. The voyage had passed the point of no return. He could last another month . . . he could. He flopped to his side and buried his face against an arm to escape the overwhelming smell of closely packed human beings. It did not help. The stench clung to his coveralls, to his own body, refusing to be washed away even in the shower. The odor permeated every centimeter of the ship. The *Dovewing* was not designed to carry passengers in her holds. The air filtering system could not handle the mass of humanity crammed into the vessel. There were too many people.

His eyes opened to stare at the gray walls. He imagined animal heads outlined in the chipped paint. *Too many people.* He felt them pressing in around him, the hull bending under their writhing weight. Inward the walls bulged, ever inward, trying to crush him beneath their imposing mass.

His mouth dried, filled with cotton. His throat scratched like a thorn branch raked up and down its sides. His pulse drummed up from his chest in a thunderous booming that filled his temples with a deafening roar. Deep within him a scream grew. It pushed upward to his throat. His lips trembled, parting to release the knotted desperation consuming him.

—Easy, Daulo, easy. Take a deep breath.

He did, filling his lungs and slowly exhaling.

—Another one.

Again he breathed deeply and exhaled. It steadied him, allowing him to fight back the claustrophobia, at least for the moment.

—Now think about Anizi, the life you'll find there, the rich, virgin soil waiting to be tilled.

*The soil,* Daulo repeated, letting thoughts of fresh rich soil and growing things bloom within his head. *And the sky, wide open, stretching clear and clean above me.*

—And the sky . . . warm breezes and light morning rains to water the earth.

The images were good, calming the panic that clenched within his chest. *Only a month more, I can make it.*

—No doubt about it, Daulo. Just keep thinking of Anizi and the life that awaits you.

*It will be good, won't it? Everything you've promised me?*

—More land than Earth ever offered. All it lacks is a man to love and care for it.

The thoughts of fields filled with grain, orchards heavy with ripening fruit, comforted him, releasing the last of the squeezing tension. Daulo Neith smiled. It was a simple man's dream, but then he was a simple man. *Jonal.*

—Yes.

*Thank you. I don't know how I would have made this far without your help.*

—We're in this together, remember?

He knew, almost remembered everything Jonal Cassell had told him about Pao Santis and his psycho-re conditioning. One day he would truly remember it all. Until then, he was grateful for Jonal's presence and the images he conjured of Anizi.

—It sounds as bad as Tula. We'll never make it.

Yerik Belen was another matter, Daulo thought.

246

t Jonal said he was necessary too. Exactly why es-
ped him, but Jonal said he would understand, and
trusted Jonal.

—We can make it. We have to work together within
e system, at least in the beginning, until we under-
nd what we're facing. That's where you made your
stake, Yerik, driving me to go against the system.
e won't make the same mistake this time.

Daulo was uncertain he comprehended everything
nal and Yerik discussed. He did understand that one
y Jonal, Yerik, and he would merge and a man
eater than any of them separately would be born.
e possibility excited him. Both Jonal and Yerik knew
re than he; he wanted that knowledge.

—A farmer! Yerik Belen stuck in the brain of a
rmer. Santis and Mazour will pay for this!

Daulo closed his mind to Yerik's ragings. His voice
s always weaker than Jonal's. It was simple to close
rik off. However, often Jonal's voice was more in-
nse than his own thoughts. That frightened him. He
d not want to be lost when the merger of their per-
nalities came.

—You won't be. All three of us will be one, a single
tity.

He believed Jonal, yet the unknown remained
ghtening. He glanced about the cabin again, feeling
close around him.

—A walk will help, Daulo. Go to the recreation room.
ere's more space. It's easier for you to breathe.
*And look for Nari.*

—Always look for Nari. One day, we'll find her.

Nari, a half-formed image, feelings of love and need,
indefinable longing for something almost remem-
red, that belonged to him. A memory Santis could
t erase, Jonal once explained to him. He wanted more
an partial memories. He wanted the gauzy curtains
rted to reveal the face that haunted his dreams, that
ft him hungering when he woke.

*I'll find her,* he thought to himself, not to the voice

247

that shared his head. He swung over the edge of th
bunk and climbed down to walk to the cabin's hatch
*I'll find her.*

The mess bell blared from the intercom. Daulo Neitl
looked up, forgetting for a moment his cabin was o
first shift this week. He shook his head and swiveled
from the light screen he played. His opponent opposit
him at the table glanced up, and he shrugged his shoul
ders helplessly. "Chow bell. I have to concede th
game."

The girl nodded and immediately forgot him as on
in the line of waiting players took his chair and begar
another game.

Daulo walked from the recreation room and moved
down a tunnel corridor toward the dining hall with a
quarter of the level's passengers. He tried to ignore th
discouraged hopelessness within him, achieving littl
success. The hollow sinking feeling was always ther
after one of his searches for Nari. With each failure
the emptiness increased.

—You'll find her, Daulo. It will take time, but you'l
find her.

He reached the entrance to the dining hall an
stopped. His gaze took in the lines stretching befor
the servo-units, the tables overflowing with humanity
His stomach churned, twinges of claustrophobic pani
returning.

He turned and ran back down the tunnel corridor
fleeing the ocean of pressing bodies that sought to swa
low him. In a slow trot, he ran, at first to dispel th
ever-present fear, then because he lost himself in th
pumping rhythm of his legs. Heads turned to stare a
him in disbelief, but he did not care; he ran. For th
first time since boarding the *Dovewing,* he felt free. H
paid no attention to the path he traveled, darting dow
one corridor this direction, then down another at th
next "Y" junction. If he lost himself in the maze

tunnel corridors, finding his way back to the cabin would help consume the endless hours of monotony.

Abruptly, he stopped. A liftshaft stood at the end of the corridor he entered. He moved toward it, uncertain. Ship regulations confined colonists to their assigned levels. *What harm could there be?* He could float up, take a peek, then find a dropshaft and return to this level before he was noticed. Sucking in a deep breath, he stepped into the shaft.

The excitement of a child venturing into forbidden territory raced through him as he rose not one but two levels, then stepped outside. No one waited to halt him, so he walked down the tunnel corridor opening before him. To his disappointment, it led to a level of cabins identical to those of his own level. He turned to retrace his steps to the shaft. The adventure had lasted long enough. It was time to return to his cabin.

His gaze fell on small lettering stenciled on the wall of the corridor—OBSERVATION BAY. A red arrow pointed down a "Y" conjunction in the opposite direction he headed.

*The Tommy John!*

—You remember?

*Almost,* he told Jonal. Hazy images flittered through his mind, unrecognizable, but familiar. He attempted to seize them, force recognition into his brain. They evaded him.

—Don't push it, Daulo. It will take time, but it will come.

He nodded, realizing Jonal was right. The memories were there, he could feel them. When the time was right, they would be his. He looked at the sign again and stepped down the corridor.

The flashing lights of the tachyon display were visible through the bay's open entrance. The kaleidoscopic display called to something hidden within him, pulling him forward. Cautiously, he stopped at the door and peered in. No one was inside the dark room. He stepped inside and sank into one of the chairs. His gaze focused on the circular window and the fascinating universe beyond the ship's hull.

"Beautiful, isn't it?" A woman's voice floated softly behind him.

He twisted around to see a young, auburn-haired woman step from the shadows at the rear of the bay. He froze, his pulse racing wildly.

"You're from one of the other levels," she said as a statement rather than as a question. "The coverall color is a giveaway. We wear green on this level."

*Nari?* He nodded, unable to speak or take his eyes from the woman. She came closer; the light from the observation window danced across her face. It *was* Nari!

Memories crowded into his skull; half-formed images took shape and solidified. The *Tommy John* ...Kara's apartment...a poker game...the night before their reconditioning...He trembled, trying to accept the rush that swept through his head. Tears welled in his eyes.

—Enough. Take it easy. Too much of this at one time can throw you into shock.

Jonal stepped in, cutting off the flood of memories. Daulo gasped, grateful, realizing *he* might have been engulfed by the tidal wave. Yet at the same time, he wanted them to continue, flow into his head until he comprehended everything. Most of all he wanted to know all that was possible about this woman who approached, this women who had dwelled only in his dreams until now.

—You know enough, Daulo. A little at a time is the way we have to do this. Do you understand that?

He did. For the first time he truly understood. The blast of memory also brought realization. He was Yerik Belen—Jonal Cassell—Daulo Neith. They were one and the same. And Jonal Cassell stood as the safety valve. His Cassell personality slowly fed him information belonging to his other two personalities, allow

250

ing him time to assimilate one memory before releasing another.

—Daulo Neith must be preserved to save all of us. Too great a dose of Belen or myself and we might lose you. Remember, Santis and her agents will be watching your every step.

He understood. He, Daulo Neith, was the newest, the least stable, and could be erased by either of the other two personalities. Neither Cassell nor Belen could afford that. Santis's field agents would be watching for any hint of the re-emergence of either personality. They needed him and his skills to survive on Anizi.

—When the merger comes, we will be one, a whole. Not three separate voices in one mind.

"There's no reason to be afraid." Nari sat beside him, apparently mistaking the rush of memories for fear. "I won't turn you in. To be honest, it's nice to have company in here for a change. Most people on this level pay little attention to the bay."

All the love that had been Jonal Cassell's was now his. He struggled against the desire to reach out and take her into his arms, to show her the love they thought lost still belonged to them. They had cheated Santis and her psycho-reconditioning machines. They had won. They had a lifetime ahead of them.

—You won, Daulo. She doesn't recognize you. This isn't Nari, but Santis's program. You must help Nari break free. I've given you enough . . . that is, if she can be freed.

*She can!* Hope he shared with Jonal Cassell rose to fill him. *She can, I know it!*

"I'm not afraid," he said. "You just startled me. I thought the bay was empty."

"Sorry." She smiled a smile that belonged to Nari Hullen. "But I normally have this to myself. It's the only privacy I can find aboard the ship."

"That's why I came in," he said, his mind pondering the possibilities of getting through to Nari, all the while repressing the urge to kiss and hold her. "Down on M Level, there's no place to get away from all the bodies. They keep pressing in."

She nodded with understanding. "Yet, you can never touch one or know what is going on in their heads."

Within his new memories he found the keys ... "something we can hold on to." If Nari still lived within this stranger's mind, he would free her.

"What's your name?" she asked.

"Tommy John," he said, hoping.

"Tommy John?" She stared at him, but didn't. For an instant he could almost feel her mind moving in the distance, searching. Then, her eyes rolled to the tag on his coveralls. "Can't hide behind an alias, Daulo Neith, not with your name scrawled on your chest."

He laughed, in spite of the sinking in his stomach. "Can't blame me for trying, can you?"

"I told you I wasn't going to turn you in," she said. She glanced up at the chronometer above the observation window. "But you really can't stay here too long. A cleaning crew makes its rounds about this time in the evening. If they find you here ..."

Her voice trailed off. He did not want to leave, not now after he found her again. But to be discovered would be a disaster. Santis's agents would learn he had met with Nari. In tachyon space there were no psycho-reconditioning units. The problem would be eliminated by a more permanent means.

"You're probably right," he said. "I just thought it would be interesting to come up here and mingle a bit. To break the monotony, you know."

"Mingle?" The distant expression returned to her face. A puzzled frown wrinkled her forehead. She stared at him for a long moment, like a woman in a trance. "Mingle?"

—That's enough for now. Don't push it. You can almost see the cracks ... feel the memories seeping to the surface.

"Do you know the way to the dropshaft?" she said, as though awakening from a deep sleep.

He shook his head, then listened while she gave
hasty directions. He suppressed his want to stay, to pry
at those cracks he felt running across her reconditioning
program. But he was pushing his luck as it was.
To be caught now would destroy any possibilities that
might exist. He rose and started toward the exit.

"Daulo Neith," she called after him. "Will you be
back?"

He turned and grinned. "If you're here."

"Tomorrow evening," she said, "at seven, after the
cleaning crew has left."

"Tomorrow evening," he confirmed. "I'll be here."

When he turned to leave again, she called out once
more. "Sameh Dery, my name is Sameh Dery."

"Sameh Dery," he said, "tomorrow at seven p.m."

She smiled and he turned once again, leaving her
alone in the observation bay.

—You're both insane. If they catch you, they'll kill
us. Leave her alone. Our survival is what is important.

Daulo Neith still did not understand why Yerik
Helen was needed. But he knew enough now to trust
Venal's decisions.

—He's right, Daulo, you have to be careful. One
mistake and it will be your last.

*I know. They'll be watching me. It won't be easy.* He
climbed into his bunk and closed his eyes. *But I . . . we
can do it.*

—If you two are stupid enough to go through with
this, there's nothing I can do, but help.

—Protect your own neck, Yerik?

—What else?

*Then we work together,* Daulo said to his mental
companions. The cabin no longer pressed in. He could
feel the universe expanding about him. *We find the
Nari Hullen that's hiding in Sameh Dery.*

—We can do it.

*Keep chipping away at the cracks we create until she
remembers.* He knew it would work. Eventually Nari

Hullen would live again. He felt it; he staked his life on it.

—Always within the system, never arousing the agency's suspicions.

When Nari was his once again, and the opportunity arose, they could slip off-planet to a world that would shelter them, allow them to live that lifetime together.

—There might be others we can reach, open their minds to reality.

Jonal was right, he thought. If he could reach others, he would. But *first* came Nari. He smiled. *Sameh Dery, tomorrow, seven in the evening.*

## About the author:

A native *Texican*, Geo W. Proctor was raised in the pine woods and red clay country of East Texas, on his parents' farm for breeding and training thoroughbred race horses. Before beginning his writing career, he worked briefly as a television cameraman and spent five years as a reporter with a major Dallas daily newspaper.

A longtime enthusiast of science fiction and fantasy, Proctor made his first story sale in 1972. Also a "weekend painter," he has sold paintings which appeared in a national fantasy periodical.

Proctor and his wife Lana presently live in Arlington, Texas, a suburb between Dallas and Fort Worth.